PRAISE FOR R.C. STEPHENS

"A sexy NHL player, a sassy heroine, and a heartfelt romance that kept me engaged from beginning to end!" — *NYT* **bestseller Mia Sheridan on Big Stick.**

"I knew in Big Stick I would love Oli's story, and after getting to know this sexy giant in the pages of Butt Ending, I now think I love him more than Myles... so, therefore, I claim them both!" - A.M. Madden USA Today Bestselling Author, on Butt Ending.

"Myles and Flynn's chemistry is ice-melting hot in this fast-paced, friends-to-lovers romance sure to warm your heart. Another R.C. Stephens SCORE!" - Julie A. Richman, USA Today Bestseller on Big Stick.

DIRTY SWEDISH PLAYER

R.C. STEPHENS

PROLOGUE

"Nils, come in here," Mother called from the family room where I sat peacefully on the couch watching the game. I don't know why I'm even here. When she phoned earlier today and asked me to come see her, she sounded . . . sad? I shouldn't care, not after the way she left me behind, but I do. I always do. No matter how shitty she treats me, I love her.

"Nils, did you hear me?"

I thought if I ignored her long enough, maybe she'd stop calling my name and let me watch the game in peace—apparently not. The season just started for the NHL. I planned to spend my free time this afternoon watching the game, not hanging out with Mother and her new family.

"She isn't going to give up. You might as well see what she wants," my stepfather, Steve, says dryly from beside me. He doesn't really feel like my stepfather, since I've only known him a year. I scratch my head, wondering if she got a divorce from Father, back in Sweden. I wonder if Steve has had this exact thought.

I shake my head. It's none of my business what Mother does.

"You're right," I say, forcing a smile. "They are one of my favorite teams," I say, realizing it's not much.

"Mine too," he agrees.

I hate to think that I'm still holding a grudge about Mother not sending for me sooner. She was living it up here in America, while I survived a shitty existence with my violent alcoholic father. In the letters Mom wrote to me, I understood she was living with a man who didn't want to deal with some abused adolescent boy from a shithole back in Sweden. I was angry when I arrived in this country, but then Steve noticed my hockey skills and called in a favor. I wanted to hate him. The anger that I harbored back in Hogsby while waiting for my mother to save me still burns inside me like an ember. I just don't let it flare, reminding myself that I'm in college on a champion hockey team trying to secure my future. I take deep breaths.

I'm happy Steve doesn't talk too much. It made it easy to live with him.

"Nils," Mother calls out again. *Fucking hell*. Steve eyes me, his lip quirking on one side.

I get off the couch and walk through the very large house. Mother is in the kitchen, cooking dinner with Steve's daughter, Sierra. She has been living with her aunt in Chicago, so we just met today. I can't understand why she chose to move to Chicago and not live in this amazing house.

I walk into the bright kitchen with gray, sleek cabinets and modern trim. The stone counters look shiny and expensive, like they jumped out of a magazine. The fridge alone is probably big enough to feed all the people of our small town back in Sweden.

"Yes, Mother," I say blandly in English, since Mother says its rude to speak Swedish when Sierra and Steve are around.

"Can you be a little more pleasant?"

She gives me a chastising grin, and turns her attention to Sierra. Mom rolls her eyes and her lips tip up at the corners, as if her and Sierra are sharing a private joke.

"I am." I shrug. *I agreed to come for dinner, didn't I?* She should be happy with that.

"Sierra, sweetheart, would you mind giving me a moment

alone with Nils?" she says, rubbing Sierra's arm gently. She's even affectionate with this girl. The mother I knew spent most of her days out of the house, working or spending time with her few friends in town. Mothering wasn't at the top of her list of things to do. Although, I can't say I blame her. I also did what I could to stay far away from Father.

Sierra eyes me and her cheeks flush as she leaves the room. I smile briefly and take a seat at the kitchen table across from Mother. By the look on her face, I already know she wants something.

"She is such a lovely girl, isn't she?" Mother asks.

"Uh . . . I guess. I've only just met her," I counter.

"Yes, I know, but she's a pretty little thing," she continues. *Okay she is cute, I guess.* I'm not really into her type. She looks like a good girl with those thick-framed glasses, and Steve is always saying what a good student she is. I have to do well in my classes to stay on the college hockey team, but I couldn't care less about school.

"Steve is so happy she agreed to move back here to go to Minnesota State, and I'm proud of you, too, Nils. Thank goodness Steve was able to convince the recruiters to come and see you." Her lips spread wide and she bats her lashes.

"Thanks for reminding me every chance you get," I say. *Fuck.* This is worse than torture.

"Don't be like that." She places her hand over mine.

"Okay," I answer, because arguing with her gets me nowhere. I stare into crisp blue eyes that mirror my own. "What's going on?"

Mother takes a deep breath. I dart my gaze around the kitchen, pots and pans cooking on the stove. I don't remember her preparing food when she was home, yet she moved to America and became wife of the year.

"Nils, I need a favor." *Of course she does.*

"You have my attention." I sit back in my chair and cross my arms in front of my chest. Mother peeks over her shoulder, I guess to see if the coast is clear. She turns to me and straightens her spine. Mom moves closer, as if she wants to share a secret. "She's having some trouble adjusting at school. She hasn't made friends and Steve is unhappy about this," she says.

Sierra attends Minnesota State because her father is the Dean of the College of Arts and Humanities. I don't see her around since I spend most of my time with friends I've made on the hockey team.

"I'm hoping you can help her out. She had a hard time in Chicago, and he's worried about her. She's very shy," she says. I figured as much; Sierra didn't even make eye contact when I said hello.

"What do you mean help her?" I ask.

"Befriend her. Maybe you could introduce her to some of your buddies on the hockey team? She just needs someone to give her a little push." She bites her lip, a tell-tale sign that she has a scheme brewing in that warped brain of hers. She pulls her gaze from me like she's deep in thought. "I have a much better idea." She grins wide and puts her pointer finger up in the air. I already know I'm not going to like this.

"What is it?" I ask. "I'm no therapist. I can't teach his daughter to be outgoing. Besides, why would he want her hanging around the hockey team? Most of the guys only care about having sex. Is that what he wants for his daughter?" I grimace. I know Steve likes to get what he wants, and he can be pompous and self-righteous.

"No, no, you are right." She presses two fingers to her lips, and it looks like she's deep in thought.

Shit. What will she come up with now?

"I have the perfect idea." She claps her hands. Her English is better than mine, but she still has a heavy Swedish accent. "You pretend to be Sierra's boyfriend. This way, boys don't come onto her because she will be under your protection. You are popular. Introduce her to other girls so she can make friends. It's perfect."

I jerk out of the chair. "Hell no. That is not perfect. Messed up is more like it. You want me to pretend I am dating my step-sister?" Of all the crazy shit this woman has done in her life, this has got to be at the top of the list.

"Nils." She stands and pushes my shoulder, urging me to sit back down. "Think about it. Nobody knows she's your stepsister. You have only just met each other. You are not blood, and this would help her so much. She has a hard life. I want to see her smile."

Dammit, I can't believe how sincere my mother sounds about helping this girl.

She cups my chin and directs me to look at her. "I brought you to this country. I've given you a good life. I'm asking for a favor. And let's not forget that it would make Steve happy," she says. The ember inside me ignites. My gaze flails wildly from side to side. My instinct is to stand and fling the chair into the wall and watch it break into pieces. I picture Mom's eyes wide and filled with hurt and maybe fear. I don't want her to fear me, per se, but maybe the idea that I am exactly like my old man. Angry. And I am so damn angry at this woman, who seems to think of everyone but me. I clench and unclench my fists. I won't lose my temper today.

I won't lose my temper today. Repeating the mantra helps, to a point.

"Is that all you care about? Making Steve happy. Fucking hell, I am your son," I hiss. *Don't you care what makes me happy?* The words die on my tongue.

"And I love you," she places her hand over my clenched fist. Memories of my attempts to save her from my father's wrath cross my mind. Something eases in my chest. "Sierra is very smart; maybe she can help you with your homework. You know, fix the English on your assignments." Mom sweetens the deal with those words and any anger I feel releases. She's thinking of me, too. I could use the help with my classes. It's only fall semester and I'm already struggling.

"If I agree, we call it even, you stop throwing Steve's help in my face," I say, my tone angrier than I mean it to be.

"Agreed. You do this and Steve will be grateful. We can call it even." She squeals and gives me a hug.

I turn around and roll my eyes. "It's a deal," I say, heading back to the family room. Even though Mom was acting as if she just came up with the idea, I know better. She had this planned before I arrived. Steve is one weird fuck. Why would he want his goody two-shoes daughter to hang around someone like me?

I take a seat on the couch in front of the TV. I would ask Steve what I missed, but fewer words are better with him.

"Your mom spoke to you about Sierra?" Steve cocks a brow. It's as if he already knows I said yes. He must know how persuasive Mother can be when she wants something.

"Yes, I will help her." I nod.

"Thanks. I do appreciate it," he says.

"Yeah. Okay." I shrug, and return to watching the game. I wonder what his daughter will have to say about all of this. She can't possibly think it's a good idea.

Sierra walks down the stairs and takes a seat in the armchair off the side of the room.

"Nils has agreed, dear. This will be really good for you. You're book smart but not street smart. Nils will be a good teacher," Steve says, and I want to hit him on the head. Why does he speak to his daughter in such a demeaning way? *I don't like it.* It reminds me of my father back home.

"Dad," she says with a chiding voice.

"Oh, don't be shy. Nils is family," he says. The poor girl's cheeks turn pink. She's timid. Another thought pops in my head. How would she look coming completely undone? My eyes rake over her body. I shake my head. Don't think of her in that way.

I want to ease her embarrassment. "No worries. You will be my pretend girlfriend. I know lots of people. You make friends then we can break up."

She nods and stands quickly. "Oh, I thought we'd be just friends," she says.

"My mother thought it would be safer if I say you're my girlfriend. Guys on the hockey team are only interested in sex. This way, you have my protection," I explain.

"Thank you, Nils," Steve says, looking to me with an appreciative nod.

"Um, wouldn't that be weird?" Sierra asks.

Yes, it will be, but stop being so difficult.

"No, it's better—"

"He's right," Steve cuts in. "Make friends with the girls. Hockey jocks aren't for you," Steve says.

Am I supposed to be insulted?

"Daddy, that's . . ."

"You focus on doing well at school," Steve says with a commanding tone. He likes to be in control of everything, which I now see includes his daughter's personal life.

"But, Daddy, I want to have a life, too," she says.

My stomach sinks. I feel bad for her. *What have you been through?*

No, stop it. It doesn't matter.

I sweep my gaze over her, cataloguing everything: her pretty face, beautiful round brown eyes with flecks of gold behind thick red glasses. Her tits are on the larger side, and she has a flat stomach leading to curvy hips.

What am I doing?

I need to keep my gaze at a respectable level. The way she looks makes it hard not to check her out. She isn't my type, but hell, my body reacts to her in animalistic way. Like I'm a predator and she's my prey.

Shit!

Checking out my stepsister is all wrong. So why does it feel so right?

CHAPTER ONE

N ils
Present

"THIS PLACE IS BORING." I SWIVEL MY HEAD AND LOOK AT MY buddy, Matt.

"Fuck, man, tell me about it," he slurs. "Maybe we should go to one of the regular clubs."

I shouldn't. Coach has been riding me about cutting down on the partying and fucking around. He seems to think it's having a negative impact on my already out-of-control anger. I don't think I have an anger problem, but the coach and senior managers have warned me that I will get benched if I keep getting into too many fights on the ice.

"Hello." Matt waves his hand in my face. "Earth to Nils." He chuckles. Fuck, he's so drunk.

"Fuck off." I swat his arm. "We should pick up some chicks and go back to my place." My house is big and empty.

We both turn our heads to look around the bar. It's an old dive on a bad street but it serves the purpose. I get out of my house to blow off steam while maintaining a low profile, away from the public eye.

There are a few patrons around the bar. Some are playing pool at a table in the back corner, and there's a table with two chicks sitting and drinking beer.

"They're kinda cute," I say, tilting my chin to the ladies. One of them notices me eyeing her and smiles, then she whispers to her friend and they both grin wide. The blonde one lifts her hand and waves. Her brunette friend smiles and then gives us a small wave, too.

Bingo.

"Nils, don't call them over." Matt's voice is pleading even through his lack of sobriety. "I promised Coach I'd keep an eye on you," he says, defeat leaking from his tone.

"I don't know about you, but I want to get my dick wet," I say, unapologetically.

"Can you take them to the bathroom then? If we bring them back to your place it will turn into an all-night thing. We'll have a shit practice tomorrow," Matt slurs. Fuck, this is funny. He's struggling to keep his head straight, yet he knows to try to keep me in line. Coach must have threatened him really good.

"How can you be so reasonable when you're this drunk?" I say. His head hangs between his shoulders and when he lifts it to look at me, it seems like his whole upper body is rocking from side to side.

I snort laugh. He places his head on the bar and groans. I get up and walk over to the girls with my signature grin and swagger.

I stumble and sway. Fuck, I don't have swagger. They still wave me over. Their grins tell me they are pleased with my arrival at their table.

"Hello, there, handsome," Blonde greets me.

Definitely a good start.

"Hey beautiful. May I sit with you two?" I ask politely.

"Yes," she says, shifting her seat over. I grab a chair from the empty table next to them. My eyes drop to her rack. *Nice tits*.

I take a seat. The waitress comes over. "Drinks on my tab. Whatever they want," I mutter. How did I get so shit-faced already? "Beer for me."

The chicks order some drinks. Blonde leans over and runs her hand up my arm. "Love your tats. What does this one mean?"

"It's a falcon," I say. Fuck, isn't it obvious?

"It's so sexy. I love it." Brunette smirks and her eyes gleam.

"Thanks," I answer.

She scoots up and brings her chair from across the table to the other side of me. She runs her hands up my arm. Being sandwiched between two chicks is heaven. Having their hands on me causes my dick to stiffen. Our encounter is meaningless, but them touching me makes me feel wanted for the briefest of moments.

"I really want to kiss you," I say, looking at Blonde.

"Yes, please," she says, all breathy. I lean forward and capture her lips right here in the bar. I should take her somewhere private as our tongues mingle. I suck her bottom lip and she moans. Her hands drop to my lap where she begins to rub the bulge in my jeans. No . . . wait a minute. I open my eyes. That's her friend's hand.

"I want to kiss him, too," she says. "I'm jelly."

Fuck yeah. Jackpot.

"Should we go somewhere more private?" I ask.

Blonde nods. Did she tell me her name? I don't remember it if she did. I turn to Matt who is watching the baseball game on TV. His gaze catches mine and he shakes his head, but he keeps quiet. I appreciate him not cock blocking me.

I walk toward the men's bathroom and open the door. "Hello. Anyone in here?" I holler. I don't wait for an answer. "All clear."

They follow me into the handicap stall. Blonde steps forward first, pressing herself against me. A small groan escapes me. I dip my lips, kissing her slow at first. Taking her response as a green light, my hand comes up to caress her breast.

"I want him, too," Brunette says, moving closer. She peppers soft kisses down my neck. With my eyes shut, I'm not sure which lady works my jeans down my legs but my cock springing free—swollen and ready—makes them both stop what they are doing.

My eyes open. Both women are staring at my dick. Blonde smirks devilishly and licks her lips.

"Fuck yesss," Brunette hisses as she grips me in her hand, pumping my cock. My head falls back against the concrete wall. Blonde gets to work pushing Brunette's jeans and panties in one fell swoop. She then dips her fingers between Brunette's thighs causing her to moan all deep and throaty. My balls harden. Blonde then removes her jeans and panties. She plunges her pointer finger in her mouth sucking it like a lollipop then dipping it between her legs and rubbing herself.

"Fuck yessss," I hiss, my hips grinding into Brunette's fist.

"I'm ready," Blonde says, grinning devilishly. In the bright light of the bathroom I see now that she looks older than me.

"Me, too," Brunette says, with a wide smile that spreads from cheek to cheek. I glance at Brunette's bare pussy. My dick aches, causing a growl to escape my lips.

The women move closer. "Spread your legs. Both of you," I murmur, dipping a finger from each of my hands inside their pussies. Brunette curses under her breath. Blonde's gaze drops to my fingers, watching me pump her. Her breath turns ragged; her lashes flutter closed, her mouth forming a perfect O. *This is perfect.*

Brunette fists my dick and blonde cups my balls. I suck in a harsh breath. Fuck, don't blow your load now.

"Easy there." I pull my finger out of Blonde and move their hands off my dick. I stop pumping inside Brunette, too. I need both hands to get a condom. No matter how sloshed I am, I stay responsible. Don't need any little Karlssons running around.

They watch as I sheath my swollen cock.

"This is our lucky night," Brunette says to Blonde.

"Kiss each other," I demand. Blonde licks her lips as she leans toward Brunette. Their lips lock and Brunette's fingers come up and mess with Blonde's hair. They have the sexiest open-mouthed kiss I have ever seen. My cock bobs as I rub myself. That tingly feeling emerges in my spine as my balls tighten. Fuck. *Deep breath.* I move Brunette away from Blonde and turn her to face the wall. She places her palms flat against it. My hand slowly caresses the globes of her ass; it's firm, and perfect. I enter her from behind, pumping inside her.

A flash of a camera blinds me. Alarm bells ring in my head.

"What are you doing? No pics," I murmur, swatting my hands at Blonde's phone.

"Come on. Do you know how long we've waited for this? Our shot with you?" she asks, and it sinks in. *They know who I am.* With my cock inside Brunette, I just want to get off. I confiscate Blonde's phone, crushing it inside my closed palm. I grip Brunette's hip firmly in my free hand and use it as leverage to thrust deeper. She moans, and my dick jerks inside her. It's hard to hold her hip and the phone. It falls from my hand, crashing to the floor and bouncing into the next stall.

"Fuck," she mutters. I come, grunting my release.

The bathroom door swings open, smacking a wall. "Hey. Sandy. You better not be in there." Some dude pounds on the stall door. The lock doesn't look strong enough to hold.

I look between the two chicks. "Are either of you Sandy?" I ask, hoping I'm smart enough to whisper.

Blonde raises her hand. *Phew.* At least I didn't fuck her.

"Who is that?" I ask her.

"Her boyfriend," Brunette answers.

"Sandy, I can fucking hear you, slut," the man growls.

Fuck. Lifting my jeans up my ass, I don't even have time to get the condom off when the dude smashes the door open. He pulls me out by the collar of my T-shirt. He's a big fucking guy but I'm big, too. I'm just intoxicated. Still, I've been getting into bar fights since I was a teenager back in Hogsby.

I rip his hands off me and back him out of the stall.

"Motherfucker," he curses. He's wearing a leather biker jacket and he has a red bandana on his head. A camera flashes.

"Would you stop taking pictures?" I snap at Blonde.

The dude punches me in the face. It's my fucking fault for taking my eyes off him.

Piercing pain shoots through my eye and down my cheek.

"You shouldn't have done that," I say. He swings again. I duck, closing the space between us. My anger rains on him as I punch him over and over. Adrenaline spikes my veins, as darkness clouds my vision, blocking out the rest of the world. This is what I crave. The fight. Feeling this high. I can't explain it. I'm just wired this way.

"Nils, stop. Nils you're going to fucking kill him." Matt's voice resonates somewhere in my mind, but I am too far gone, consumed by and drowning in my anger. It flows through my veins, igniting a fire that feels so good.

Someone is pulling me off the guy. He's curled in a ball on the floor, his arms up protecting his face. My breath is heavy as the darkness clears and I see Matt, the bartender, and another big guy, holding me back.

"I hope they don't call the cops," Matt mutters, but it's too fucking late.

When I look up, the cops are standing there, ready to read me my rights as I get arrested along with Blonde's boyfriend.

MY FIRST TIME IN THE BACK OF A COP CAR. I CAN'T BREATHE. After getting fingerprinted and placed in a holding cell, I'm given the opportunity to make one phone call. My best friend Myles is at the top of my list. His wife, Flynn, is a lawyer, and will know who to call to get me out of this mess.

Back in the holding cell, my head pounds as the reality of my poor decisions weighs heavily on my shoulders. If I get charged with a criminal offense, I could be suspended from the NHL. What would I do with myself then? Those girls set me up, but I didn't need to fall for their stupid advances. When something is too good to be true, it usually is. Sitting and waiting on my fate makes me crazy. I pace the cell. I dig my nails into my scalp. All I need is a second chance.

CHAPTER TWO

S ierra

RUNNING DOWN THE STREET WITH MY BACKPACK ON MY BACK and a coffee mug in hand isn't the way I pictured my morning going. My cell rings. I reach into my jeans pocket to see the mechanic's name on my screen.

"Hello," I say, panting as the unusually humid September air has me sweating.

"Sierra, this is Holt from the garage," a man says. My friend Ami from the station recommended him and said he was honest and reasonably priced.

"Hi, Holt. Please tell me you have good news?" I ask, holding my breath. My little red Toyota is an older car, but it gets me from A to B.

"Your exhaust pipe is punctured. It can potentially leak carbon monoxide, gas and AC freon. You must have hit a damn high curb because it's punctured badly in a number of spots. It's going to cost you a grand for the pipe, and another couple hundred to refill the freon that leaked," he explains.

"I guess that means I can't still drive the car without fixing it?" I ask, hope leaking from my every word.

He laughs sympathetically. "You could drive the car as is but if you are leaking gas and freon it will cause you a fortune to refill every time and there is the carbon monoxide threat," he reminds me dashing my hope. "Wish I had better news for ya."

Gah! No AC in the car. I freaking hate the humid Chicago summers. I much preferred the weather back home in Minnesota. Too much heat makes me want to crawl out of my own skin and the bigger, more pressing, problem is the lack of funds in my bank account. Now that I got fired I need to use the little money I have on groceries. It wasn't much to begin with. I had planned on eating ramen noodles at least once a day until I found a new job.

"Sierra, you there?" Holt asks, breaking through my thoughts as to how I will pay him.

"I'm here. I lost my job last night. Not sure how I can pay you right now. I need to find something new," I explain, trying to think of a solution. I don't have one. I need to go job hunting ASAP.

"Ah! Gotcha. Well, you're more than welcome to pick your car up or you can leave it with me. I've got space on the lot. If you think you'll have the money soon?"

"Please keep the car there this weekend and let me see what I can do," I say, hoping to buy some time. One of the reasons I got the car to begin with was that I hated the hot weather and needed my AC blasting all the time.

"You have a nice day," Holt says.

"You, too," I answer and end the call. At least he's keeping the car with him. Getting stuck in a hot car with city traffic in this humidity would be a nightmare.

My forehead is dripping sweat as I near campus and rush to make it to my class on time. It's good I only have one class on Thursdays.

My mind keeps going back to the station where I was an

assistant on set for the evening and late-night news. I was basically everyone's gopher. I didn't mind the job so much when Sloane worked there, but since she's been gone it has completely sucked. Still, I needed the job to pay my rent, car, bills, and food.

After getting fired, I was driving home when an asshole cut me off and I ran up a curb. They say bad things happen in threes; I'm just waiting for the shoe to drop on number three.

After class, I head back outside and my cell rings. Sloane's name lights up my screen.

"Hello."

"Sierra, good, hope I caught you after class," she says, speaking quickly.

"You did. What's up?" I stop walking back to my apartment and wait to hear what she has to say. I don't like walking on the street and talking on my phone. It's a distraction. Bad things can happen when distracted. Poor Sloane got mugged last year, and a girl from school was hit by a bus last week while she was texting at her stop.

"Nothing, it's just I'm having these crazy nightmares. Last night I dreamt that all the bridesmaids and groomsmen forgot to come to the rehearsal dinner. Only my mom and dad showed, and well . . . you know they're divorced, and things were very awkward. I woke startled in a cold sweat," she says, sounding a little frantic.

"You know I would never forget to come," I assure her.

"Did you ask the station for the weekend off?" she asks.

"Kind of." I wince.

"What does that mean?" she says, her voice shooting up several octaves.

"Hon, relax, take a breath. Sheesh, I've never heard you this worked up before," I say.

"I've never gotten married before," she counters.

"Everything will be perfect. I have all the time in the world to help you with whatever you need. Stay calm. You only get married once," I say, even though I am not sure I believe in marriage myself. Mom left Dad for a younger man. Dad remarried Maria, Nils's mom, and they split, too. True everlasting love just doesn't exist.

"You're right. I know you're right but after everything that happened with my parents, and my mom, well, you know she's a sex guru now. It's all a lot to digest," she says.

I answer in the only way a good friend should. "You aren't your mom, and Oli isn't your dad. Look at everything you've been through together. How many years you spent loving him and he you. You two were meant to be," I say, proud of my little speech.

"You are so right," she says, taking several deep breaths. "Okay, now tell me why you have all this time on your hands. What happened? Don't think because I am getting married you can put one past me."

I laugh. "I got fired." I should be crying, not laughing, but why cry over something I can't control?

"Shit, Sierra," she huffs.

"Cutbacks at the station. I was clearly dispensable. And I got into a little fender bender, so my car is in the shop. When it rains, it pours. But I don't want to burden you with my problems."

"You're never a burden. Let me think of something."

"Okay," I reply .

"Do you need a ride to the rehearsal dinner? I can ask . . ." She pauses.

I think I know who she was going to say. Nils Karlsson.

"I'm just going to Uber." I may be tight on cash right now, but I'd rather Uber than be stuck in a car with Nils.

"Okay, sweets. I better go," Sloane says.

"Yup. See you tonight. Everything will be perfect," I say.

"Yesss." She sighs.

"Bye."

"Bye."

I press the End button.

Sloane promised me I wouldn't have to walk down the aisle with Nils. I won't even have to sit with him. I told her the story about what happened between us back in Minnesota. She's convinced he isn't the same guy. She thinks I should try to be friends with him because he's best friends with her future husband, Oli, and it would help if we all got along, but I see the social media feeds. Nils is still the same guy: a player among women, a hot-headed fighter on the ice. Something runs hot in that man's blood and it always leads to trouble. He side-railed my life seven years ago. I don't feel like getting back on that tightrope and walking a line that I know will lead me to fall. Yes, that boy is hotter than hell, but he's a big asshole, too. I've learned first-hand what Nils Karlsson is all about, and I am not having anything to do with him.

I take the bus to Aunt Becca's. She's the reason I moved to this city to begin with. When Mom left, Dad shut down; then he met Nils's mom, Maria, and felt it would be better if they had privacy. He didn't want to deal with an awkward teenage girl who was abandoned by her mother. Aunt Becca took me in, and I went to high school here in the city. It was a far cry from my quiet suburban life back in Minneapolis, but Aunt Becca was cool and supportive.

By the time I reach her apartment, I'm tired and sticky from all this humid weather.

"What's wrong, Sierra? I know that look," she says, as I sit at her kitchen table trying to hide my glum mood. She places a glass of sweet tea in front of me and eyes me closely.

"Sloane's getting married this weekend," I begin. I don't have it in me to tell her I got fired from my job just yet. She'll want to offer me money and she doesn't have much, so I need to figure things out on my own.

"Aren't you happy for her?" she asks quizzically. She knows Sloane is one of my bestest friends.

"I'm very happy for her but her fiancé, Oli, is very good friends with Nils. He's a groomsman at the wedding and I'm going to be seeing him tonight. I don't know why he still makes me so nervous," I explain. Aunt Becca knows why I needed to come back to Chicago. Seven years ago, when I showed up on her doorstep with tear-filled eyes, she embraced me like a daughter.

"Didn't you tell me Oli is a really good guy?"

"Yes," I confirm, unsure where she is going with that question. "So what? Nils isn't."

"A person's friends say a lot about who they are. If you think Oli is a good guy then maybe he is friends with Nils because of certain positive traits Nils possesses," she explains.

Uh-uh. No way. I'm not buying that argument.

I pull my cell out of my jeans and scroll to a video that came up on my social media feed this morning. "I would believe that ... but look at this. What does this say?"

She reaches for her glasses on the counter and takes my phone out of my hand. I watch her press the replay button and my blood runs cold. With her glasses on, her hazel eyes look big and round.

"Hashtag big stick," she says, reading the caption above the video. Her cheeks flush. "Holy smokes, Sierra. That boy can move."

My jaw drops. "Is that all you have to say? This video is totally gross. He's a compulsive megalomaniac," I sputter.

"Why are you getting so upset?"

I throw my hands up in the air. "When I walked away from Minnesota seven years ago, I never expected to see him again. He ruined my life," I say, knowing I sound overly dramatic but not caring either way.

"Oh, honey, your life is just fine. Yes, he may have made some bad choices that had an impact on you, but I think it's only made you stronger. Besides, if you'd stayed in Minnesota, you would've studied something your dad wanted you to. You know how he is with wanting to control everyone and everything."

I bury my head in my hands. "You're right. I'm lucky." My

dad pays my tuition for a private university. He pays because he feels guilty about what happened with Nils, considering it was his idea. When I left, he could have completely cut me off, but he didn't and for that I am grateful.

Aunt Becca sighs. "Look, I get it. It's never fun bumping into an ex—or a fake ex. The fact that you have friends in common just adds to how much it sucks, but when life throws you lemons you make lemonade. You don't cower and run," she says, pressing her lips together in a sympathetic smile.

"Make lemonade, huh?" I smile and stand from the table to give her a hug. "Thanks, Aunt Becca.

"Anytime, sweets. Now come sit down," she says, waving me back over to the kitchen table. "I just got a whole shipment of stones in; we need to make magic."

The kitchen table is covered in exotic looking gems and wires. While I was living here, she taught me to make custom jewelry for her souvenir shop.

I take a seat at the table and we get to work. If anything, I find designing jewelry relaxes me.

"You'll be fine," she says, looking at me over her glasses.

I hope she's right because the rehearsal dinner is tonight, and my heart is already beating a mile a minute.

CHAPTER THREE

N ils

I GOT RELEASED ON BAIL. I'M BEING CHARGED WITH PUBLIC misconduct, since there isn't enough evidence for assault. The women I was with didn't say anything negative about me because they are apparently die-hard fans. Matt told the police that the guy jumped me first and smashed my face in. The bruises forming around my eye and cheek are proof enough. My attorney thinks I'll likely get off with one-year probation or community service. I head home to shower after spending the night in a crusty cell.

As I leave the bathroom, my cell rings. I'm not in the fucking mood to speak to anyone, but one of my best friends' name lights up the screen, so I answer.

"Hey man."

"Where are you? There is a fucking shit storm going down after what you pulled last night," Oli says. I texted him on my way home that I was released on bail.

"I needed to shower. I'll be there soon." My body aches and my head is pounding.

"You better get here fast. Coach knows what went down. It's all over the internet." His voice is taut and clipped.

What? The internet? How? My stomach sinks.

"Hmm?"

"There's a video circulating of you fucking some random chick . . . in a bathroom," Oli booms. My world stills as his words process. Fuck, I thought she may have gotten a picture. All I cared about was getting off. I was too drunk to care. A video? Fuck me. Adrenaline spikes in my veins, causing me to feel dizzy. I grab the wall. This is even worse than I thought. Those chicks from the bar set me up. I don't remember seeing them before. The usual bunnies hang out at the clubs we usually do.

"Karlsson, why would you pull shit like that? Weren't you out with Matt?" The mention of my teammate causes remorse to blanket me like a sheet of armor. Fuck, I feel sick. My stomach churns in a bad way.

"I just wanted to get laid, not cause a shit storm," I say.

"Look at your damn phone then get the hell down to the arena. We have practice. I just wanted to warn you that Coach has been talking to the senior managers for the past half hour. You're in big shit," he says.

I've finally done it. I've fucked up so bad that they are going to boot my ass from the team. After all my hard work. I will be a loser like my father.

"Thanks for the warning. I owe you." I sigh.

"Yeah, man. This is way over the top, even for you. Fuck, Nils, my rehearsal dinner is tonight. You're a fucking grooms-man. My wedding is two days' away. This is not the kind of drama I need right now," Oli continues. "As for the team . . . we haven't even started the season. We need to make our mark in a positive way."

"You're right." I rake fingers through my hair, defeat sitting heavy on my chest. "I'm going to get ready and head over. I'll apologize. I'll smooth it over and I will definitely be at your rehearsal dinner tonight. You know I'll be there for you, right?" I ask, my chest feeling tight. Oli has been a good friend, and I don't have many friends.

"Nils, I don't think you get how much shit you're in. Just get down here," Oli says flatly.

I head downstairs and make a protein shake, and head to the arena.

~

"KARLSSON," COACH'S ANGRY VOICE BOOMS AND STOPS ME IN my tracks.

I turn.

"Get in my office now!" He snarls. His face is red, his lips are pinched, and his brows are furrowed. He may actually have steam puffing from his nostrils.

I don't think I've fucked up this badly, ever.

I enter his office. Mike Wilson, one of the senior managers, is sitting in a chair. Daria Jacks, one of the media relations advisors, sits in the chair next to him.

Fucking hell.

"You've really messed shit up, Karlsson," Mike's eyes narrow to slits as he stares me down. "Public fucking misconduct."

"I'm sorry. I didn't know they knew who I was," my voice is wobbly and strident. "I haven't been accused. The defense attorney is going to try to strike a deal with the DA."

"I'm disappointed, Karlsson," Coach says. "We've given you chance after chance because you bring it on the ice, but fuck . . . you get into too many damn fights. Having you sitting in a penalty box isn't worth our while. And now, with this latest stunt . . ." Coach swipes a hand over his mouth.

I've never seen him like this—fuming, disappointed, and maybe even defeated. He's been more than a coach to me. He's been a father figure.

"Coach, I'm sorry. It won't—"

"Karlsson, we're thinking of terminating your contract," Mike says point-blank as he stands.

My heart skips a beat.

The middle-aged man stands and puts his hands in his pockets as he paces back and forth. His thick brows are drawn tight. He looks like he's contemplating the end of the world. That being my professional career.

"You're a liability to the team. Your teammates are beginning to settle down. Some already have. They are having babies and that's a good thing. It creates a nice wholesome image for the Blackhawks. You're throwing away a career that other guys would die for. You just don't appreciate what you have, and if you're accused, you can be suspended from the NHL," Mike goes on.

Fuck, he's right. I don't know how to stop the stupid shit I do.

"I fucked up. I'll do better. No more drinking. No more women. Please don't terminate my contract. One more chance. My attorney is hoping I get off with some community service." I'm clearly not beneath begging as my heart pounds in my chest. "Please, Coach. Hockey is all I have," I plead, knowing how pathetic I sound. The guys on the team have become my family. I spend holidays with Oli, Myles, and Dave. If I get fired, what will I do? I know the guys won't end our friendship, but if I'm not their team mate it won't be the same, and what would I do with my life?

Panic beats hot and heavy inside me. Coach's lips pinch together, he can't even look me in the eyes. He stares at Mike and some sort of understanding passes between them.

Daria, the media relations advisor, stands. "You need a new image, Nils, a complete makeover," she says, waving her manicured nails in my face. Her long dark hair sways down her back as she speaks animatedly.

"I agree," I say, without knowing what she wants.

She laughs and shakes her head. "You need to stop drinking.

You need to stop going to clubs. You need to lay low. Get a girlfriend and settle down." She says it like that's an easy thing to do. I can't imagine how that's going to happen. I've never wanted something serious with a woman.

Wait. That's a lie. I fucked up my chances at settling down with the only girl I ever wanted. *Sierra.* I always fuck up; it's expected of me.

"Will do. No drinking and find a chick," I agree. Even though I'm not sure how this is going to go down.

"Just a minute here, Karlsson," Mike holds up a hand. "If we agree to this, you're on probation. One fuck up and you're out." He points his thumb towards the door. "Do you understand? That means no fighting on the ice and no fuckups off the ice. We want you to attend anger management with a therapist approved by one of our MDs."

Fuck, they have me by the nuts.

"Okay, Mike." I grind my jaw as my anger rises. I want to punch him in the face.

"I mean it, Nils. You're a liability. We aren't going to keep you around unless you can prove your worth. And I don't need to tell you the consequences if you do get terminated," he says. I know . . . I won't find a job with another team. I'll be considered too high-risk, and that's if I don't get suspended by the NHL.

"Deal." I nod.

Coach walks over and shakes my hand. "Now get your ass ready for practice."

I stand to leave.

"Nils," Daria calls after me.

I turn. She saunters over to me in her tight, little black dress that clings to her body like a glove. "I'll be sticking around to watch you. Get moving on the relationship front. We need to clean up your social media image ASAP," she says assuredly, but her cheeks flush. Why is she flushing? We've spoken before. "I'm thinking some quiet nights in with a lady. Take some couple shots show the public your budding romance, be consistent and for goodness sakes show commitment. Oh!" she presses her pointer finger to her lips then points it at me. "Please make sure you have a really good story about how you met the girl and what made you fall for each other. We need to go hardcore if we are going to make this work." She gives me an assured nod.

Is she for fucking real?

Is she offering herself up for the job? Not only is she not my type, but I'm not messing with someone who works for the team. Her eyes drop to my junk. *What the fuck?* I have the urge to cup myself just to keep her from checking me out. *This is fucking weird.*

"Sure thing. Get a girlfriend and post about all kinds of cheesy shit on social media." I force a smile.

She lifts her gaze from my crotch. "Good. Glad you're paying attention."

How am I supposed to find a girl to fall in love with so easily?

"Of course." I nod. My job is on the fucking line.

"You have yourself a good day." She turns away. Okay, so I had that wrong. She wasn't offering herself up as a sacrificial lamb.

"Yeah, you too," I mutter. I head to the locker room to get ready for practice.

After practice, Matt comes up to me and asks me how I am doing. He tells me Coach gave him shit and took him off babysitting duty. I tell him the managers put me on probation and want me to find a chick to settle down with.

"It should be easy man," he says, clearly reading my distress over the situation.

"I don't attract women that want to settle down. Women with dollar signs in their eyes are after me, or the ones that want to score with an NHL player," I say, as we make our way back to the locker rooms.

"It's a tough life, Karlsson," he claps me on the back. I was hoping for some better advice from him.

I'm taking off my gear next to my locker when Oli walks over to me with Myles, his best friend and soon to be brother-in-law.

"What happened with Coach?" Oli asks.

"I've got to tone shit down. I'm on probation. They want me to find a girlfriend." I scoff.

"Okay, well you're coming to the rehearsal dinner tonight, right?" he asks, for the tenth time.

"Yeah, man. Told you I wouldn't miss it," I say, with my brows pinched.

Myles laughs, chuckling so hard his shoulders vibrate. I glare at him.

"He's nervous." He points his thumb at Oli. "He's meeting Sloane's mother tonight for the first time. He wants everything to go over smoothly. Sloane's been on edge and Quinn hasn't been sleeping through the night," Myles explains, talking about Oli's six-month-old daughter.

"Ah! Got it," I say, as if I now understand why Oli is acting like a loon. Who cares if he's meeting his future mother-in-law?

"Sloane has some friends coming tonight. They are bridesmaids; you'll be walking with one of them. Maybe you can meet someone tonight," Oli suggests, as if it's no big deal to meet a girl and settle down. He has clearly forgotten all about his days as a bachelor. I don't think I even know how to be in a relationship.

"Don't worry, man." Myles claps me on the shoulder. He must have read my distress.

"Yeah okay." I nod. I have to meet a woman and go for therapy. No problem at all.

It should be as simple as a power play.

CHAPTER FOUR

S ierra

SINCE MOM LEFT WHEN I WAS LITTLE, I ALWAYS PICTURED myself having a different mom and dad. A picture-perfect couple who fell in love in the most romantic way possible and built a life together.

My fantasy doesn't exist. I've basically given up on love, which is an ironic thing to think as I stand at the entrance to the hall where Sloane and Oli will exchange vows this weekend.

Walking into a party alone is my pet peeve, but it seems to be a consistent pattern with me. My high school persona of "loner with no friends or boyfriend" seems to follow me wherever I go.

I smooth out the jumpsuit my roommate, Sunny, lent me. It's a fitted royal blue number with a cut-out exposing my back. I figured it would be perfect for a rehearsal dinner.

Sloane is one of the few friends I've made since moving back to Chicago from Minnesota. She's marrying her long-time crush and the love of her life, Oliver Russell, forward for the Chicago

Blackhawks. Most of the team will be here tonight because they are groomsmen.

Hanging around famous hockey players makes me anxious. More like one specific hockey player makes me nervous. Every time Nils and I are in the same place, he tries to talk to me. He thinks his apology will matter. It won't. Whatever happened between us happened long ago. I don't want to dredge up the past, even though seeing him again reminds me that my wounds haven't healed over yet.

I scan the room. This is one heck of a fancy place. The wedding hall has a glass wall that opens to an outdoor garden for the ceremony. A couple of tables are set up in the large hall; I'm assuming they're for tonight's dinner. Only family, bridesmaids, and groomsmen are attending the rehearsal dinner. I'm glad we get to practice walking down the aisle because I've had nightmares two nights in a row about stumbling over my own feet and making a spectacle of myself.

The thought makes my gaze drop to my beige stilettos. *Please keep me steady.*

"Sierra! I'm so glad you're on time." Sloane walks up to me in a form-fitting, off-white dress. Her dark hair is lifted off her neck and she's wearing eye make-up that make her green eyes look slanted and cat like. She only had a baby six months ago and her figure is exactly what it was before she had Quinn. "Everyone is late." She waves her hand in front of her face like she's fanning herself. "Flynn just got the kids into the car and there are only a few guys from the team here. Why can't they be on time? Why?" Her lips tremble and her eyes look glossy.

"Sloane, take it easy." I take a step toward her and rub her back. "Everything is going to be fine. You look beautiful, by the way." I smile. "Where's the little munchkin?" I ask, looking around the room.

"Oli is burping her while walking around. I just finished breastfeeding her because I didn't want to leak all over my dress." Her gaze drops to her boobs. "Phew, I'm good. Quinn is tired and cranky and I'm starting to sweat." She waves her arms beside her as if they are wings flapping in the air while breathing fast.

"Deep breath. You and Oli have got this. You and Oli love each other so much. This is just sealing the deal." I wink, hoping to alleviate her nerves.

She touches her stomach and her mouth turns down in a grimace, as she leans into my ear. "My mom and dad are going to be in the same room together for the first time since my mom left. I know my dad will keep his cool but who knows what can come flying out of Mom's mouth? I don't want her freaking him the hell out. He needs to marry us," she says, exhaling then inhaling quickly.

Sloane's mom is a sex guru and her father is a pastor. This should go over well. Not.

"Sweetie, slow your breathing down before you hyperventilate. Trust me, I've done that to myself and it doesn't feel great. Just introduce me to your mom. I'll keep her busy throughout dinner. Who knows? Maybe she'll have some good dating tips." I wink.

Sloane's eyes widen and she places a hand on my shoulder. "Babe, you need a good man after that cheating ex of yours, but trust me when I say you don't want my mom's help," she sighs.

"You're right," I shrug, remembering when Sloane came to work one day saying that her mom told her she had a hostile vagina because she was still a virgin. It sounded out there in left field.

"Thanks so much," Sloane's voice brings me back to reality and reminds me that I just offered to babysit her mom. "You don't know how much this means to me. Let me just head over to the seating cards and change Mom to your table." She walks away like she's on a mission.

I walk deeper into the hall. Sloane warned me that Nils would be here tonight. She knows why I like to keep my distance. She promised I wouldn't have to walk down the aisle with him, so that's a definite bonus.

A waitress walks by with champagne and I indulge in a glass. I'm not much of a drinker.

"Thank you." I smile to the waitress and sip the very crisp and fruity champagne. Geez, this is good stuff.

Some guys I recognize from the team walk in, and behind them, I spot Nils in a white button down shirt. The cuffs of his sleeves are rolled up, revealing sinewy forearms and tattoos. He even looks hot in his slim fitting dress pants. My blood thrums quickly through my veins. I adjust the neckline of my jumpsuit, ignoring the prickle of sweat down my spine. Sloane was right about the room feeling a little too warm. I quickly turn away, so he won't think I'm ogling him. That would be the last thing I need tonight.

I take a few slow breaths. *Do not go and hyperventilate now. That boy does not need to see that he still has an effect on you.* My inner dialogue is useless. I'm feeling woozy.

"Oh, there she is." Sloane's voice pulls me from my anxious state, reminding me that I need to play babysitter now. I turn around. A woman in her mid-fifties wearing some sort of white smock with wild black hair stands beside her.

"Hi." I smile.

"Mom, this is my friend Sierra. Sierra, this is my mom, Carol," Sloane says.

"Honey, you know I don't go by Carol anymore," her mom says in a chiding tone.

Sloane frowns.

"It's Mata now." Her mom smiles to me.

"Right, Mata," Sloane repeats, like she's chewing on a jaw breaker.

"Pleasure to meet you," I say, offering my hand to shake. She grips my hand and doesn't give it back. Instead, she closes her eyes and hums.

Sloane rolls her eyes. *Why did I offer to babysit this woman all night?*

"You're very uptight," her mom says, staring at me. I swallow my champagne wrong and cough.

"Darn it," Sloane curses as she slaps my back. "You okay? Say something." She smacks me again—hard. My body jolts forward.

"I'm good. I'm good." I hold up my hand to stop Sloane's assault. I take a small sip of the champagne to get rid of the scratch in my throat.

"Okay, phew." Sloane palms her chest.

Out of the corner of my eye, I watch Nils walk by. I swallow hard, feeling butterflies flutter in my belly. I pull my attention away fast, my gaze landing on Mata watching me. Our eyes meet and she nods her head and blinks once.

"Well, if you two are good, I better go find the wedding planner," Sloane says, looking between her mom and me.

"All good," I say my voice too high pitched.

"Me, too," her mom says. She speaks slowly, almost like she is emphasizing each syllable. Mata turns her attention on me, and I gulp, my heart beating rapidly in my chest. "Why don't we take a seat at a table?" she suggests.

"Sure. Would you like some champagne?" I ask, because I know I'll be needing another glass.

"Not yet. Come." She takes me by the shoulder and guides me to our table. I sit beside her ramrod straight. What am I supposed to say to this woman? I have no good conversation starter off the top of my head. I'm not using to dealing with a mother. The only mother figure I had was Nils's mom and that was short lived.

We sit in uncomfortable silence. Flynn walks over to the table and I stand to hug her.

"Hey there, beautiful," she says. Her smile is wide and warm.

"You're looking good, too." I grin and look down at her twins Patty and Kev holding hands.

"Flynn, this is Mata. Sloane's mom," I say.

"Oh. Oh . . ." Flynn's brows draw together as it seems recognition strikes. "Um . . ." She presses her pointer finger to her lips her brows furrowing.

"You look confused dear," Mata says. "Sloane must have mentioned my name was Carol. I go by Mata now," Sloane's mother clarifies. She stands from her seat and envelops Flynn in a hug. "I've heard so much about you." Her eyes drop to Flynn's chest, which is voluptuous, like mine, and then back up to her eyes. She nods and it's totally weird and freaky.

Flynn's blue eyes turn round. "Uh . . . it's very nice to finally meet you. This is going to be a great weekend," she says awkwardly. I'm guessing that in her mind she is looking for a way to run far away from Mata.

"It's lovely that you and my daughter will be sisters now," Mata says slowly. Flynn nods to the rhythm of Mata's slow cadence.

"It's very exciting. I was praying for it for a long time and the day is coming soon," Flynn palms connect and the warmth from her smile touches her blue eyes.

"Yes." Mata nods and sits back down. She places her hands on the table, lacing her fingers together.

Flynn gives me a "what the fuck" look. I shrug. What else can I do?

"Well, I'll catch you both later," Flynn says, taking Kev's hand. She dashes off to the next table where her husband, Myles, is sitting with some guys from the team.

Mata turns to me and watches me carefully. "So, tell me about yourself, Sierra."

"I'm working on my Bachelor of Architecture. This is my last year. I'm originally from Minnesota, but I've been living . . ." Mata shakes her head.

"No, no, no," she says. "Those are simple facts, not who you are."

"Um . . ." I'm just as speechless as Flynn was moments ago.

"You're insecure. Why is that? You're beautiful," Mata says

matter-of-factly, then she just sits and watches me. I'm beginning to think she's very stoned or that I have bigger mommy issues than I imagined.

"I, uh . . ." I adjust my glasses which have slid down my nose.

"It's okay; you don't have to share. We've only just met. Your aura tells me you have trouble achieving orgasm. Why do you think that is?" she asks easily, causing my jaw to drop. My chin tilts down and I stare at her, dumbfounded. I glance over my shoulder to see if anyone heard. There are tables all around us filled with guests but no one seems to be paying us any attention

"Oh, come on. It's just sex. It's a natural part of our being. We were made to get off," she continues. I choke on my saliva and break into a coughing fit.

"Um, maybe we should keep this PG," I say, blushing. I haven't had a chance to meet everyone yet. Sloane has some family visiting from out of town for the wedding. I don't need her entire family to know about my lackluster sex life. I look to my left to see a young boy, who looks no more than a tween, watching us, and judging by his wide smile, I'm guessing he heard the whole conversation. Just great.

"I can whisper," Mata says redirecting my attention to her. "I don't believe in chance. If you were seated next to me, it was for a reason. Let me help you."

Yeah, we were seated together because I told your daughter I would keep you away from your ex-husband. Big mistake. I should make a run for it.

I smile. *Sloane owes me big time.* "Okay. I haven't had the best of luck when it comes to men," I admit quietly. The last thing I need is for Nils to walk by and hear my confession. I sip my champagne.

"I got the feeling your vagina was singular," she says, throwing me off again. I make sure to swallow my champagne down the right tube this time.

"What do you mean by that?" I ask with all seriousness. If you can't beat them, join them.

"You want one man," she states simply.

"Yes, well . . . I'm a monogamous person," I agree. "But still, even when I've been in monogamous relationships, I can't seem to, you know . . ." I shake my head a little, hoping she gets the gist of what I'm saying. I place my hand over my mouth. I hope the entire table hasn't heard about my orgasm issues. "Please, whatever you say next, please whisper."

Mata laughs. "Okay." She looks around the table.

"Hi, Aunt Carol." A woman about my age walks up to Mata's chair.

"My name is Mata now, dear," she explains then waves like she's the queen. Yup. Definitely stoned off her ass. She pulls her attention from the woman and turns back to me. The woman frowns. "I'm hungry. Are you hungry?" Her green eyes are indeed bloodshot. Sloane is not going to like this. On the positive side, the woman is super mellow, so I doubt she will be starting up any fights.

"They've started to bring out appetizers," I say, noticing the table next to ours has been served their soup and salad.

"Oh good." She rubs her hands together just as the waitress places a squash soup in front of us. We eat our soup and I lean into her.

"What did you mean before?" I ask.

"About what?" she says. She's so high.

"About my vagina being singular," I say so quietly, I hope she heard me.

"Right," she says, putting a spoonful of soup in her mouth.

She glances over to the next table, and I follow it. When my gaze lands on Nils, my heart stops. He's watching us, or maybe, watching me. I glance away. I don't need him thinking anything when it comes to me.

When we first saw each other here in Chicago, I'd been invited to Flynn's backyard Fourth of July party. I knew Myles and Nils were on the same team, but I hadn't expected to see him there that day.

That was fifteen months ago. He's tried to talk to me since—
that's the hazard of having friends in common. He wanted to
explain himself about what happened back in Minnesota, but I
didn't want to hear it. He was an angry boy and that angry boy
turned into a man with a bad temper.

I watch the games. I see him getting into fights. Old habits
die hard. I don't want anything to do with him. Except, I follow
the team on Twitter. The sex tape that was posted was totally
gross. Then someone zeroed in on his goods and now there is a
pic of his dick circulating with the hashtag: bigstick. I can't help
that my curiosity has been piqued. A big stick could probably
lead to a hell of a lot of orgasms, but I don't truly know that to
be the case. I've never had one.

"I may be high right now, but I am a perceptive woman,"
Mata says pulling me from my thoughts. "You ogled him before.
I watched your blood pressure rise. He's got his eyes on you and
he looks flushed. If you two get together, I'm pretty sure he will
make you orgasm," she says so definitively. The thought of Nils
making me orgasm makes my skin burn. I hate to have this kind
of reaction because I know what an asshole he is.

"He's my stepbrother," I mutter quietly. Or, my ex-step-
brother. Nonetheless, my inappropriate thoughts are just that—
completely unacceptable.

"Really? So, you two grew up together?" she asks curiously.

"Not exactly."

"Care to elaborate?" She persists.

"His mom married my dad. She came from Sweden and
married my father my freshman year of high school. They didn't
want me around and so I moved to Chicago to live with my aunt
on my mom's side, but then my aunt got sick. It was hard for her
to keep me around. I went back home my freshman year of
college," I say as my pointer finger circles the top of my champagne glass. Memories of that year bombard my mind. Nils and
me hanging out in the library where I tutored him. Him coming
by my dorm room looking sexier than any guy ever should.

There were always girls around vying for his attention but when we hung out together they seemed to have melted into the background. He did a better job than I thought he would as my fake boyfriend.

"And?" Mata's voice breaks me free from my reverie.

"Sorry," I shake my head. "Where was I?"

"Freshman year of college," she says, surprising me.

"Right." I nod. I don't want to get into those details. "My dad is a professor at the college back home and he really wanted me to attend the U of M. Nils came to Minnesota the year before from Sweden. He was attending the same college as me, but he lived in a dorm for the hockey players. We'd only known each other a few months when things imploded," I say.

"Give me more details," she insists, her eyes gleaming with curiosity.

"I'm not really comfortable sharing our past. Besides, he isn't a nice person. There is no way he can be it for me," I say with total honesty.

"Fair enough. Maybe I'm wrong." She shrugs.

What the hell. Seriously? That is her intuitive guru advice?

After dinner, we practice walking down the aisle. Flynn is the maid of honor and Myles is the best man, so they walk together with the twins between them. Then comes Dave and Kelsey.

"Okay, doll. You walk to the center and meet your beau," the wedding planner gives me a nudge. I look up to see Nils standing across from me.

You've got to be kidding me.

This is the third bad thing. The fucking shoe just dropped.

I don't want to cause a scene. Sloane is feeling nervous enough as it is.

I bite my lip and walk toward him. When we reach the center of the aisle, I am supposed to link hands with him. Nils takes my arm and laces it with his.

"You're looking good, sis." He smirks.

"I'm not your sis," I bite back. My father separated from his mother last year. He didn't do it legally, though, because she didn't get her papers yet and he didn't want to ruin her chances. Dad can be a jerk, but I guess there's a heart in his chest.

"I wouldn't know. Haven't spoken to Mom in years," he says, surprising me. His words hit home. I haven't spoken to my own mom since eighth grade.

"Sorry." I find myself apologizing. I don't know what for.

"It's good to see you." He raises his brows; his gaze sweeps over my body.

My insides shake from nerves but that's not all. I find Nils attractive-- still.

"Wish I could say the same," I answer dryly. It's bitchy, but what he did to me was the lowest of the low and I don't want to give off the vibe that I think he's fucking gorgeous.

"About that. I really want to . . ." He trails off when we reach the bride and groom and we have to separate to different sides. His jaw pulses as he continues to watch me. I try to ignore his eyes on me and focus on the wedding planner as she instructs Sloane and Oli on what to do.

After the rehearsal, there is a dessert table set-up. Sloane's mother has taken a pile of cakes, so I figure she'll be busy for a while. Besides, I don't see that woman starting anything with anyone right now. She looks too burnt out.

"Hey, can we talk a minute?" Nils catches me putting some fruit on a plate.

"I don't think that's a good idea," I answer curtly.

"I just want to say I'm sorry," he says, surprising me. *When did he grow a conscience?*

"It's a little late," I answer. The reality is, I should have never put myself in the position I did. I knew he was toxic, and I went against my better judgement. Yet, I became a stronger person thanks to him. What doesn't kill you makes you stronger. I have Nils to thank for the harsh lesson.

"Look, we have friends in common. I just want to set things straight between us. I'm not the same guy I used to be." He swipes a hand over his mouth. "I'm a stupid asshole. I seriously don't know what's wrong with me," he whispers, and I get the feeling he's being sincere, so I give him my attention. "I didn't mean to fuck things up that night," he says, and my stomach twists into horrible, tight knots. "I really didn't. I don't know. I always seem to drink too much and then I do stupid shit I don't mean, and I hurt people I care about." He stares me straight in the eyes. His royal blues cut me deep. I feel a sincerity from him I've never felt before. It makes me curious.

Wait! Did he just say he cares about me? Don't tell me he's high, too?

"Why apologize now?" I ask. I'm no longer the young girl with poor self-esteem. I see my worth.

"Maybe I'm growing up and realizing my mistakes," he says. I notice how much better his English is even though I shouldn't care.

"And I would believe that if I hadn't seen the video of you piss-drunk and fucking those girls in the bathroom last night. Saw it twice, Facebook and Twitter. Real classy." I smirk.

He has the decency to wince.

A part of me feels bad for being so harsh. Maybe the sting of his betrayal still hurts even though it's been years.

I walk away and head straight to the ladies' room, needing space, and just like years ago, I don't turn back.

CHAPTER FIVE

Nils

"WHOA." MYLES CLAPS ME ON THE BACK. "WHAT DID YOU DO now?" He tilts his chin to Sierra and then looks my way. I watch as she stalks away. Her curvy hips sway in that outfit she's wearing. It's a little on the conservative side but with Sierra it usually is. Still, my dick gets a little too excited at the sight of her.

I rub my temples. "I don't know, man. I guess being myself has that affect."

She leaves the wedding hall and I wonder if she's coming back.

"Hey, did you even hear what I said?" Myles waves a hand in front of my face to get my attention.

Her raven hair sways down her back and I can't peel my eyes away.

"Sorry. What were you saying?" I drag my gaze from Sierra to Myles and will myself to stop thinking of her.

Myles smirks as if he's privy to some secret. "I was saying

that she could be a good option for cleaning up your image. She looks like a sexy librarian."

"Hey, who are you calling sexy?" Flynn arches a brow at her husband.

I chuckle. "Busted."

"F-you," he says and looks around the room, probably for his kids.

"They're hanging with Sloane and Quinn," Flynn says, crossing her arms over her chest. "Don't try to distract me. Who looks like a sexy librarian?"

As big and badass as Myles is on the ice, he is a wuss when it comes to his wife. The guy is totally pussy whipped. It's pathetic.

"I was actually suggesting Sierra would be a good option for Nils. The senior managers are riding his case about finding a serious girlfriend and cleaning up his image," Myles explains. "I was simply suggesting Sierra has that good-girl vibe." Myles is trying to dig himself out, but it seems he's just getting into a deeper hole.

I should feel embarrassed about Flynn knowing about the sex tape, but I can't say that her husband was much better before she came to town and tamed his ass.

"She's a really nice girl, but isn't there history between you guys?" Flynn narrows her eyes on me.

"Yeah, there is." I rub at the scruff on my chin.

Fuck. Sierra must have told her the story, which means she told Sloane, too. For some reason, I get the vibe Myles and Oli aren't in the know. I prefer it that way. It's one thing to play the field and another to be a total asshole. I was definitely the latter to Sierra.

Myles gives me a questioning look.

"It was a long time ago. I was a jerk. I just tried apologizing to her, but it didn't go over well," I explain.

"Man, I don't know what happened between you two, but I know that look. I saw your face as you watched her leaving and you didn't even hear what I was saying."

"Cut that shit out. I'm not pining for her or anything. She's just a blast from the past. I was wrapping my head around seeing her again is all."

"Right," Myles says.

"What's going on?" Oli walks over and asks.

"I think Sierra is a good option for Nils," Myles says to him.

"Fuck yeah. Totally man." Oli gives me a fist pump. I leave him hanging.

"No, not happening. Trust me," I say. No way am I explaining what happened and why.

"I don't know. You were pretty mean to her but maybe it could work," Flynn says.

My eyebrows raise. "Are you kidding me?"

"Look you need to stop doing stupid shit. What you pulled last night was gross and you seriously need to get yourself tested." She cringes, and I do, too.

"I just got tested. Clean as a whistle." Leave it to Flynn to say what's on her mind.

"But honestly, I don't think you're a cruel guy. You're a good friend to us. You care for your teammates on and off the ice. You just need to tone the anger down and stop being so douchie."

"Gee, thanks." My lips twist with mock offense. "I'm headed for anger management therapy."

"That could be a good thing, man," Oli says. "It's not something I advertise but I did therapy when I was trying to win Sloane over. I had issues and she was slipping between my fingers."

"What?" Flynn asks, her eyes widening and her mouth falling open. She's Oli's twin sister and probably thought she knew everything about his life.

He looks to his sister and shrugs with a guilty look on his face.

"Thanks, man. I'm kind of hoping to deal with some shit from the past," I admit. I was always an angry kid and had a temper. Playing hockey was a good way to relieve tension.

"Of course." Oli shrugs. "You need to clean up your act. None of us want to see you booted from the team. You got a lot of good years ahead of you in the NHL. Don't go fucking it up."

"Truth," I agree, nodding. I just hope my attorney will convince the DA not to press charges.

"You had to see how he was checking her out," Myles says to Flynn, his lips tugged up at the corners. Asshole is enjoying this.

"Really?" she says excitedly.

For fuck's sake.

"I can hear you. You know?" I stare between them and Flynn giggles. They may have a point. I've always had the hots for Sierra. I've just burned that bridge down. There's no way I could build a new one.

"Man, she's had a rough week. Sloane said she got fired from her job and smashed her car, so don't do anything to upset her," Oli says.

"Sorry to hear that, but I don't want her," I reassure him, feeling like I need to make a better argument to convince this crowd. "I just feel . . . I don't know . . . guilty?"

"Amen. That is a start, " Flynn chimes.

Myles gives her a quizzical look.

"What?" she says innocently. "I know what he did. You don't."

"Whatever he did is in the past," Oli answers his sister. "If he wants her today, then I was going to suggest volunteering at the AMHA offices. Sierra volunteers there, and if you're looking to clean up your image, it's a really good place to start. See? Two birds, one stone." Oli shakes his head. "I swear I hate that expression."

I laugh. "Wait. What is AMHA?"

"America's Mental Health Association. I hung out there for a day when I was trying to get into Sloane's good graces, and here we are," Oli says with a wide smile.

"Yeah, man, thanks for the tip. It's not a bad idea to volunteer, but I sure as hell am not trying to get into Sierra's good graces. I don't want to end up at my own rehearsal dinner," I say, looking at my three friends who are each in a relationship and very much in love. I get the feeling they are not understanding where I am coming from.

"Karlsson, just get your image cleaned up." Myles claps me on the back. "Don't worry about falling for someone, because when it happens, you'll have no control anyway. Peace." He takes Flynn's hand and presses a kiss to her lips. "Let's go find our kids."

Oli shrugs. "He's right. I'm damn happy." He smiles wide. "I'm going to find my future wife." He turns and walks away.

I'm left standing alone by the dessert table. I turn my head and a woman with wild hair is piling cake onto a plate. Sierra was sitting beside her. I think she's Sloane's long-lost mom or something. She reaches into her shirt and pulls out a joint. My eyes grow wide. She lifts it in the air. "Wanna share?"

"Uh . . . no thanks." My voice is a little high pitched. I dash away from her like the place is on fire. I don't need any more bad press or rumors being spread.

I head over to sit beside Matt. "I'm really sorry about last night."

"No worries. I told you I needed a night out. My bad judgement is on me," he says.

"Thanks, man."

"So, what are you going to do about your situation? Do you think you'll be charged?" he asks.

"My attorney is optimistic, and I've got some ideas up my sleeve to clean shit up." I press my lips together the weight of my actions feel heavy on my shoulders. I reach for a bottle of whiskey on the table, then pull my hand away. "I have some bad habits to break."

Matt laughs and shakes his head. "I'm not babysitting you anymore. You're on your own."

"Don't I know it." I quickly glance at the next table and notice Sierra is seated beside the wild-haired woman again. Sierra's lips are moving and the woman's hands are flailing animat-edly. Sierra pushes her red-framed glasses up her nose. It reminds me of a time when she used to tutor me in college. She would explain something and her glasses would slide down her nose. She would push them back up, and I would stare at her pretty hazel eyes. Sometimes, she would catch me watching her, but she never called me on it. There wasn't anything to call me on anyway. She was just different for me, interesting.

She turns her head and our eyes lock. I quickly look around the room hoping to seem nonchalant but something tells me I've failed terribly. *Why am I drawn to her like a moth to a flame?* What is it about her? And why the hell didn't she come to me if she needed help with money? Holy shit, that's it. I get up and walk over to her table. This may be the dumbest idea ever, and she may slap me in the face, but it's a no brainer. Now I just need to convince Sierra of that.

CHAPTER SIX

S ierra

I GLANCE OVER TO MATA AGAIN. HER EYES ARE BLOODSHOT, her pupils are dilated and she looks spacey. "Are you okay?"

Her head lolls as she turns to face me. "Totally. Just smoked another joint. Feeling good."

Nils walks toward us. *Shit!* What does he want now?

He stops behind my chair and leans forward. "Can I talk to you for a minute?"

"Uh, sorry. I'm just hanging with Mata here," I answer, even though we clearly aren't conversing since Mata looks like she's staring into space.

"I'm good. Go ahead." She turns to look at me, her chin tilted down, her face lingering too close to mine.

Just great. She chooses now to talk.

"Okay for a minute," I say, pinching my lips.

Nils smiles, his full lips tilting at the corners. His eyes are clear blue, like the sky on a sunny day. He holds my chair out for me then extends a hand for me to go first. I'm surprised he's such a gentleman. The Nils I remember was all brute force.

I walk a few feet away from the table and stop. I look at him expectantly.

"Maybe we can go out to the lobby to speak," he suggests.

"Okay." I shrug. My hands tremble. I hate that he makes me feel so nervous. I still can't believe he apologized, or said he cared about me. Why does that cause excitement to bubble inside me? I feel like a traitor to myself.

He walks beside me, and when we reach the corridor where there is a couch and coffee table he pauses, and stares at my face intently. It's unnerving. "I've got a proposition."

I snort-chuckle. "You've got to be kidding me?"

"Just hear me out," he says, tucking his hands into the front pocket of his pants.

"Why do I feel like I need to take a seat for this?" I take a seat on the couch. Nils sits, too, keeping a cushion space between us.

He watches me like I'm a wild animal getting ready to run, or maybe it's just my mind jumping to conclusions.

"I'm not going to sugarcoat it," he begins, and I shift in my seat. "I messed up with that sex tape and now I'm on probation with the team. I may be accused of public misconduct, which means I could face suspension from the NHL. I need to clean up my act."

"I'm sorry to hear that, but I don't know what you want from me," I retort.

"The senior managers want me to find a girlfriend and settle down to clean up my image. There is no way I can find a girlfriend so fast. You would be perfect. I want you to be my fake girlfriend." His blue eyes gleam, his lip quirks on one side and his nose slightly scrunches.

"You've got to be freaking kidding me." I shoot to my feet. "We tried this before and it worked out terribly." I place my arm on the arm rest and stand. I take one step.

"I'll pay you," he says loudly, stopping me from taking another step. I stare into his eyes. "I'll pay you," he repeats. "You can treat it like a job. I messed up in the past, but I've learned from my mistakes. I don't plan on having a repeat, and honestly —you would be perfect, Sierra. You are beautiful and smart. My fans would eat it up." He continues waving his hand in the air. "Just picture the headlines . . . badass Nils Karlsson gets tamed by architectural student Sierra Cole."

"How do you know what I do?" My brows pinch together.

"I asked Sloane." He shrugs with a cocky smirk.

"Why not just find a girl you like, Nils? Wouldn't that make more sense?" I cross my arms over my chest.

"No, it wouldn't. I don't meet the right women. Honestly, the women I meet in bars or clubs are puck bunnies. They treat me like I'm a piece of meat. They don't have feelings. They have dollar signs in their eyes when they see me. I haven't been a saint, but this really does make sense, Sierra," he says, looking at me with puppy-dog eyes.

For crying out loud. Why does he have to be so adorable and persuasive? And damn, the way my name rolls off his tongue is pure seduction on its own.

"I see your hesitation, and I don't want to sound like a jerk, but I heard you lost your job." He scrunches his face.

I want to tell him to fuck off, but then I wonder how much he would be willing to pay me.

"How much would you pay?" I ask, trying to sound nonchalant.

"I'll give you two grand a month. Hopefully, we can pull it off for at least three—maybe four—months. Enough time to get Coach off my back and this horrible sex tape forgotten." He sighs.

"Three grand a month, and no kissing this time," I counter.

His right brow arches and his blue eyes gleam. I can't believe I've agreed to do this, but I've lost my income and messed up my car, and that kind of money is sounding super appealing right now. It could be the answer to all my problems.

"Yes to the three grand, but we'll need to kiss. I have to post pics of me and you on all my social media sites," he explains. "That part can't be negotiable."

"Fine, but just closed-mouth kisses and make them quick. No lingering," I demand.

He chuckles and shakes his head. "I gotta say, this negotiation is very different from last time."

"I'm not the same broken girl," I say.

"I never thought you were broken," he answers softly. "If anything, I was an idiot."

His words cause a tumultuous wave to rise inside me. "We keep this professional, Nils. Seriously, there have to be boundaries. I have my schoolwork to do," I explain.

"Four dates a week, and you come to some home games," he says.

"Three dates a week and yes to the home games." I smile. After all, I love hockey.

He laughs. "When did you become a ball-breaker?"

"When I realized you have to be tough in this world or you get walked all over," I answer.

Darkness clouds his eyes. He nods, showing me he understands my meaning.

"Tomorrow is our first date. I'll pick you up around noon," he says.

"It's Friday. I have a class in the morning and need to get some work done," I answer. I had planned to do some job hunting, but now I can put it off for a little bit.

"I have practice in the morning. Maybe we can start with lunch? Give me your cell number and address," he says.

I don't move. He's being a domineering a-hole assuming I'll clear my schedule for him.

I cock my brow. "I said I was busy."

"You've got to be kidding me. You're my employee," he argues, rightfully so.

He has agreed to give me way more money that I could have made working part time.

"Now please give me your cell number and address; that's basic info," he says.

"You haven't paid me yet." I raise my brows and stare him down.

His lips quirk on one side. "Give me your email address. I'm wiring the first payment now."

Holy shit. Butterflies swim in my stomach.

I give him my email and he types some stuff on his phone. Within minutes, I get a notification on my screen that a transfer has been sent. This. Is. Happening. Inside, I am squealing. I won't need to look for a job right away. I can pay to have my car fixed. This is gold.

I get to work transferring the funds to my account.

I look up to Nils, unable to hide my smile. I actually feel like kissing him I am so excited, but I keep my cool.

"Now give me your phone number and address, and please, do not tell anyone about this business deal. The last thing I need is more bad press," he says.

"So, you want me to act like your girlfriend at the wedding this weekend? Our friends will know it isn't real," I say.

"We aren't going to act like we are totally in love. Things have to progress. We can start with some dates before we make it official and I make you my girl," he answers. His words cause my blood to warm.

His girl.

But would he even know how to treat a woman? The man is volatile.

"I see your mind running off with you. If you're thinking I don't know what to do, I do. I was there when Myles fell for Flynn and Oli fell for Sloane. I can imitate what they did," he says.

"Okay, if you think you can, that's fine. I don't mind helping you out with some tips. I love chocolate and flowers." I wink playfully.

"Got it." He nods.

"I was joking," I say.

"Well, it's still good to know," he says, and his words cause my tummy to clench as I think of a clean-shaven Nils picking me up for a date with chocolate and flowers. *Oh, no.* I cannot be thinking of him in that way. *This is a job, Sierra.*

"Okay, so what now?" I ask.

"Just don't go falling in love with me." He raises and lowers his brows.

I snort. "Not in this lifetime."

"Goodnight." He stands and looks me in the eyes. With his close proximity and the spicy scent of his cologne, my breath catches.

"Good night, Nils." I step on my tip toes and lean up to press a kiss to his cheek. It's a bold move for me, but I want him to see that I am up to the task and that he doesn't affect me at all.

When I pull away from him, I can't read what he's thinking, but he definitely seems surprised.

I head back to the hall. Most of the guests have left.

I take my phone and open the Uber app. Nils is still standing beside me. "I can give you a ride home. This way I can see where you live. And I still want your phone number," he says.

"A ride would be great. Thanks," I say. Then I give him my number.

I say good night to Sloane, Oli, and Flynn. Nils and I head out together. Sloane looks at me like I've grown two heads, and Flynn looks just as confused, but I am grateful they don't call me on it.

I follow Nils to his SUV and get into the passenger seat. The spicy scent that wafted my way when I kissed his cheek is all over his car. He smells so good, big trouble because I realize I'm attracted to Nils.

CHAPTER SEVEN

Nils

"The DA is dropping the charges." My lawyer's voice comes through the phone.

"YESSS!" I shout rubbing a hand over my mouth. "Thank you so much." I just stepped out of the shower and I have a white towel wrapped around my waist but it doesn't stop me from placing the phone on the counter and flossing.

"Nils, are you there?" His voice is loud enough to be heard without it on speaker.

I pick the phone back up. "Yes, sorry. It's just such a relief." I breathe easy for the first time in days.

"Stay out of trouble now," he says.

"Will do."

We end the call and I scream at the top of my lungs. What a fucking close call. I could have had a criminal record. I'm still on probation with the team, but as it stands now, I won't get suspended from the NHL. Which means, I'm staying on the straight and narrow.

I call Daria, since she is keeping tabs on me and reports back to the managers. Coach cancelled practice this morning in honor of Oli's upcoming nuptials.

"Hello." She sounds chipper.

"Hey, it's Nils." I rub the scruff on my chin.

"You being good?" she asks, sounding too cheerful for first thing in the morning.

"I've been staying out of trouble. I got my eyes on a potential woman," I answer.

"Good. You aren't the first professional athlete to fuck up, and you won't be the last," she says.

"I wish there was some device to erase my memory or the memory of everyone who's seen that awful video." I sigh.

"It's bad, but not terrible. Puck bunny enthusiasm is way up, which isn't a good thing. We don't want you hooking up, but you're being considered a superhero among men. The comments on Twitter are freaking hilarious," she says. I wince. I may get around, but having everyone in the state of Illinois seeing my junk is downright invasive.

"Just great," I say dryly.

"Aw, come on. All I'm saying is that it's not going to be that hard to change the public's perception of you as long as you're committed to doing this right," she says.

"Actually, that's the reason for my call. I want to volunteer my time to the AMHA. If I'm going to do good deeds, I might as well start by helping people. Right?" I say. It's a win–win. Volunteering will clean up my image and I can even play it up that Sierra has made me into a better man.

"Music to my ears," she singsongs. "I'll give them a call and try to set something up."

"Thanks, Daria." I say.

"No worries. Don't forget your first anger-management session is this morning. And I'd like to hear more about the potential girlfriend candidate. Hopefully she isn't a bunny." She laughs.

"I'm getting ready for the anger-management appointment now. And the woman I'm interested in is definitely not a bunny. She's an architectural student I met last night at Oli's rehearsal dinner. I gave her a ride home. It was all PG; you'd approve," I say.

"Good. You're a catch. Honestly. What that video shows is that you are able to hit it home, even intoxicated. And . . . I can't believe I'm going to say this." It sounds like she is muttering to herself. "That big stick is going to work for you. Even the good girls like those."

I choke on the saliva that's stuck in my throat. "Are you fucking kidding me?"

"No, I kid you not. Go check out Hockey Hot Spot on Twitter and read the tweets. Hashtag 'bigstick' has gone viral. Nobody gives a shit about you being a fumbling ass. What they care about is that the legends are true," she says.

"So, you're saying my dick is all over the internet?" I ask dumbfounded. It was one thing having an out of focus sex tape circulating.

"People used the sex tape to zero in. I know that can be kind of embarrassing, but you should really be proud. You must have good genes," she says.

My genes fucking suck. I don't want to be anything like my father.

"You better head out for your anger-management session. You can't be late. Keep me posted on your new friend. Maybe meet up for coffee with her or make some romantic gesture," she suggests.

I rub at the scruff on my jaw, not liking the news about my dick going viral. Some things should remain private. I have myself to blame. "I'll think of something. You have yourself a good day."

"You too, big stick." She giggles into the phone.

For fuck's sake. I end the call.

I head out to my Jeep and blast music, but I'm just not feeling like myself. Sierra enters my mind. She looked so sexy in that pant-thing she was wearing last night. The way she pushes those thick-framed glasses of hers up her tiny button nose always gives me a hard-on. I need to adjust myself. I don't understand my attraction to her. She isn't my type, she's too good and pure for me and yet I want her. I hate the way she watched me with such skepticism. Her hazel eyes glancing at me as if I was a bomb ready to detonate. I've given her good reason to fear my wishy-washy asshole personality before, but she needs to know that was in the past.

I find a parking spot in front of the building of my new therapist's office. I get out of the car and open the door to the building.

I check in with the receptionist. The waiting area is pretty busy and I hate the idea of being recognized in a place like this even though I made a public statement about being sorry for my actions saying I would seek treatment. My therapist is a young guy named Fisher. He asks me a slew of personal questions about my childhood. Talking about my alcoholic father and abandonment isn't as easy as I thought it would be and I find myself answering one word answers.

"Tell me something that makes you angry," he says, holding a pen in his hand and a notepad on his lap.

"When idiots piss me off," I answer.

He chuckles. "What makes you feel passionate?"

"Uh sex?" I say.

"Other than sex," he grins and begins to write a whole lot of shit on his notepad.

"I don't know."

"What makes you happy?" he asks.

What is with these weird fucking questions?

I smile. "When my team wins a game."

He smiles, too, and writes on his damn paper.

"What are you writing there? Am I incurable?" I ask tilting my chin to his paper.

He shakes his head. "You're just fine. These are just get to know you questions."

He then goes on to tell me he is a little unconventional. He'd like to have phone conversations instead of regular in office sessions, and then he says, "I'm sure you're a busy guy, but we need to understand what gets your anger going."

"Fair enough. Phone calls would be great." I smile, knowing I need to play nice.

"So, unless you have any questions for me, we will be meeting in a couple weeks." He waits, staring at me with an easy smile.

"No questions," I say twiddling my thumbs in my lap.

He stands and walks to the door with a slight bounce in his step. "It was great meeting you. I'll be getting in touch soon." He waits for me to leave. Wasn't I supposed to have a full hour to figure out my life? I guess the movies have it wrong.

I stand, taking the cue.

"Bye, Fisher," I say, and leave feeling very awkward. I walk to my SUV. Inside my car, I check my phone to see I have a few text messages from Daria. She's arranged for me to head over to the AMHA after my appointment. I need to find a woman named Zelda.

I enter the AMHA into my GPS. It's close to ten a.m. Traffic is light and I make it there in no time. Scoring street parking is an added bonus.

I enter the building and walk over to an information desk. The woman instructs me to head up to the third floor. I walk around, asking people where I can find a woman named Zelda. The young woman I ask smiles at me and points to the left, where I see an office door with the name *Zelda Ealson* on it. A middle-aged woman sits behind her desk. I give a little knock on the door to alert her I'm here.

She stands and walks up to me with a professional smile. "Mr. Karlsson. So happy you could make it. Pleasure to meet you."

I shake her hand. "Pleasure is all mine." I smile back.

"Have a seat." She points to the one chair opposite her desk. The office is small, and I have little leg space.

"It's pretty cramped in here, sorry." She frowns. "We have two floors in the building, but it isn't quite enough space. We're only a local office," she explains. "Daria mentioned you are interested in doing some volunteer work?"

"Yes, I am," I say, feeling very out of my element. "What can I do?" I've never been about giving back. I learned early in life that I needed to fend for myself to get by. I made my way into the NHL where I make a shit-ton of money, but I've never thought about helping others.

"I have a few ideas up my sleeve." She smiles with a blush. The sex tape comes to mind. I curse inwardly, hoping she hasn't seen it too, or the many dick pics that are apparently circulating social media.

"Sure. I'm all ears," I answer with a friendly smile.

"Great. Firstly, we are going to be running a local fundraiser. We have a lot of departments here, one of them being our youth helpline. We have volunteers who come in to run the line, but we also have paid social workers who monitor the high-risk calls . . . threats of suicide, drug addiction, and overdose," she explains.

I cringe. As fucked up as I was as a kid, I never turned to those things or had those thoughts. Just the thought alone makes my blood turn cold. I was high-risk for trouble, but hockey kept me grounded. What about all the youth out there who have no one and don't have something to fall back on?

"What can I do? I want to help," I say, and I mean every word. Something about the conversation sparks a ripple of emotion in me. Passion?

Fisher had asked me what I was passionate about. I had nothing. After talking with Zelda for a few minutes, I'm feeling overwhelmed, excited, and sympathetic. Fucking passionate that no kid should have to feel bad or low.

"Good. For starters, I'm hoping you can be the face of the campaign. A representative of sorts. I read a little into your background." She winces. "Coming from a small town. Teaching yourself how to skate. Stealing your first pair of skates." She blushes about the last part and looks apologetic.

"It's fine. I haven't kept that part of my life a secret. I want to help you out here. This is important to me." The words feel weird and stringy on my tongue, but they are truthful.

"We can get a photographer in for some shots. We will also be running some televised commercials during mental health week. We have a few large sponsors—Spartan, KTV, LGM and Fido Foods. It would be great to have you speak on the commercials."

"I haven't experienced mental health issues," I say. At least, I don't think I have. "Unless anger falls under that category."

I laugh. Zelda looks at me sympathetically.

"You've struggled, but that isn't the focus. The focus here is an open dialogue about mental illness," she says.

Something hits me. The fucking sex tape. She doesn't know about it or else she wouldn't want me to be her face. I bite my lip. How do I say this politely? My manners stink.

"Ma'am, with all due respect, I don't think I'm the right person. I've recently caused a shit storm . . . um . . . I mean, I've been viewed negatively in the media and—"

"Nils—may I call you Nils?"

"Yeah." I sit back uncomfortably, rubbing my sweaty hands up and down my jeans.

"I've seen it," she says flatly. My cheeks burn. *Fuck me.* Is there someone in the city who hasn't seen the fucking tape? "I don't care about it. You're here now. You clearly want to clean your rep. We've all made mistakes, you're living with consequences, and trying to make yourself better,"

"How much did Daria reveal?" I ask. My jaw is wound so tight I think it may snap.

"She begged," Zelda says, and her lips tug down. The corners of her eyes crease sympathetically. "It doesn't matter. We need you like you need us. You can help us bring in the needed funds to make a real difference."

"I'm in." I nod.

"I appreciate that. I also thought it would be good if you could run some of the high-school-age programming we have. A lot of the kids in the city look up to you as a hockey player. Having you as a mental health advocate will get their attention. Your teammate, Oli, conducted a few lessons and it went very well. The feedback we got from the teachers was phenomenal."

"Sign me up." I pat her desk for effect.

"Great. I'll need you to train for a few hours. One of the volunteers who has been with us for many years is in right now. I'd like to introduce you and maybe you can get started today?"

"My schedule is clear for the next couple of hours." I grin. Before I leave her office, I write the AMHA a healthy cheque, knowing it's going to a good cause. Zelda is speechless for a few moments before she thanks me profusely.

I follow her down a long narrow hall. She reaches a cubicle.

"Sierra?" She begins. My heart picks up pace at the mention of her name. "I have Nils Karlsson from the Chicago Black-hawks here. He'll be volunteering with the high-school-age groups and will need to be trained." *Sierra will be training me. This is so perfect.* I can't see her since Zelda is blocking my view of her small cubicle. "He also just made a very generous contribution to the AMHA. Please let Stacey know to include his name in the weekly newsletter." She says giving me her back.

"Um . . . no, please. I . . . uh, don't want to be mentioned. Can we keep that part quiet?" I ask.

Zelda turns to me with her brows raised and a crease in her forehead. "Do you not want to be recognized for your charity work? I thought you were trying to clean up your image?"

"Um . . . not that way. I, uh . . . did that because I thought it was important. Not because . . ." I'm at a loss of words.

"Fair enough, Mr. Karlsson. It was a pleasure meeting you. Sierra will take it from here. I'll be in touch about the ad campaigns." Zelda gives me a firm handshake and leaves. I take a step into the cubicle to see Sierra.

She stands abruptly from her desk and adjust her glasses. Her dark hair is in a messy bun on her head. She's wearing a heather grey T-shirt and a pair of light blue jeans, and she looks completely adorable. I remember the first night I saw her at our parents' house. She was cute then. I had to remind myself repeatedly that she was my stepsister. I wasn't supposed to look at her that way.

"Nils. I wasn't expecting to see you here?" Her tone is accusatory, as if I'm here to destroy her life. Her brows are furrowed and she's looking at me like she doesn't know what my angle is.

"I'm here because I want to volunteer," I say. "Besides, shouldn't you pretend to be excited to see me, fake girlfriend?"

She rolls her eyes. "You're incorrigible."

"I'm not. I'm reforming myself," I say.

She laughs.

"What? I can't take back the past, but I can change who I am going forward."

"If you say so." She shrugs and pinches her lips together staring at me as if I'm feeding her a line. I don't know why but what she thinks of me matters, and I don't like that she thinks poorly of me—not that I can blame her.

"Follow me. We train in the School Intake Center. It's much roomier than my little cubicle," she explains, and she turns back to her desk and picks up a folder. My eyes drop to her ass. Shit. I should not have looked. Her ass is perfect. It's round and her hips are curved. Sexy AF.

"Lead the way." I extend my hand for her to go first. I don't let my eyes drop to her ass again. She can't be anything more than my fake girlfriend.

For the rest of the afternoon, I listen as Sierra goes through the basics. When we get to the gritty details about bullying and teen suicide, my blood runs cold and I shiver. She pauses to watch me for a moment, and something softens in her gaze, she gulps as her cheeks flush, but then she blinks twice and it gets locked down just as quickly as her emotions rise.

"Okay, let's see how much you've learned. Stand up front and give me a mock lesson," she says.

"Do I look like I can be a teacher or role model?" My self-doubt is running pretty high right now. *How did I volunteer for this?*

Her gaze sweeps over me from top to bottom causing nerves to build inside me. I want to know what she thinks of me. I want her to see me as something more than a jock who gets around. "Hey, I'm not the one who hired you. Zelda thinks you'd be good for the kids and she's rarely wrong." Her words do little to stifle my insecurities, but I can't hold it against her after the way I treated her back in college.

"I don't know anything about kids or how to be a role model," I admit. Fuck. She must really love hearing those words from my mouth. I'm waiting for her to just rub it in.

"No, I guess you don't, but I just taught you what to say. You basically need to follow a script like you would for a commercial," she says, referencing a commercial I did a couple years back.

"You saw it?" I ask, my tone laced with surprise.

She laughs. "Don't flatter yourself. Everyone saw it."

Fuck. This girl really hates me.

I get up and walk to the front of the classroom, where there are whiteboards and blackboards. I say everything she taught me. I'm here to do better, but I know I need to change the way I think of myself before I can change the way others see me.

Sierra watches me intently. She definitely isn't the same girl who left Minnesota seven years ago with her head bowed. She's more confident, and surer of herself. That makes me happy.

Fisher's words ring in my head. *"What makes you happy?"*

Seeing Sierra doing well makes me happy.

I finish my lesson, and then I ask, "How did I do?" I wait nervously because suddenly, her opinion fucking matters.

"Honestly?" she asks. "You nailed it." Her brows are creased. I feel just as surprised.

"I nailed it?" I ask, needing the confirmation.

"Yeah." She nods narrowing her eyes on me like she's

processing some sort of complicated math equation. "Send me
your schedule and I'll pencil you in on the days we have high
school kids coming through," she says, and she leaves the office.

"Sierra, wait!" I call after her and she turns to me. I don't
know what I wanted to say; I just don't want her to leave. "Uh . .
. sorry. Nothing. I'll send you my schedule," I mutter like an
idiot.

She nods.

"Actually, wait." I look at the watch on my wrist. It's noon.
"We have a lunch date," I smirk. "You aren't canceling on me."
She flinches and it takes me a second to catch on. "You said you
had an early morning class today. I'm guessing that was bullshit."

"Volunteering. . . class . . . it's basically the same thing," she
answers with a cool bravado like I just didn't catch her in a lie.

"I need you to take us seriously. I'm paying you enough, that's
for sure," I say.

Her shoulders deflate. "You're right. I'm sorry. I will take this
job very seriously." Her words sting me for some unknown
reason.

"When are you finished here?"

She looks at her watch. "I'm done. Will this be considered
one of our dates?"

Fuck. I've never had to work hard for a girl to go out with
me. She's throwing me off my game. She really doesn't want to
spend time with me.

"Yes," I answer, gritting my teeth. Does she realize that most
women trip over my feet?

"Okay, then. Let me just grab my purse from my cubicle," she
says, and she saunters away.

I watch her hips sway, feeling very confused. It shouldn't
matter to me what she thinks of me. Only, it does.

I shouldn't be attracted to her, but I am.

CHAPTER EIGHT

S ierra

NILS DRIVES DOWN THE STREET FROM THE AMHA. "WHAT are you in the mood to eat?"

"I'm not picky. I don't like hamburgers, though," I say.

"Are you kidding me? Who doesn't eat hamburgers?"

"Me," I say flatly.

"Okay, no hamburgers." He gives me a side glance and his lips purse together. "Can you at least pretend to like me? I mean, for the sake of our deal. If you keep rolling your eyes and acting all irritated, this will never work."

I exhale. "You're right. I'm sorry. I'm being a bad employee. I'll do better," I say, giving him a full-wattage smile. *He sure is paying me enough to pretend to like him.*

He shakes his head, but he's smiling.

"You're different," I say to him.

"Different how?"

"I mean different than you were back in Minnesota as a freshman in college. You were angry back then. You had a chip on your shoulder; you were always scowling. Getting a smile out of you was nearly impossible," I say. Shoot! Now he's going to think I wanted his smiles back then.

"I had come from Hogsby the year before. My life wasn't a walk in the park. I was angry with my mom for leaving me to fend for myself against my father so long. I was adjusting to a new country and language, dealing with a new family, and the pressure to make it in hockey. I had nothing back then, Sierra," he says.

My heart sinks. I never thought about it that way. All I saw was a popular guy with his nose in the air who thought he was too good to be with me.

"Your rough edges have smoothed out somewhat," I say. I don't have a better compliment. Sitting here in the car with him makes me nervous. He's still the hot, popular guy who's now a famous hockey player, and I'm still a bookish nerd.

"To a certain extent. I still get angry and make bad choices but the steam that burns inside me has fizzled a bit. I have a stable job I can't lose and good friends. I have to thank Oli for suggesting the AMHA," he says. "Have you been volunteering there long?"

"Two years," I say. "They do a lot of important work. When I went to high school here in the city there were a lot of at-risk kids. Some of them just needed a fighting chance at a better life. The AMHA helps keep some of them on track."

"It must have been hard for you to go from a rich suburban life in Minnesota to a city school," he says. We stop at a red light and he turns his head to look at me. I meet his gaze and something uneasy shifts inside me. His blue eyes, clear and intense, make my heart gallop.

"It was hard, but I'm sure you know how controlling my dad can be. He was on my case about everything. He just didn't understand me, and I was angry, too." I think of a scowling Nils back in college and my heart softens. "I was angry at my mom for leaving me behind. I was angry that my father didn't know how to deal with me. I was angry that he sent me to Chicago my freshman year because he didn't want me around. I was this awkward kid and it was hard to make friends," I say, surprised that I revealed so much to him. Although maybe I shouldn't be. Back in Minnesota, when he became my fake boyfriend, I spent a lot of time with him having deep conversations just like this. Something about our pasts felt similar and we had this connection. This feeling of being left behind that we could both relate to. Well, we did . . . until he pulled a one-eighty and became the biggest jerk on the planet.

"Neither of us had it easy," he says.

I remember the many times Dad and I fought about course selections, or what he wanted me to do with my life. Dad didn't want me to be my own person. He wanted everything his way or the highway. Sometimes I didn't blame Mom for leaving. I just wished she had taken me with her.

"At least you coming out here allowed you to take architecture and you're definitely not shy anymore."

I sink into my seat and watch the traffic.

"No, I guess I've worked past it. I still have my self-doubt." A blush creeps up my cheeks.

"I have my self-doubt, too," he says softly, staring out to the traffic on the road. His words hit me in the chest. He seems so self-assured. He gives me a quick side glance. "Don't look so shocked."

"Sorry," I smile impishly. "The first time I left for Chicago was because my father told me it would be better for me there. Then, in college when things imploded between us, I wanted to leave. Dear old dad didn't fight me because he saw an opportunity to get rid of me all over again He had your mom and they wanted their privacy."

A loud hiss escapes him, and he mutters something in Swedish. "I thought you chose to leave," he says. "I didn't know he told you to go the first time or the second time. That makes me so angry." He grits his teeth, and his knuckles whiten as he grips the steering wheel.

"My mother didn't bring me from Sweden for the same reason. She wanted time alone with your dad. I learned that reality my senior year of high school when I arrived," he explains.

My stomach knots.

"I don't like thinking of the past," I say, as I watch his jaw pulse and his hold on the steering wheel tighten. "It makes me feel bad. I tend to focus on the future, and the good things I have in my life. My Aunt Becca taught me that."

He lets out a long breath and it looks like he deflates. "You're right. I just hate that our parents are this way."

"Me, too," I agree.

"Is the Chicken Nest okay for lunch? I need to eat healthy since the season starts in a couple weeks," he asks, changing the subject.

"Yeah, it's fine."

We reach the restaurant and Nils parks the car. We head in and he grabs hold of my hand. I cock a brow and look at him.

"What?" he asks, innocently. "Hand-holding is obvious, Sierra."

I don't argue.

A hostess seats us at a table and Nils orders a half-roasted chicken with baked potato and sour cream. I get the chicken salad.

"No more depressing talk," he says. "Tell me about yourself."

I roll my eyes. "Do we really have to do this?"

"Yes, fake girlfriend, we do. I need to know everything about you." He grins wide. He's so handsome and . . .troubled. Something inside me softens, and the usual anger I feel towards him deflates somewhat. When I don't say anything, he repeats himself. "Start talking . . . tell me about yourself."

He *is* paying me, so I should act professionally. "I go to the Chicago College of Architecture. I'm in my fifth year. I live off campus," I say. "I have a roommate named Sunny. She goes to University of Chicago. We've been living together for the past three years."

"Tell me what you do for fun," he says.

"Fun? Well, I've been in school, plus I volunteer. I've also had to work to support myself. It doesn't leave too much time for fun." I shrug, and heat claws at my cheeks.

The waitress comes and places our orders in front of us.

"Where did you say you worked?" he asks, then he takes a large bite of his meal. I imagine a guy his size needs to eat a lot.

"I worked for a TV station. It's where I met Sloane," I explain.

He doesn't say anything; he just digs into his meal. "Sorry, I'm starved."

I eat my salad quietly. The silence feels comfortable. Sitting here, chatting with him feels like déjà vu, reminding me of an easier time back in college in Minnesota when he was my fake boyfriend and I was his tutor. At least before things got shot to hell.

"Have you had any recent boyfriends?" he asks. "The only reason I'm asking is because sometimes old flames come out of nowhere and like to make a big deal about knowing someone famous. I'm not saying I'm famous but as a player for the Black-hawks, I'm in the public eye."

"No boyfriend . . . well . . ." I tilt my head from side to side. "There was someone. We dated, and he cheated on me. I can't imagine him being a problem. I've been on dates. Had a more serious boyfriend a couple years ago, an architectural student in my class. We were just very different. We dated a year, but it didn't work out."

"I don't like cheaters," Nils says, throwing me off.

I don't know why but they aren't the words I expect from him.

"I may have gotten around, but I would never cheat. I know we didn't mention anything last night, but I need you to be very discreet if you're going to hook up with someone. I can't ask you to become celibate or anything." He grins mischievously, and I swallow my salad down the wrong tube.

I cough. I sip my water from the straw and take a breath.

"You good?" he asks.

I nod. I'm not sure what else to say. I'm not telling him that I don't get laid on the regular like him.

"Will you be hooking up with women on the side?" I ask. "I honestly didn't consider all this."

"No. I won't be hooking up. I can't afford to make any mistakes. My NHL career is on the line, Sierra," he says.

I repeat the way he says my name with that heavy accent in my head.

Sierra. Sierra. Sierra.

I picture him hovering above me. It doesn't help my case that I saw his dick pic online. Normally I find dick pics gross, but his is beautiful, long and thick. I take another sip of water to cool me down.

"I understand. You don't need to worry about me. I won't be hooking up with people on the side. It isn't my style. You said it yourself; this is serious for you. I always take my job seriously," I assure him.

"I do appreciate it." He smiles, and it's a warm smile that touches his blue eyes and makes me feel tingly all over.

"Of course."

With the table cleared the waitress comes by and asks if we want dessert. Neither of us do, and so she places the bill on the center of the table. Nils insists on paying. He drives me home and stops in front of my apartment.

"Lean over to me," he says. With the car in park his hands are free and I freeze, my eyes getting a deer in the head light look for sure.

His eyes glow with amusement. "Relax, I just want to take a selfie," he says and I release the breath I must have been holding. *Jerk.*

We lean into each other. He shows me the picture to get my approval. Our heads are tilted toward each other. He's photogenic, with his tanned skin and sky-blue eyes. I look like his tutor with my straight hair and glasses.

"I like it," he says.

"Okay, fine," I concede.

He loads it up to Twitter with the caption.

#mynewspecialgirl

Afternoon lunch with a kickass woman.

He presses the tweet button. My heart flutters. His caption is sweet as hell. I remember what Aunt Becca said about him having good traits. Maybe he does. He donated money to the AMHA, he seems like a good friend to his teammates, and he's being sweet with me.

This is really freaking bad because my old crush on him hasn't died. It should've after he acted so shitty, but I guess old habits die hard. Now I need to make sure of one thing . . . I can't allow myself to fall for Nils Karlsson all over again.

CHAPTER NINE

S ierra

I'M LYING IN BED WORKING ON A SKETCH WHEN MY CELL rings. Sloane's name lights up the screen.

"Hey, babe," I answer.

"Oh, good, I'm glad I caught you. I only have a minute because I'm nursing Quinn. I just wanted to say thank you for babysitting Mom last night. You saved me," she says.

"It was nothing. Don't mention it."

"I felt really bad that the wedding planner placed with you Nils. Thanks so much for being so cool about it. After everything that boy did to you—"

"It's fine," I say. I don't want to make her feel guilty when I've agreed to spend time with him anyway.

"Really?" I hear the surprise in her tone.

"Yeah, yeah, totally," I answer, feeling bad about withholding such juicy info from my best friend.

"Okay, cool. I know he can be a little on the wild side, but he is a good guy, Sierra. I want to say something, and please don't hate me for it, but Nils and Oli are really good friends. Is there any way you would be okay hanging out with him some more?" Her voice is shaky and her tone a little high pitched. "I mean, we try not to invite you guys over at the same time. I saw your reaction to him years ago at Flynn's party. I don't want to put you in a bad position. It's just sometimes really hard—"

"To choose sides." I finish the sentence for her. My stomach sinks. I feel like a terrible friend for deceiving her right now. She would definitely keep the secret. Nils asked me not to tell anyone about our arrangement, but I can't hide it from Sloane.

"I need to tell you something."

"Okaaay." She drags out the word, sounding confused.

"I kind of agreed to be Nils's fake girlfriend," I confess, speaking very fast.

"What the . . . of all things holy, what on earth does that mean? Did my mom give you drugs? Are you high?"

"I'm not high. This needs to stay a secret, Sloane. Like, please don't tell anyone. Nils is on probation. Senior managers have threatened to end his contract. He needs to show he's serious and settling down. That he's putting the wild life behind him," I explain.

"And what, you suddenly care what happens to him?" She scoffs. Can't say I blame her.

"He's paying me three G's a month. It's a job."

"I don't understand. He's paying you for sex?" Her words cause me to jolt up in bed.

"No, I'm not going to sleep with him. Geez. It's just for show for a few months so his rep will get cleaned up," I say.

"And then what?"

"Then we break up," I state the obvious.

"This is a little messed up, don't you think? I mean, given your past when he was your fake boyfriend—"

"Don't remind me," I sigh. "This is good, trust me. I lost my job and I need my car fixed."

"Honey, if you need money, I could lend it to you," she says. I hear Quinn beginning to whine in the background.

"I don't want to borrow money. This way, I earn the money myself and help Nils along the way. It makes sense," I say.

"You're okay with this? I mean what he did was cruel. Can you really see yourself spending time with him?"

"Trust me, I've been mulling over the same thing since he asked me. I was angry for a long time, but then my aunt made me realize that if it weren't for Nils's shitty behavior I would have stayed in Minnesota where my dad would be controlling my life. I wouldn't be on the road to becoming an architect," I say, working on my sketch. "There was a reason I moved away from Minnesota. My dad isn't an easy man and I probably wouldn't have been able to afford paying for my degree on my own." My words make me realize what a pushover I was back then. "It was my dad's guilt that got him to support my career choice. Sometimes bad things happen, but they are part of a greater plan," I end my speech.

"You've convinced me babe . . . OMG! Did you see the sex tape?"

"Yes." I blush.

"Your fake boyfriend is equipped to deliver in the bedroom. Are you allowed to have fake sex? Wait, I think real sex would be better. Hashtag big stick, Sierra," she says.

I burst out laughing.

"I don't even know what to say to that," I answer.

"I may be getting married, but I don't live in seclusion. Fuck, he does have a big dick. It's kind of awkward. I don't think I'll ever look at him the same again. I feel kind of bad," she says.

"Why bad? He set himself up for that mess."

"Aw, come on . . . no one wants their private parts exposed for the whole world to see," Sloane says sympathetically.

"Have you read all the comments on those tweets? He's going to have an easier time getting lucky now than he did before, and prior to hashtag big stick, it was a walk in the park for him," I say, twirling a piece of my hair.

"You have a point, but I get the feeling he's down on himself," she says.

"He came by the AMHA today. Made a big donation and volunteered his time. I don't want to be making arguments about Nils being a good guy, but he did seem to care about his role at the AMHA. I'll give him that."

"See? He isn't so bad. He's had a rough go. You know better than anyone what that's like," she says.

"Aw. Now you're hitting below the belt." I scoff. Truth is, she's totally right. Nils and I share a broken past.

"I won't go there. But I'll say that hashtag big stick is no joke." She laughs.

A vision of his dick pic enters my mind and all I can think about is Mata's suggestion that Nils and I would be good together. Thinking about all the orgasms he could deliver with his big stick makes my body heat.

"I can tell you firsthand a big stick can be loads of fun. Why do you think I'm marrying Oli?"

"That is TMI. You love Oli and he loves you. You aren't marrying him for his big stick. And we need to stop talking about it because it is starting to feel too warm in here." I touch my cheeks, they're flaming hot.

She laughs. "My prudish friend."

"I can't argue that," I counter.

"Okay. I'm glad we had time to talk. This weekend is going to be hectic. My dad is staying with us and Mom is checked into a hotel in the city. They're coming to dinner tonight. Do you think you want to come? Your fake boyfriend will be there."

"Do you invite him for every family thing you do?" I ask.

"Yes, hon. I've always wanted to invite you, too, but I knew he was a sore spot for you. Though, now that you two are a fake couple, it totally works," she says, and I ponder her words.

"I'm not sure how to act around the rest of the gang. This thing with Nils is new."

"It will be fine. I wouldn't be surprised if Nils told Oli, Myles, and Dave. They're good guys; they would take his secret to the grave," she says.

"It would be a relief if they knew," I admit.

"Either way, you're in. Right?" she asks, and Quinn's whining becomes louder.

"I'm in. Thanks for including me."

"Mom also really liked you," she adds. *Oh dear. I hope I'm not put on Mata duty again.*

"Your mom is sweet," I say, through clenched teeth.

She scoffs. "Always so polite. Mom was high as a kite at the rehearsal. I'm expecting the same thing tonight. Please don't let her convince you to get high with her."

"You know it isn't my thing," I assure her.

"Right, okay," she answers.

"Bye, babe."

"Bye."

I'm about to hang up when Sloane shouts, "Just try not to think of his big stick too much."

My eyes become round saucers. "You're a terrible person. You know that?"

She knows I'm playing with her, but I don't exactly want to be thinking of Nils and his big stick every time I look at him.

"I'm bad to the bone," she says. "Bye, again."

She ends the call.

She leaves me thinking of a hot Swedish player with a big stick.

CHAPTER TEN

Nils

I'M DRIVING TO THE ARENA WHEN MY PHONE RINGS. I PRESS the answer button on my steering wheel without looking at the number.

"Heellooo," I say.

"Nils, good. I'm glad I caught you. This is Fisher," he says. Just great. It isn't even nine a.m. yet and I have to deal with anger management.

"Hi, Fisher. "

"I was thinking . . ."

I keep my sarcasm to myself. "I'm all ears."

"Coach sent me some of the games from last season. I just wanted to get the gist of what angers you, and why you tend to fight on the ice."

"Okayyyy."

"I also asked Coach if you get along with your teammates and it seems that you do. In fact, he says you're close friends with a lot of them," he continues.

I want to ask him if it's professional of him to check up on me behind my back, but I hold my tongue. "I do get along with them."

"So, you get angry with people from other teams?"

I snicker. "That's usually the case with hockey."

"I understand that, but you fight more than your team mates and it seems according to the footage I've seen that you take the fights a little too far."

He has a point. I get angry and see black. My adrenaline spikes and I lose control. Admitting those words out loud is too hard. "I fight with assholes. It's not me who takes things too far." My words carry no conviction. They are a copout.

"I watched your plays. I've watched you fight. You don't like when other players try to intimidate you. And I get that because no one likes it. But what strikes me as odd is that players on other teams know, and please excuse my analogy, that you are a hot head," he says. *Fucking hell.* "They try to draw reaction penalties out of you and you fall for it every time," he says. Anger builds in my chest, as my blood runs faster through my veins, feeding the anger inside me.

"Look doc. . . " I grit my jaw, trying to stop the expletive words trying to escape me. "I don't need some fucking know it all to tell me I'm a fucking idiot. I know that some players have beef with me. I'm a strong player and it's to their benefit to get me in that penalty box. Problem is that I fucking love the high of a fight. I like defending my teammates, knowing that I can. I don't put up with any shit because I don't have to." I grip the steering wheel in a vise grip and quickly glance in the rearview mirror. My face is beat red.

"You've still got to learn to rein in your anger," he says.

I know that, Einstein. "I'm short-fused. Doesn't take much to set me off."

"Why do you think that is?"

"Um . . . well, my dad has a short temper. Used to get drunk and slap my mom around. He was abusive to me, too. Probably get my short-circuit from him," I say.

"Did he hit you, Nils?" His voice softens.

My jaw is about to snap, it's wound so tight. "Yes," I answer firmly. "Hitting wasn't always enough. He poured boiling water on me once when he was angry, and he put a few cigarettes out on my arm." I laugh it off. Maybe because I am surprised I just said those words out loud. I've never gone into detail about the abuse before.

"Sorry. That sounds terrible," he says softly.

"It was. It's not something I like to talk about or remember," I say curtly, feeling sweaty and anxious.

"Did you ever witness your father hitting your mother?" he asks.

My patience is waning. I've had fucking enough of this conversation. I take a deep intake of breath. My fucking job is on the line. "Many times," I answer, grinding my jaw. My blood boils at the memory.

"And how did it make you feel?"

"Fucking angry," I grit out. "Fuck. It doesn't take a genius to put two and two together." The minute the words leave my mouth, I instantly regret them. "Shit. I'm sorry."

I apologize, not only because my job is on the line, but because I'm not blind to see what he just did there.

"You aren't angry because you got genes from your dad. You're angry because you felt helpless when your dad hit you and your mom."

"If you say so." My harsh grip on the steering wheel loosens and I stretch my neck from side to side. "Shit, doc, this is a little intense for a morning call. I'm driving."

"I'm glad we cracked your code. How about you come to my office early Monday morning and we talk about those feelings some more?"

"My good friend is getting married this weekend. Is it possible we make the appointment for Tuesday instead?"

"You got it. See you then, Nils. Don't be so hard on yourself. We're going to get you under control faster than you think," he says.

His words bring me some relief, like a heavy weight has lifted from my chest. He's a professional and he doesn't think I'm a lost cause.

"Enjoy the wedding," he says.

"Thanks, Fisher. Bye now," I croak.

"Bye."

He ends the call and I head into practice.

As I get ready for dinner at Oli and Sloane's tonight, I remember that I need to call Sierra. She doesn't have my number, and it's not like she would call me anyway. She tolerates me because she needs the money, which makes me feel bad because it was never my intention to take advantage of her bad situation. And maybe a part of me remembered our first fake relationship and I wanted to feel just a small piece of the serenity I felt when we hung out together back in the day.

"Hello," I say.

"Nils," she says, sounding unhappy to hear my voice.

I chuckle. "Don't sound too excited there."

"Sorry. Hi, Nils," she repeats, sounding chipper.

"Okay, cut the crap. You don't like me, I get it. Oli mentioned that you're coming to dinner tonight. Do you need a ride?" I ask.

"That would be great, thank you. My car is spending the weekend at the mechanic."

"No problem. Does an hour work?" I ask.

"I'll be ready," she says. A male voice laughing in the background causes my blood to boil.

"Who is that?" I ask too quickly. *Shit!* I don't need her

thinking I care if she has a guy over. Maybe she decided to hook up on the side and be discreet. My gut churns at the idea.

"It's Sunny's boyfriend. He's over here a lot."

"Right, okay." I rake my fingers through my wet hair. "See you in an hour then."

I stop at the grocery store to pick up chocolate and flowers. Might as well start off as the model fake boyfriend.

Reaching her door, I'm internally laughing at myself. I'm not a chocolate and flowers kind of guy.

A pretty blonde opens the door. Her jaw drops.

"Holy shit," she says, and smacks a hand over her lips.

"What is it, babe?" A guy says from behind the blonde. He makes his way to the door.

"Holy shit," he says. "Nils fucking Karlsson. What an honor." He extends a hand to shake mine.

"Nice to meet you. Sorry, I have my hands full." I smirk.

"I'm Sunny, Sierra's roommate. This is my boyfriend Declan."

"Good to meet you both." I nod.

"Sierra," she shouts. "Nils Karlsson is here."

It's funny how she says my full name.

Sierra walks toward me, and my eyes rake over her body, clad in a tight pair of black jeans and a red loose tank top. It hides the size of her boobs, but I like that it's modest. She pushes her glasses up her nose, and my heart does this funny thing in my chest.

Her warm hazel eyes gleam as she takes in the chocolate and flowers. "Thank you so much. This is so sweet." She bats her lashes and gives me a peck on the cheek. She's a bad actress. I'm wondering if her friend Sunny can tell, too.

She walks into the kitchen wearing a pair of heels, and her ass sways with the movement. I force my eyes back up to a respectable level. A moment later, she walks back to the door.

"All ready," she says, grabbing her purse off a hook at the front entrance.

"You two have fun." Sunny smiles wide. Declan's arm rests on her shoulder.

"I just want to say I'm a huge fan." He waves his other hand in the air.

"Thank you," I smile to him and shake his hand, then Sunny's. "It was nice meeting you. Have a good night."

The door closes, and I offer Sierra my hand. She just looks at it.

"What?" I ask.

"What?" she repeats. "There's no one in the hall watching us." She walks toward the elevator.

I roll my eyes. She's become one sassy chick. I'm digging it.

"Your roommate seems nice," I say. *Can you maybe show the same enthusiasm she just did toward me?*

She nods. "Sunny is great. She's younger but totally responsible and easy to live with."

"Cool."

We head out to my Tesla Roadster.

"Whoa. Nice ride, Nils," she says, sounding impressed.

"Thanks, it's my contribution to saving the environment and I do enjoy driving her." Another indulgence to make myself feel good. Now, I wonder if dumping so much cash into a car was smart. What if my hockey career ends next week?

I open the passenger door for her and she gets in the car. I walk around the car and get in.

I pull into traffic. "Did you give her a name?" she asks, pulling me from my thoughts. Her wide grin eases the tension I feel inside.

"No. I'm not into naming cars," I say.

"What are you into then?" she asks. She looks at me like she's genuinely interested.

"Hockey is number one, but that's obvious. I play some golf in the off-season. I ended up switching my major to math after you left."

"You did?"

"My English was shit. Without you helping me, I would have never made it. Math is a universal language; it's straightforward. It makes sense, if you know what I mean?"

"I actually do. I take math courses as part of my Bachelor of Architecture. The calculus always gets me—that and all the computer science courses."

"I can definitely help you with Calculus. At least, I can if I'm in town," I say.

"Right. What happens when you're not in town? Am I still obligated to give you three dates?" she asks. Her words feel like a sword through the heart. Why I want her to really care is beyond me.

"Yes, we can make those dates into phone calls." Since we're stopped at a red light, I take a minute to look at her, my right brow cocked in challenge.

"Fair enough," she agrees. "But what will we talk about? It's not like we are really dating." This woman . . . she frustrates me.

"You should really stop mentioning the fake aspect of our relationship. If the public is going to buy into us as a couple, we need to get to know each other." The light turns green and I drive.

My eyes dart quickly from the road and meet hers. "I told Sloane about our little arrangement," she blurts.

My brows practically hit my forehead. "Seriously? Not cool." I'm just playing with her.

"Shoot, I'm sorry, Nils. I had to tell someone, and I knew I could trust Sloane." Her tone is so apologetic as she squirms in her seat.

I laugh.

"What's so funny?"

"Myles and Oli know too, which means that Flynn knows. We have a lot of people in the know right now. They're like my family and I trust them but please don't tell anyone else."

She punches me in the arm.

"Ow." I use one hand to rub my arm. "Don't you know it's unsafe to hit a person while driving?"

"That's what you get for making me feel bad," she says, and I quickly glance to see her pouty lips turned down. That mouth of hers looks luscious. I fantasize about her sliding over the console and pressing those luscious lips of hers to mine.

"Sorry, babe," I say.

"What in ever-loving hell, Nils? Do not call me babe. I'm not one of your whores." She scoffs, sits back in her seat, and shakes her head repeatedly.

"Sorry. I need a term of endearment. For the record, I know you aren't a whore. Far from it. I respect you, Sierra. I want you to know that," I say, and I watch her shiver for the briefest of moments.

I pull into Oli and Sloane's driveway. I walk around the car to open Sierra's door but she beats me to it and leaves the car. We walk to the door side by side and she rings the doorbell, but no one comes to answer the door.

"Sloane said dinner was tonight, right?" Sierra turns to me and asks.

"Definitely."

After we wait a few minutes, Oli finally comes to the door cradling a crying Quinn. His hair is mussed and he has spit up on his dark shirt.

"Hey. Come in," he says, rocking the baby back and forth.

"Hey." I give him a half bro hug and smile to the crying baby. She looks at me and stops crying. "Hey there, Quinn," I coo. I'm not good at baby stuff but I've watched my friends interact with their kids before, and it seems that making little funny voices works. Oli gives Sierra a peck on the cheek.

"Glad you could make it," he says to her sounding out of breath.

"Thank you." She smiles. "Hi, Quinn." Sierra takes the baby's hand. Quinn smiles at her, too.

Oli's brows furrow and he looks down at his baby girl. "Seriously? You stop crying for them?" he says, and he turns her, so she is upright and facing me.

I take her hand, bounce it up and down. Quinn gives me a giggle. "What can I say? I'm good with the ladies."

"No way my girl is ever going to date a hockey player." Oli scoffs.

"Yeah, man." I nod. "Can't say I blame you on that."

"Follow me," he says. We follow him to the kitchen. They moved to this mansion three months ago, since Oli's apartment was cramped with all the baby toys they'd bought Quinn.

"Oh hey, Nils, Sierra," Sloane says, walking over and giving me a peck on the cheek and Sierra a hug. She dashes back to the stove where she has lots of pots full of bubbling liquids. One of them is boiling over.

"Shit," she curses.

"Baby, we got to stop with that," Oli says.

"Don't start parenting me now. The guests are starting to arrive, and dinner isn't fully cooked," Sloane says. She looks like she is sweating. Her short hair stuck to her face like she just finished a workout.

"Sorry, man. I told her to hire waitresses and order catering, but she refused. Would you mind holding Quinn so I can help out?" Oli asks.

"Um . . . me?" I turn around to see if he meant Sierra. He surely wouldn't want me to hold his cute little baby.

"Nils." His voice is distressed. "Please."

"Oh, okay. Sure, yeah . . ." He passes Quinn, but it's awkward, because where do my hands go?

Oli moves my hands. "Just like that. She should be comfortable. If she gets tired, she likes to be turned around so her head is on your shoulder."

"Ookay." I hold little Quinn facing outward. "What now?"

The doorbell rings.

"I'll get it," Sierra chimes.

I stand off to the side. Oli has a pot in his hand that's boiling over and he's walking it to the sink. I've time-warped onto another planet.

"Maybe take her over to the couch," Oli suggests. "She has a bunch of toys in the family room."

I feel nervous about dropping her. I head over to the family room, where a chair thing, play mat and swing, along with other little toys, takes up most of the floor space. I lean forward and try to place Quinn in the chair that has dolls hanging in an arch above it, but the minute she leaves my arms she begins to wail.

"Okay, okay." I pick her back up and do a rocking dance.

"OMG, you're so adorable. This reminds me of that *Friends* episode where Ross and Rachel sing 'Baby Got Back' to baby Emma," Sierra says, smiling wide her voice too excited. At least she's happy about something. She starts to rap those infamous lyrics while shaking her fine behind.

"You totally sound like Sir Mix-A-Lot." I laugh, her beat and energy are contagious. I find myself moving my hips and shaking my ass.

Mata walks into the family room. "Nice. This is my kind of jive," she says, moving her arms in a wave motion. Both Sierra and I stop dancing. "Oh, don't stop on my account," she says. Suddenly, Quinn starts crying.

"Just sing and dance, Nils," Sierra urges me, doing some rolling thing with her hand and shaking her fine ass. Quinn eats it up. "She loves it. Aren't you a cute baby? You're so cute," Sierra chimes, using a baby voice while dancing in front of Quinn.

"Thanks, you guys." Sloane walks into the family room and wipes away the wisps of hair sticking to her face. "Now I know who to call when I need a babysitter." She pauses, and her finger comes up to her lips. "Wait a sec. Were you just singing 'Baby Got Back' to my baby?"

Sierra and I both freeze.

"They were," Mata answers.

Thanks, lady.

I think Sloane is about to go off on Sierra and me when she

bursts into laughter. "Keep it up. I have more things to take care of in the kitchen," she says, and I release a lungful of air.

Sierra shrugs and starts up her song and dance again.

I never introduced myself to her last night so I figure now is as good a time as any. "Hello. I'm Nils, Oli's friend," I say to Sloane's mom. Oli gave me the lowdown about her transformation from Carol to Mata.

"Nice to meet you." She nods. Dave and Kelsey walk in with their three kids, who are all under the age of six.

"Hey, man. That's a nice look on you." Dave winks.

"I agree." Sierra laughs. "I can see it now. Lots of little Karlssons running around."

Sierra is joking, but suddenly Dave looks between me and her and gets an odd look on his face. He doesn't know about our fake relationship. I feel bad not including him but too many people know as it is.

Kelsey comes up to me and kisses my cheek. "Don't listen to him," she says, ushering her kids toward the toys. She gives Sierra a hug.

Myles and Flynn show up next with their twins.

"Oh, man. I said find a girlfriend, not make a family overnight." Myles chuckles.

"Ha ha. You're too damn funny," I say. I glance over at Sierra. The apples of her cheeks are bright red.

"Damn is a curse word," Flynn whispers to me, and I wince. "The other day, I was on the phone and said 'shit' accidentally," she whispers. "Kev and Patty started a competition of who could say shit more. Then I had to drop them off at pre-school. Who knows what they said there?" She rolls her eyes.

I laugh. I'm about to say, "Shit, that sucks," but think twice.

"Hey, any of you ladies want to take Quinn?" I ask, looking between Kelsey, Flynn, and Sierra. They look to each other and answer 'no' in unison. "Thought so."

"Aw, come on. You look totally adorable. And little Quinny looks happy," Kelsey says.

"I can't argue on both counts." I chuckle. I turn to Dave. "Hey, Dave!" I shout. "Your wife just told me I'm adorable."

He checks to see who is looking at him and then, deciding the coast is clear, he gives me his middle finger. Fuck. I love these guys.

The doorbell rings again. I blow out a breath. My hands are tired from holding Quinn, which is weird, but I guess I'm using muscles I don't normally use.

"I'll get it," Kelsey offers.

I take a seat. Quinn sits in my lap and Dave kneels in front of me, making goo-goo faces and singing some song he must know from his own kids.

"Got to admit I didn't see you as a guy who likes to hang with kids," Sierra says.

"Isn't he sweet?" Kelsey asks. "Quinny is loving attention from Nils."

"Ah, here it is," Mata says, pulling a joint out of her purse. She waves it up in the air. "I'll step out back. Anyone want to join me?"

Sloane's dad, Pastor Carmichael, walks into the family room. "Put that thing away, Carol. This is a room full of kids," he chides her like you would a young child.

Carol—I mean, Mata, stands from the couch and digs into her purse. She pulls out a lighter. "Last call . . . who's in?" She holds the joint up. *Sloane's mom is something else.*

"We're good," Dave says, as if he's speaking for everyone.

"Alright then." She saunters barefoot through the kitchen and out the back door.

"I can't believe she's so liberal about it." Flynn says.

"What was that woman holding, Mommy?" Patty asks.

"Um . . ." Flynn's blue eyes turn wide as saucers and she glances around the room with a dear-in—headlights look on her face.

"She needs that to make her head okay," Myles explains.

Flynn gives him a look that I think says, 'you're dead.'
"Really?"

He lifts his hands in the air. "What did you want me to say?"

Flynn clearly doesn't have an answer.

Myles shouts, "Who wants a piggyback ride?"

All the kids cheer that they do, but of course, Myles chooses
Patty. He's clearly trying to make everyone forget about the
joint.

Sloane comes out of the kitchen with a smile. She looks
exhausted. "Dinner is ready. Let's go to the dining room."

"Ah . . . guys, how do I stand up now?" I ask. I'm still holding
Quinn. Sierra hears my call for help, and I swear it looks like
she's thinking twice about helping me out. I cuss in my head.

"Please." It comes out as a whimper.

"Oh, fine." She walks over to me with open arms. She leans
forward, showing me the slightest bit of cleavage down her
tank top.

"Thank you." I stand, shaking out my stiff arms.

"Here you go." She passes her back to me. Quinn looks up to
me and smiles. Why does she have to be so cute?

"Come, little one." I open my arms to her, and she leans
forward like she actually wants to come to me. It feels nice to be
wanted.

"Well, look at that." Sierra giggles and makes all kind of silly
faces to Quinn. The baby giggles.

Mata walks back into the room. Her eyes are bloodshot. "Oh,
hi." She looks to Sierra.

"Hi, Mata." Sierra waves awkwardly, then she shifts on her
feet. There's something about Sierra that is just so perfect.

"You look nice," Mata says, eyeing Sierra up and down.

"Thank you." Sierra follows her gaze then crosses her arms in
front of her chest.

"We better get to the table," I say to both ladies.

When we enter the dining room, Sloane takes Quinn from

my arms and places her in a high chair. Sierra and I get seated between Mata and Pastor Carmichael.

Mata looks at me, then bursts into giggles.

From across the table, Sloane's eyes turn wide. "You've puffed the magic dragon already? I can't believe you couldn't wait until later." Her tone is incredulous, bleeding the hurt she must be feeling. It makes me think of all the times my own mother didn't think of me and my feelings when she made decisions.

"Where is the magic dragon?" Dave's son, Kayden, asks. *Oh shit. That can't be good. What do you explain to a kid?*

Dave looks to Kelsey and Kelsey shrugs.

"That's just a saying; it doesn't mean anything," he says to his son.

"Mom, I want a magic dragon," Kev says to Flynn.

Sloane sits in her chair and holds her temples.

"Everything is fine," Oli whispers to his future wife.

"Let's start with grace," Sloane's father says, and then he goes on to lead us in prayer.

From there, the brisket gets passed around. The mashed potatoes are the next thing I put on my plate.

"Everything is delicious," I tell Sloane. Oli agrees and so does everyone else.

We all eat a hearty meal, and after dinner, we all pitch in to help Sloane clean up. Oli tells her that since she cooked, she should go relax. The ladies leave to the other room with her, and then it's me and the guys in the kitchen.

"How are things going?" Myles asks me, as I wrap some left-over food.

"Good as they can be," I say.

"You guys make a cute couple," Dave says.

"Ah thanks, man," I answer, the guilt about lying to my friend rises inside me like indigestion.

"Oh, just tell him, Karlsson," Oli says.

"Fine." I give Dave the rundown on my fake relationship.

"But you two seriously have chemistry," Dave says.

"I second that," Oli shrugs.

"I third that," Myles says.

"It would never work. Trust me. She hates me. If I wasn't paying her, she wouldn't want to spend a minute with me," I admit, the words burn as they exit my lips.

Dave snickers. "I'm calling it that you and her are going to be a thing by the end of the month."

"Don't be ridiculous. She and I are like black and white. Saint and devil. Good and bad," I say, running out of analogies.

"Fuck. I get it, man. But, hey, you can clean up your act. We all did. It isn't beneath you," Myles says, clapping me on the back.

"Hear, hear," Oli agrees.

"Thanks, guys. I do appreciate the vote of confidence. My therapist doesn't think I'm a lost cause either, which gives me hope," I say.

"Man, I went through emotional abuse—not physical—but honestly, being with Flynn has mellowed me out. She gives me equilibrium," Myles says.

"It would be nice to feel like my life was stable, but I'm in a fake relationship. I just need to clean my name up and all will be good. I need is hockey and good friends," I say.

"To good friends," Oli says, placing a row of shot glasses and whiskey on the counter.

I pass, because I'm not drinking right now, but the three guys take a shot.

We help Oli set up dessert and call the women and kids, along with Sloane's parents, back to the dining room.

"I'll be back in a minute." Mata turns and walks out the back door with her purse slung on her shoulder.

Sloane fingers grip her scalp and she tugs on her hair.

Sierra walks over to her friend and drapes an arm around her shoulder. "She is who she is. She's an adult. What can you do?"

"I guess you're right," Sloane says solemnly. "It's just that this is my special weekend. Can't she think of my wants and needs for once?" Sloane's eyes fill with tears.

"My mom walked out the door when I was in eighth grade and never looked back. I don't understand why some people act the way they do. I just try to focus on myself and what makes me happy. You have Oli and Quinn, you are an amazing mother. Focus on all the good you have. Stressing over her is a lost cause."

Sloane hugs Sierra and mumbles something.

Her words hit me in the center of my chest. I know all about self-centered moms. Something about Sierra's longing and pain for an absent mother makes me want to hold her in my arms. Soothe her and tell her everything will be okay.

Dave and Myles set more fruit platters and pastries on the table.

"Babe, you did such a nice job," Oli says, laying a juicy one on Sloane. Sloane swats at him and then looks at her dad, who has his head bowed.

"Thank you," Sloane mouths to Oli quietly. Her sadness has vanished and her eyes gleam. The way they look at each other, all gooey-eyed. I've never felt like that about anyone or had them look that way at me.

I pull my attention away from the loving couple and my gaze connects with Sierra's. I swallow hard as warmth floods my heart. Her chest rises and falls fast. *Is she feeling something, too?*

Feeling overwhelmed, I pull my stare and focus on the large dessert selection.

Sloane says she's heading up to put Quinn in her crib, since the baby has her eyes closed in her high chair. Flynn takes Kev and Patty to bed upstairs, too. Kelsey leaves the room to get her kids situated on the couches in the family room.

It leaves me and the guys with Sierra and Sloane's parents at the table. Since Mata walked back into the house, her eyes are small and pupils are dilated and she's smiling to herself. Her ex-husband keeps tugging on the collar of his shirt like he's trying to loosen it and his cheeks are flushed. The guys are just chilling.

"What should we talk about?" Mata asks, looking around the table and breaking the silence.

No one answers.

"Well, how about we discuss ways of causing titillating orgasms without penetration?" Mata says.

I swallow the piece of watermelon I was eating wrong. I cough, and curses ring around the table.

Sloane's father stands. "Carol, what is wrong with you?" His eyes are wide and his tone is chiding.

"Nothing, relax. Maybe you can learn something." She shrugs.

"I'm going to bed." He throws his napkin on the table. "Thank you for hosting a lovely dinner, Oli. Tell my daughter I love her. See you in the morning."

Oli clears his throat. "Sure thing, Pastor Carmichael."

"Good, now that he's gone, we can get to the good stuff." Mata rubs her hands together.

"Nils, why don't we start with you. Your uh . . . penis has been circulating the internet, so we all know what you're packing but it doesn't mean you know how to hit it home," she says.

My jaw drops, and I stare at this woman like she's grown two heads. Beside me, Sierra curses under her breath.

Oli groans loudly and rubs his eyes. I look to him for help. It's his fucking mother-in-law-to-be, but he appears to be stunned into silence.

"Ah, Mata, this is probably not the right setting for this type of conversation." Sierra comes to my rescue.

"I think you're wrong, dear. These men have young, passionate wives. It's my duty to make sure they are doing things right. I took an oath."

For fuck's sake.

"Quinn is asleep. What is going on here?" Sloane walks into the room and stares at us with confusion on her face. I turn to look at the guys and I burst into laughter. Hardcore, tears-spilling-down-my-face laughter.

Oli follows suit and so do Myles and Dave. We are all laughing like idiots and Sloane is smiling, trying to maybe figure out if Mata slipped some of her weed in our food.

Oli stands from the table. "Let's head into the family room." He walks over to his fiancée, drapes an arm over her shoulders, and kisses her on the lips. She sinks into him.

We all follow them into the family room. No one mentions Mata's crazy suggestions. I'm still reeling that she has seen my dick, but what can I do? The damage has been done. Kelsey and Dave get their kids ready to leave, and Myles and Flynn decide to spend the night since their kids are asleep upstairs. It leaves me and Sierra on the couch.

"We should get going," I say, to Sierra. Her head is perched on the arm of the couch.

"Yes, I'm exhausted." She stands and stretcher her arms above her head her back arching like a feline. *What would she look like arching off a bed as I make her come? Nope. Don't think it.*

I turn my attention to Oli and Sloane, "You two have a busy weekend ahead."

"They sure do," Mata cuts in. I pray the woman will keep that trap of hers shut.

We each hug Sloane and Oli and say our goodbyes. Mata leaves at the same time as us.

"Mom, where is your ride?" Sloane asks.

"Oh!" The woman stares in front of her like she was expecting a horse-drawn carriage to materialize.

"I can give her a ride," I offer. So much for getting Sierra alone. *Wait.* Why do I want her alone?

"Thanks, man." Oli pats my shoulder, looking relieved to get rid of his future mother-in-law.

We all leave the house together. If I'm not mistaken, Sierra looks terrified, and the truth is, so am I.

CHAPTER ELEVEN

S ierra

WE REACH THE STOP SIGN AT THE END OF OLI AND SLOANE'S street. Nils raises his chin and looks in his rear-view mirror, then he glances at me.

"She's fast asleep. I don't know where to take her," he says.

I turn to check on her. "That can't be right. We literally just left Oli and Sloane's," I say. But Mata is clearly asleep. Her head hanging on her shoulders, her breaths slow and easy.

"I'll call Oli," he says, and he pulls Oli's number up and presses the talk button. A loud ringing noise vibrates through the car.

"Don't use Bluetooth," I whisper.

He gives me a quizzical look.

"It's better she stays asleep. We don't want to poke the beast." I say, leaning into his ear. He smells fresh and clean, like a rain shower in spring.

"You're right," he says. He transfers the call to his phone and a moment later, he is asking Oli what hotel to drop Mata off at. He ends the call with Oli and plugs a name into his GPS.

I turn around again to make sure Mata is, in fact, sleeping. She still has her head hanging off to the side and her eyes are closed.

"It's good she's out. I was seriously scared what she would come up with here in the car," he says.

"Yeah." I agree. I don't add that I was freaking the hell out. The woman knows I've never orgasmed. She clearly doesn't have a filter. "We shouldn't talk. I don't want to be rude but it's probably safer she stays asleep."

He runs fingers through his hair. "Good idea."

The car is silent for the next twenty minutes as we head back into the city. We pull up to Mata's hotel, which is not too far away from my apartment.

"What do we do now?" Nils asks, looking at me. Mata is dead asleep, hunched over in his back seat.

"Um . . ." I turn to the back seat. "Mata, we're at your hotel." I raise my voice a little.

"You need to be louder," Nils says, watching me with a smirk on those full lips of his.

Right. Okay.

"Mata, wake up. We're here," I say even louder.

She doesn't move. A light snore escapes her.

"I'll get out and give her a shake," Nils says. He's laughing to himself. He cuts the engine and walks around his SUV to the passenger side of the backseat. He opens the door. "The air should get her up."

I can't help but realize all the trouble he's going through to get Mata home. He seems like a good friend to Oli and Sloane. The guy I remember had lots of friends, but none of them seemed close to him.

"Mata. Wake up," he says, and his voice is strong and bold. I jolt from the unexpected firmness.

"Huh, what?" She lifts her head. "Oh, where am I?" She looks to Nils and then to me in the front seat. She sits up and her eyes dart left right left right .

"I gave you a ride to your hotel," Nils explains.

Her eyes drop to his crotch. "Right, you're the friend with the big package."

Adrenaline spikes in my veins as I prepare for impending danger. She will blurt something about me. I just know it. "You can get out here. This is where you're staying. Have a good night," I say slowly, hoping she says goodbye and leaves.

"I don't remember my room number. And where did I put my key?" She sifts through her purse. A minute passes and she looks up to Nils. "Be a doll and come inside with me? I need a new key."

Why on earth does she need his help?

She begins to slowly shift off the seat. Her movements are stilted and off-balance. "Sierra, why don't you come here and give me a hand?" Nils says through gritted teeth and wide eyes. *Shit. Fuck. Shit.* This night is going down the shitter real fast.

"Okay." I practically screech. My tone is so high-pitched. I leave the car and give Mata a hand. Nils takes her purse and I offer her my arm for support.

"I'm sorry. That last glass of wine did me in. Weed and wine don't mix well for me," she says. "It fucks me up really badly."

Then, why did you drink it? I scream in my head.

I snort. Oops.

Nils gives me a look of warning. I press my lips together, hard.

"No worries," I finally say.

"Shit, does she have weed in here?" Nils asks, looking at Mata's purse which he's holding. He drops it on the ground as if it's on fire. "I can't get into any more trouble."

I pick up the purse.

"I'll go to jail for you." I wink. Then I look to make sure there are no cops around.

We walk to the front desk. Mata mumbles her information

and is given a key. I want to say bye to her—NOW. But I get the feeling she needs help to her room.

"Relax, would you?" Nils says to me quietly behind her back.

"Easy for you to say. You clearly aren't fazed by the fact that the whole city of Chicago has seen your private parts," I chide.

He laughs and covers his mouth with his hand. "I can't believe you just said private parts. What, are you in kindergarten?"

I glare at him.

"Ready." Mata waves her key card.

"Did you need us to take you to the elevator?" I ask sweetly.

"No." She pauses, and I let out a breath. "I need you to take me to my room. I'll get lost in this big hotel. I just know it," she says.

How on earth does this woman give lectures all over the world but she can't even make it to her room?

I'm holding my breath again. I want to laugh and cry and run for dear life. A quick glance at Nils and I see his eyes are round saucers.

The elevator door pings, and we enter with her. I hope she is on one of the lower floors. I don't know how much more of her I can take.

"Eleven, please. Or was it thirteen?" she asks, swaying.

"Eleven," Nils clarifies.

I press the button, willing the powers that be to keep this woman's mouth shut.

Nils leans into me and whispers. " Would you relax?" He winks.

Right. Yeah. Relax. Okay.

We make it to the door, and she presses the card against the key car lock. Okay. This is almost over, and I've survived.

"Thanks, kids. You two have a good night." She waves like the queen, just like she did at the rehearsal dinner. She walks through the door and . . . please shut the damn door. She pauses and presses a finger to her lips. FUUUCK.

"You, with the big cock, should help her." She points to me and I shut my eyes. Yup, I'm going down—*timber*. "I don't mean with your big stick; I mean with your hands and mouth. Take it slow and steady. She's never had an orgasm," she says, and my world comes crashing down.

I don't know what is happening. Hands on each of my shoulders grounds me.

"Open your eyes," Nils says, his voice soft and tender.

Why? Why me?

"I can't," I whine. "Is she gone?"

"Yes," he answers.

I open my eyes, pull out of his grasp, and charge down the hallway back to the elevator. He catches up to me.

"Can you wipe your ears clean? I mean, like, erase whatever it is she just said," I plead.

"Okay." He shrugs just like that. No dickish comments. *Nothing.*

He presses the call button for the elevator, and we stand in silence.

"Don't take her seriously," Nils says. "If I took everything people said about me seriously, I'd probably have to be committed." He laughs. The elevator door opens and we step inside.

"Thanks. I appreciate you saying that," I say. *When did he stop being a jerk?*

"Sure." We step off the elevator and walk through the lobby. I just want this night to end.

"Oh! Don't you look like a lovely couple," says a man standing behind a table in the hotel lobby with a wide smile. He's standing beside a table littered with brochures.

"Thank you," Nils answers.

I turn and give him a WTF look. He smiles at me and puts his finger on my nose like I'm adorable.

"Are you married?" the man asks him.

"Yes, two years, going strong," Nils answers, wrapping his arm around my shoulders.

"Great. Would you be interested in time-sharing? We're affiliated with many hotel destinations around the world. We have both couple and family resorts. We are now offering a free evening dinner cruise on Lake Michigan. You get a free dinner and all you have to do is listen to a small seminar that will be given on the boat," he says.

"Cool. Sign us up," Nils says.

Did Nils smoke some of Mata's weed? He must be high.

I raise my hand. "Uh . . . I don't think so."

"Oh, come on, honey. It'll be fun," Nils says, with a smile resembling the Cheshire cat's.

"Great. There is a cruise tomorrow night. Would that work?" the man asks.

"No, sorry. Our good friends are getting married this weekend," I say curtly. Then I give Nils a look to make sure he doesn't say another word. He covers his mouth with his hand, but I can still see his lips tugging up at the corners.

"Okay, I can book you in for next Sunday then," the man suggests.

"Perfect," Nils says.

"No. Not perfect," I protest.

"The cruise is a lot of fun. It's mostly couples your age and older. Oops. I forgot to ask about your annual income. Does your combined annual income exceed eighty thousand dollars? I'm sorry for asking, but it's one of the criteria required."

"Sorry. We are poor." I link my arm with Nils. "Okay. Let's go home, honey." I emphasize the *honey*. I figure it's the only way of getting Nils out of here and ending this crazy night.

"Very funny." He shakes his head at me. "I'm Nils Karlsson. I play for the Blackhawks," he says to the sales rep.

The guy winces. "Sorry, my apology. I don't have time to watch hockey but of course I've heard of the team."

"No worries." Nils nods.

I'm never getting home.

"So, I'll sign you two up for next Sunday. It's really a nice time. You'll love it," the man says. He asks Nils to fill out some paperwork and tells us to enjoy our night.

I stalk off to the exit. Nils catches up to me quickly.

"You know you may have started a rumor that we are married now?" I snap.

"Yeah, sorry about that. I don't know where that lie came from. Maybe people will talk about my possible marriage instead of my dick. It would be an improvement," he smirks devilishly.

"Not cool. I signed up to be a fake girlfriend not a fake wife," I cross my arms over my chest.

He places his palm over his heart. "I'm sorry. I didn't mean it. It just came flying out of my mouth. Consider it one of our three dates for the week. Doesn't it seem like something a couple would love to do?" He's freaking serious.

I don't even know what to say.

"Whatever. If it's considered one of our dates, then fine," I snap. I can't remember my schedule off-hand, but I hope I don't have any assignments due that Monday.

"Cool." He presses his key fob to unlock his car and we get in.

He pulls into traffic. A few minutes later and we are in front of my apartment. "Thanks for the ride," I say.

"Wait. Can we take another pic? I should post something about tonight," he says.

"Yeah." I lean in so that I'm close to him. He gives me a quick kiss on the cheek and my skin burns where his lips touch me. A flash goes off. I want to complain about the kiss, but I agreed to it. I suddenly begin to think I'm in way over my head. I'm attracted to Nils.

He posts the picture.

"Holy crap, our last pic has thousands of likes," he says. He starts to read off some comments, most of them saying what a lucky girl I am. Then he says, "Stupid bitch doesn't deserve you." He pauses to look at me. "Don't worry. There will always be haters."

"I guess," I say. I really didn't think this whole thing through. A job at a coffee shop would have given me a third of the salary but it would have been less of a headache.

"See you tomorrow night," he says, and I could swear his eyes drop to my lips. "Do you need a ride to the wedding?"

"Uh . . . yeah, sure. Thanks. I won't be getting my car back until Monday," I explain. "Wait, actually . . . Sloane asked if I can get there early for family pictures."

"Yeah, me too," he says. "So, I'll get you around two, yeah?"

"Perfect. Thanks." My hand lingers on the door handle a minute. I take him in. He has the brooding bad boy look down to a T, and I find it so hot. He isn't my typical type, yet looking at him sets my blood on fire. "Have a good night, Nils."

Our eyes lock, something in his eyes is too intense, too . . . emotional?

"You have a good night, too," he says with a raspy voice and a killer smile.

I may be attracted to him but that's all it is, attraction, not feelings. Old habits die hard and if there's one thing I consider myself it's a fast learner. I've been burned once. There's no way I'm going down that road again.

CHAPTER TWELVE

P ast

WE WALK INTO THE FRAT HOUSE, HOLDING HANDS. SOME OF Nils's friends who live here throw a party every other day. Nils doesn't like to party often, since he has to work hard physically for the hockey team, but he needs to make an appearance once in a while to please his fans.

His eyes roll down my body. I wasn't sure what to wear tonight but his mom took me shopping and bought me this black Bodycon dress. She's been much better to me now than she was my freshman year of high school. Her and Dad were all touchy-feely back then. Now, their love affair has simmered down, and she's been acting a lot nicer to me. I don't usually wear such tight clothing, but she assured me it was the right thing to wear. She's a beautiful, well-dressed woman, so I figure she knows what she's talking about. I also kind of liked getting her opinion; she's the only mother figure I have. Aunt Becca was great to live with, but going clothes shopping wasn't her thing.

"This dress is different," Nils finally says.

"Different good or different bad?" I ask.

He adjusts his crotch. He does that on occasion.

"Just different," he says blandly. It doesn't help my self-esteem, which is severely lacking. "Come." He nods for me to follow and I do.

Nils stops and turns to look at me. I walk with my arms crossed over my torso, my shoulders hunched, and my head down.

"Don't do that," he says, taking my hand.

I'm forced to release the little fortress I had covering my body. "Don't what?"

"Cover yourself up. You're beautiful. Own it." He winks. His words cause this weird fluttering thing to happen in my stomach. *Wait a minute.* I stop walking and push my glasses up my nose. Did he just call me beautiful? *OMG!* He did. He totally did.

He's staring at me and I have a stupid smile on my face. I wipe it away. "Sorry."

This is the fifth party I am attending as his fake girlfriend. I've met a few guys from the team, and some girls who are kind of like groupies who like to hang out around them.

"Nils, Sierra. What's up?" A guy named Tobin walks up to us and gives Nils a fist pump. Then he checks me out. He nods, bobbing his head appreciatively.

"Looking good, woman."

"Fuck off," Nils berates him with that heavy accent of his. Where I am all awkward, shaking limbs, Nils is brooding confidence.

Nils leans close to my ear, his lips grazing my skin. Goose bumps erupt down the back of my neck. "This is the fifth party we've been to. I'll need to kiss you in front of everyone or no one's going to buy into our little game here."

The thought of kissing Nils makes my lips tingle.

"Okay." I nod, my cheeks must be the same color as my red-rimmed glasses. I've been tutoring him for weeks now and staring at his kissable lips. He's got the angry, bad boy vibe going on but he's harmless.

He pulls me farther into the house and grabs a beer that's sitting in a bowl of ice on the table. He's already figured out I don't drink. He doesn't offer me one.

"Man, come do shots with us," a guy I haven't seen before calls him over. Still holding my hand, Nils guides us to him.

"What are you drinking?" Nils asks.

"Vodka, man. The cheap kind. What else?" The guy bursts into laughter. He's clearly drunk already.

Nils looks down to me and cocks a brow. He takes a seat on the couch and I move to sit beside him, but he loops his hands around my waist and pulls me on top of him. Butterflies dance in my belly.

I sit ramrod straight. "Relax. Trust me," he whispers. His hot breath brushing my ear causes goosebumps to trail down my spine.

"What's your friend's name?" the guy who invited us over asks.

"Sierra," Nils says. "Sierra, this is Trina, Jodi, Ruby, Kit, Deacon, and Larik." I remember that Deacon and Larik are his teammates.

The girls all mutter something along the lines of "nice to meet you," while the guys nod and smile.

"What should we play?" I think it's Ruby who asks. She is a pretty redhead. She's sitting on the floor, on the other side of the coffee table.

"Truth or dare?" Deacon suggests.

"No. Let's do something else for once. How about we spell our names backward, or something messed up, and whoever can't do it, drinks." I think it's Jodi who suggests that one. I can't believe that this is what college kids do. They play games like children—only with alcohol involved.

"Fuck this shit. That's lame," Larik scoffs. "We're playing blow and suck, and whoever fucks up, drinks."

"Yeah," Deacon cheers.

I look at Nils, not knowing what the hell they are talking about. I'm too embarrassed to say the first thing that comes to mind at the words blow and suck.

"It's no big deal. Watch," he assures me.

Deacon takes a piece of paper out of his back pocket and sticks it to his lips. Trina leans forward and sucks the paper from his mouth. She turns to Jodi and they do the same, only when it's Larik's turn, the paper falls and everyone chimes, "Drink, drink, drink."

He picks up the bottle of vodka and takes a very long pull. When he's done, he puts the paper to his lips and looks at me.

Oh. Right.

I lean forward and suck the paper from his lips. I'm pretty sure I hear Nils hiss behind me. He's putting on a good show about being my boyfriend. I turn to Nils and the paper falls, but our lips collide and hot electricity zaps through me. I've never been kissed. This is the closest I've ever come, and Nils lips are full, warm and inviting.

I blink and realize everyone in the group is shouting drink, drink. *Again.* But Nils doesn't pull away. Instead, he whispers he's going to kiss me and he does just that. His lips press softly against mine. It takes me a moment to snap out of my daze and realize what's happening, and when I do, my lips move with his. I don't know what I'm doing but whatever it is, it feels good. His tongue enters my mouth and warm tingles shoot south between my thighs. Our tongues tangle, wet and messy. I don't want this feeling to end.

Nils breaks the kiss, leaving me entranced. I adjust my glasses and stare at him, a little in awe. I lick my swollen lips. Deacon passes him the vodka bottle. Nils downs quite a few gulps then passes it to me. I take it from him, *here goes nothing*. I take a large gulp and the burn of the alcohol makes me cough. Some members of the group break out in laughter.

"One sec." I lift my pointer finger. "I can do better."

This time, I bring the bottle to my lips, expecting the burn. I gulp it down like the rest of them did.

"Whoa." I use the back of my hand to wipe my lips, which isn't very ladylike, but I'm feeling tingly and loose all over after that hot kiss.

"Let's play a new game," Jodi says.

"Yeah," Trina agrees. "Truth or dare."

Shit.

"Okay." Deacon rubs his hands together. "Trina, truth or dare?"

"Dare." She grins and rolls her eyes, as if it's obvious. They have clearly been drinking for a while because Trina is having trouble sitting upright and she's slurring her words.

"I dare you to kiss Larik—right here in front of us," he says to her.

Nils gives my shoulders a squeeze, maybe indicating that my eyes should go back into my head. He leans forward and drinks more of the vodka. Trina crawls across the floor to Larik. She takes his face with each of her palms. She leans forward, brushing her lips on his. He opens his mouth to her and they are full-out Frenching in front of us. Larik moans and grabs her ass. Trina breaks the kiss and swats him on the shoulder playfully.

"Okay, my turn," Trina says, rubbing her hands together. "Nils, I dare you to go into that closet and make out with Jodi." She smiles sweetly.

"Come on. I'm here with Sierra. That isn't cool," he says.

"Seriously? She must know you've slept with all of us," she says so easily, and my insides that had felt all gooey and happy turn with a sinking twist.

"What is wrong with you?" he snaps at Trina.

I shouldn't feel offended. He isn't my real boyfriend. I know in the back of my mind that he must have gotten around, but thinking it and hearing it are two different things.

"We're out," he says, pushing me off his lap gently. I stand and he stands with me. He takes me by the hand.

"Sorry, Sierra," one of the girls calls after us. "Maybe we can hang during the week?"

Geez. I don't think Nils's mother fully understood what she was asking of Nils when she asked him to be my fake boyfriend.

Nils pulls me by the hand toward the kitchen. There is a large punch bowl of something on the counter. Nils uses the ladle to fill himself a large plastic red cup. He pours me one, too, and passes it to me.

"Sorry. I forgot to tell you that girls can be catty bitches," he scoffs.

I snort. "Now I can see what I was missing."

"Hey, guys." A girl named Carly, who I met at the last party, walks up to us. Her speech is a little slurred, but I remember her being nice. She's a social science major, like me.

"Hi." I smile and take a long gulp of the drink Nils poured. "How have you been?"

"If you're good, I'm going to hang out with some guys on the team for a bit," Nils says to me, and I think it's because he wants me to make friends with Carly. Or maybe he's trying to get away from me. I'm hoping it's the former.

"Yeah. Sure." I smile, and he leans in and gives me a quick peck on the lips. When he walks away, Carly is grinning widely.

"So how did you guys end up together? You seem like an unlikely couple, and I heard he doesn't do relationships." Carly's question makes my stomach sink. I am definitely feeling the alcohol. I'm worried about messing up the story.

I tell her how he needed help with his classes. I was his tutor and we just hit it off. I feel bad for lying to her because she seems nice, and has good friend potential.

"You're so lucky," she sighs dreamily.

Drinking gives me a sense of bravery I haven't felt before. "Nils removed my glasses from my face during one of our study sessions and told me how beautiful I was," I explain, batting my lashes at the thought of that little fantasy coming true. She sighs.

I do, too. I may help Nils with his schoolwork, but our study sessions have always been purely platonic.

"So dreamy," she says. "You want to take a seat?" She pulls herself up on the kitchen counter, since the chairs at the table are all occupied.

I pull myself up onto the counter beside her. "Tell me about you."

"I'm from North Carolina. My family has a farm. I have three sisters and two brothers. I'm the only one attending college," she says sweetly with a southern drawl. "I don't have a hot boyfriend like you. I honestly don't even know how to flirt with a guy. Maybe you can teach me?" She waggles her brows.

Oh, Carly. If only I knew how to flirt.

"Definitely," I say. "So easy really."

I've been talking out of my ass. Dating a guy like Nils is impossible; they don't do relationships. It's on the tip of my tongue to tell her to get a fake boyfriend because real ones don't exist.

Carly leans over and refills our cups with punch.

"This is good stuff." She swirls the liquid in her cup and some spills on her jeans. "Shit."

We both burst out laughing. I may not be able to find a real boyfriend, but I feel like I am making a friend.

"Are you drunk?" Carly slurs.

"I think so." I giggle.

"We should dance," she says. I place my drink on the counter and we both jump down.

I push my glasses up my nose and allow her to pull me through the house. In the main room, a makeshift dance floor has been set up and people are dancing all over it and the furniture.

Trina is grinding on some guy. Just watching her makes my cheeks flush. She is so confident and sexy, even though she seems like a bitch, too. She spots me and gives me what feels like an evil smile.

I turn away from her like I would when the sun burns my eyes. I focus on Carly, who is swaying her hips and pumping her arms up and down. I follow her lead. It's easy when my body feels weightless. My hips move with ease, and this dress makes me feel sexy for the first time in my life.

A guy walks up to Carly and whispers in her ear. Carly nods and then leans over to me.

"That's Seth. He wants to dance with you," she says.

"Sorry. I'm here with someone," I say.

"Aw! Come on, beautiful. It's just a dance," Seth says, demanding and insistent. His tone unsettles me.

"No, thank you," I answer curtly. I lean into Carly's ear. "I'm going to find Nils."

She nods and as I walk away, I turn my head to see Carly dancing with him.

Did I overreact?

I walk around the crowded house, looking for Nils. It feels too hot and stuffy in here. I need air. I spot him on the same couch as earlier where we played drinking games. Jodi is sitting beside him with her legs crossed. Her thigh leans on his leg, and as I approach, I realize her arm is draped over his shoulder. Jealousy courses through my veins, as I come to a stop in front of them.

"What's going on here?" I ask. My voice feels light and airy and I'm unsteady on my feet.

"Nothing. What's up, baby?" His head tilts to the side.

"Don't 'baby' me," I snap, not fully understanding my own emotions.

Jodi moves in closer to him and kisses his neck. My blood turns hot and I see red.

"Whoa, trouble in paradise," some guy says from beside me. I turn to see a crowd gathered around us. My pulse picks up pace as my heart beats erratically. I take off toward the kitchen. I just need to get away from these people, from Nils. I reach the kitchen counter and brace my palms against it, trying to get my bearings.

"Sierra, fuck. Why did you take off? Nothing happened. I swear," he says, swaying a little.

"Why do you have to hang around slutty girls like that?" I ask, jealousy and anger mixing and creating a toxic cocktail inside me.

"Well, at least my parents don't force me to date them," he snarls.

A sharp intake of breath sucks the air from my lungs leaving a piercing pain in my chest. I turn to see Trina, Larik and Jodi walking into the kitchen. By Trina's smartass grin I know she's heard. Other college kids trickle into the kitchen and I see them whisper. Nils snaps his lips shut and his eyes widen.

This is okay. Maybe they didn't hear what he said.

"Nils, please," I beg softly, but I'm not sure the words have actually left my lips. Everything feels like it's playing before me in slow motion.

"It's a really funny story, you see. My mother—who never invites me over for dinner—called with an invitation." He leans forward and lifts the punch bowl directly to his lips. He looks beyond drunk; he's cold and callous. My blood runs cold in my veins as I stand, frozen. I should take off. Run out of here, but my legs aren't moving as he pins me with his gaze. "I obliged, and when I arrived, the real reason for my visit was brought to my attention. Sierra here needed some help making friends, and so as a favor to my beloved stepfather, dear old mom asked me to be Sierra's fake boyfriend."

Trina smiles widely.

"Nils, you're wasted. Maybe go to one of the rooms and sleep it off," Deacon suggests, looking to me with pity in his eyes.

"So, I spent the last few weeks pretending." He's using his hands animatedly as he speaks and knocks over an open beer bottle. "Fuck." He jeers. Standing right in front of me, he continues, "Look at her. Why would I be attracted to someone like her?" My heart shatters and whatever self-esteem I had managed to muster gets squashed.

I have no words. He is the cruel asshole I always thought him to be.

"I'm going upstairs," he slurs. He looks around the kitchen, his eyes wild. He pauses on a group of girls sitting at the kitchen table. "Who wants to join me?"

Trina stands. "Let me help you. You're wasted," she says, but she looks like she plans on helping him with a lot more than climbing stairs.

Bile rises in the back of my throat. I turn around to see Carly standing behind me.

"Carly, I . . ." I don't know how to explain myself.

"If there is one thing I can't stand, it's a liar," she says.

"And a fake," Jodi says.

I look to the people who I've slowly warmed up to these last few weeks and know that Nils just burned any bridges I've built. I pick my pride up off the floor and head outside to call a cab.

When I get back to my dorm, the first thing I do is puke. Then I pass out on my bed.

I awake the next morning, and the only thing I want to do is leave this university, this town. I don't know why I bothered coming back here anyway. I can't ever look at any of those people again. I call my Aunt Becca and she sends me a ticket to fly back to Chicago

I don't look back.

CHAPTER THIRTEEN

N ils
Present

SHIT. THIS BOW TIE ISN'T COOPERATING. I TRY AGAIN FOR THE trillionth time. I have to wear suits all the time but I've never worn a tux in my life. I have no clue how to tie the knot.

Fuck it! I don't want to be late picking up Sierra. I can't get her out of my head.

When Mata said Sierra had never orgasmed, my mind went spiraling into the past. To the night when I had taken her with me to a frat party as my fake girlfriend. We kissed. It was the hottest kiss of my life, and then we broke up.

I was developing feelings for her and that scared the shit out of me. So I drank enough alcohol to numb myself. Problem is, booze in my veins always turned me into an asshole. I did what I normally do when my guard goes up. I lashed out.

I pull into the parking lot of her apartment building and head up the elevators. I knock and wait. The door opens and my heart stops beating. She's wearing a lemon-yellow dress that hugs her curves and hits her ankles. There is a dip in the front, revealing some cleavage. My eyes travel higher and meet hazel eyes and pouty red lips. Her dark hair falls in loose ringlets down her back. Her makeup is light, but it gives her eyes a catty look.

"Hi, Nils." She waves.

I haven't said hello. I clear my throat. "You look . . ."

Her brows bunch together. I can tell I'm making her nervous and that isn't what I intend.

"Beautiful," I finally say.

Her arms come up to hug her torso.

"None of that. You shouldn't cover yourself or feel self-conscious. You look like a vixen," I say.

She bursts into laughter. "Me, a vixen? Should I loan you my glasses?"

"Don't do that," I say.

"What?" Her brows pinch together and her nose scrunches in this adorable way.

"Put yourself down. I'm telling you that you look hot as hell. Accept the compliment and own it."

Her eyes soften. "I don't know how to own it. I've always been on the curvy side. I'm not stick thin like the girls you're used to."

Her self-deprecation is all too familiar. I've been there. Not about my looks, but about my self-worth.

"You're better looking than any girl I've been with. Your curves are sexy as hell. I could go into detail of how your breasts look like the perfect handful . . ."

She socks me in the shoulder.

"Ow," I mock whine, while rubbing my shoulder.

"I appreciate what you're doing but don't talk about my breasts. It's weird." She gives me a quirky smile.

"Okay, no boob talk." I chuckle.

She rolls her eyes, "You're looking good, too, Nils. The tux suits you."

Her words hit me in the groin. I picture lifting her dress

above her ass, turning her around and taking her on the dining table.

I button my jacket and offer her my arm in a gentlemanly way. "You ready to go?"

"Yeah." She sighs, grabbing her purse. She threads her arm through mine. *Progress.*

My feelings that made me lash out and run in the past are back with a vengeance but I don't want to run for the hills now.

We head out to my Tesla and drive to the wedding hall. I drop Sierra out front and park my car.

I walk inside. Some of the guys from the team are here with their families.

We spend the next two hours getting photographed. By five-thirty, guests have begun to arrive. And by five forty-five we are all gathered by the wedding planner, since the ceremony is about to begin. Since it is such a hot day, Sloane decided to have the ceremony indoors, but she ordered live birds and enough flowers to make the indoor ceremony look like an outdoor wedding.

When it's mine and Sierra's turn to take the aisle, something shifts in my chest. I've never been in a wedding party before. Back in Hogsby, people got married in churches and it was pretty simple.

I meet Sierra in the middle of the aisle and extend my arm to her. She smiles and I wonder if she's brushed up on her acting skills or if she's feeling something, too.

With our arms linked, we walk down the aisle. Again, something weird happens in my chest. I need to talk to her and explain what happened back in college. Yeah, I've given her a half-assed apology, but what is an "I'm sorry" without an explanation? My mom had lots of apologies, Sierra deserves more than just words.

The melodic music pulls me from my thoughts as we reach the pastor standing at the head of the aisle.

Sierra and I break apart to our respective sides. Flynn whispers something in her ear, and then our eyes meet. I hold her gaze. *What am I doing?* Why can't I stop looking at her?

The ceremony is emotional. I don't understand love, but Oli and Sloane do,

and it flows from their every pore as they exchange vows. Mata remains quiet during the ceremony, and Flynn and Sierra take turns holding Quinn. When the final *I do*'s are said, everyone cheers, and the happy couple takes Quinn and walks down the aisle with bright, infectious smiles plastered on their faces.

They look happy, peaceful. Both are foreign emotions to me.

THE WEDDING PARTY IS IN FULL SWING. THANKFULLY, MATA is sitting at the head table with Sloane, Oli, Quinn, and Pastor Carmichael. Myles, Flynn, and their twins sit close by them. I honestly think Sierra would have had a coronary if she had to babysit Mata again.

Sloane put Sierra at my table with Dave, Kelsey, and their kids. Sierra has chosen to spend her time at the bar, which sucks because I've watched a bunch of guys try to hit on her. Matt walks up to her, and I watch as he chats her up. She throws her head back, laughing at something he's said, and I feel my anger rising. Of course she would like a clean-cut guy like him. He suits her.

Fuck this.

I stand from the table and stalk over to the bar. Matt needs to fuck off. I reach them without a plan. I can't exactly punch my teammate in the face. I usually like him. I also shouldn't drink alcohol, even though my temptation to drink is high.

"Hey, man." Matt lifts his hand for a fist pump.

"Hey." I pump him back, but my eyes are trained on Sierra. Her face falls when she notices me.

"Having a good time?" I ask, placing my hands in my pockets.

I've clearly cut whatever conversation she was having with Matt short. *Fine by me.*

"Well, I'll go back to my table," Matt says awkwardly. I don't take my eyes off Sierra.

"Are you drunk?" I ask her.

"You aren't my father." She giggles. *Yup.* Definitely drunk.

"Thank goodness for that." I chuckle.

She laughs, which is unexpected. "Not sure why that's funny." She covers her mouth with her hand.

"I figured since you aren't on babysitting duty with Mata, you could spend some time at the table. You know, maybe eat something since you're hitting the bar," I say. I figure she isn't usually much of a drinker.

"Holy crap, you have no idea what a relief it is not to have to watch her," she says loudly, then she snaps her mouth shut and looks around, perhaps to see if anyone of importance heard her.

I glance around. "Your secret is safe."

"Phew." She palms her chest.

"Relax. After last night, I'm keeping a safe distance myself," I say, leaning into her ear.

"That was so messed up. I got home and I was telling my roommate what happened, and she was like, 'no fucking way,' that doesn't exist," she says enthusiastically. She's clearly loose-tongued from the alcohol. I plan on milking every minute of being with a Sierra who isn't closed off.

"The shit that comes out of her mouth is too much." I roll my eyes playfully and smile.

She's laughing so hard she holds her belly.

"You have a really nice laugh, you know?"

She stops laughing, and her face pales.

"Ouch. Not the affect I wanted," I say, taking a step back.

"Sorry." She winces but then she turns to the bar, picks up her drink, and takes a long sip.

"What are you drinking?"

"Some mix of juice with vodka." She shrugs and takes

another long sip.

She didn't acknowledge my comment about coming back to the table, so I try a different tactic. "Hey, how about we hit the dance floor?" I ask. She'll probably say no, but it's worth a shot.

She looks from side to side. "Who? Me and you?"

I cover my mouth with my hand. "Yeah, well I am your fake boyfriend, and your older stepbrother," I say as a joke. I'm really beginning to hate using the excuse that I am paying her to be with me.

She punches me in the arm. "Hush, you aren't my stepbrother."

"Right. My mom fucked your dad over and now they're separated."

Her brows bunch together. "Your mom didn't mess my dad over. They weren't getting along. They fought a lot. They wanted different things from life, so they separated," she says, surprising the shit out of me. I'd assumed Mom was just being a gold-digger.

"And how do you know this?" I ask, unable to hide the surprise from my tone.

"My dad. Called to tell me they were breaking up. We had a long talk. We've been talking a little more lately. He's gone to therapy, and is trying to get his dominating tendencies under control."

"That's nice. I'm happy for you," I say, and I mean it. I don't talk with either of my parents. It fucking sucks.

"Yeah, it's been okay. You should talk to your mom. She really misses you," she says.

I swipe a hand over my mouth, processing her words. She clearly holds nothing back when under the influence.

"Dare I ask how you know?"

Her lips quirk on one side and she gives me a knowing look. "Your mom calls me all the time, silly."

I have to hide my smile at her use of the term of endearment, although knowing she's in touch with my mom stings. After everything got messed up with Sierra, her dad and my mom came down on me hard. They just wanted to blame me for shit and tell me what a loser I was. Mom told me I was a cruel loser like Dad, and that was the end of it. I walked away and haven't looked back since.

"Enough talk about our parents. Do you want to dance with me or not?" I extend my hand.

She looks at it skeptically, and then takes another long pull of her drink. She places her glass on the bar and takes my hand.

"Let's dance, boyfriend." She doesn't say fake boyfriend, and to me, that sounds like a win. *Wait!* I sure as hell don't need a real relationship. It would be too demanding with my schedule, and besides, I like variety. I clear my thoughts. Being around her is confusing.

We hold hands as we walk to the dance floor. The music is a fast beat. When we get to the center of the floor, she drops my hand and begins to move. Her hands move up and down and she gets into the groove, swaying her hips. She's so sexy and she doesn't even know it. This sweet energy pours off her in spades as we move together. My hips sway and my arm wraps around her waist drawing her closer to me. After hitting the clubs on the regular, I'm more than smooth on a dance floor. I remind myself it's a family event, so I keep it PG, but I lace my fingers with hers and move our bodies closer.

Her breath catches. "What are you doing?" she asks, smiling wide.

"Dancing with you, beautiful," I say.

Her cheeks flush.

"What? Too much?" I ask with an innocent tone. I don't know what I am doing but I like being with her, and I don't want to dig into what that means.

For almost two songs we move to our own rhythm and then the band moves to a slow song.

I cock my brow and extend my hand. "You in?"

Her lips press together.

"Don't leave me hanging," I say.

"Okay," she relents, rolling her eyes playfully.

I exhale sharply and bring her in close to me. My nose presses into her hair. *Fresh flowers.* My hand rests respectfully at her hip and we move quietly, in sync.

The song ends and she pulls away. "Wait," I say.

She waits, but I wait, too. I'm not sure what I wanted to say other than "don't stop dancing with me," which would sound crazy.

"I need a drink," she says.

"I'll come with you," I offer.

"Okay." She shrugs. I get the vibe she is wary of me right now.

She walks up to the bar. "I'll have another one of those drinks," she says to the bartender, and he seems to know what she's talking about. He smiles like he thinks she's adorable. Apparently, he isn't immune to her charm.

He passes her a drink and then looks to me. "Just tonic and ice please," I say.

"Really?" she asks.

"No drinking for me. I'm cleaning up my act," I explain.

She nods and sips her drink. "I need to sit. My feet are killing me." She lifts her dress high enough for me to see her heels.

"Lead the way." I take my drink and follow her to the table.

We reach the table, and she lifts her dress above her knees, giving me a nice view of her long, fit legs.

"Geez." She leans forward and begins to remove her heels. She opens her purse and takes out a pair of flip-flops.

"Ah. Always prepared, are you?" I ask.

"Not always." She frowns.

Shit.

We're the only ones sitting at the table. Dave is drinking with the guys—which is a rarity—and Kelsey is chasing their kids.

"Sierra. Look . . ." I begin and take a breath. She's drunk.

That's a good thing. Maybe it's easier to confess to a drunk person. *No. No. No.* I wish it were me who were drunk for this confession. But in this moment, it doesn't matter. I need her to know how I really felt about her.

"What is it?" She continues to sip her drink. She sways forward, getting close to me.

"Back in Minnesota. The night I messed everything up . . . I want you to know I didn't mean to do that. I didn't want to hurt you. It wasn't my intention to make you run," I say, and rake fingers through my hair. This apology is harder than I'd thought it would be.

She watches me intently. "What do you mean? You screwed me over in front of everyone."

She's apparently not drunk enough. I pinch the area between my eyes. "See, here's the funny thing. That night, when it all went down, I felt the need to protect myself."

Her eyes narrow on me, and she gives me a look like she thinks I'm crazy.

I hold up a hand. "Before you say anything, hear me out."

She nods. "Okay. You have my attention."

"When we kissed . . . even though it was in front of everyone and it wasn't meant to be personal but something. . . happened to me. Like inside me. . ." I struggle to find the right words. "I felt something I never felt before. I knew it was because of the kiss. Trust me. . . I'd kissed dozens of girls before you but none of them felt the way you did," I grit my jaw anticipating what she may say. How she may react to my words.

She looks like she's trying to focus on me and having a hard time. "What are you saying, Nils? I was your fake girlfriend. There were no feelings involved." She says so innocently, even though her speech is slurred.

I begin to question if this was really the right time to have this conversation. Truth is, there would have never been a good time for me. I don't like feeling vulnerable and that's exactly what I feel right now.

I grit my teeth. "We set out to have a fake relationship, but all that time studying with you, going out for pizza together, hanging out in your dorm room and the library. . . I may have developed feelings for you. When I kissed you that night, I liked you." I look her in the eyes trying to gauge what she's thinking.

Her chin tilts down, and her mouth hangs slightly open. It's weird that I'd prefer to kiss her right now than continue having this weird, confession, but I fear she would slap me if I did. Will she remember any of this? I want her to remember.

"Y-you liked me?" she asks, sounding flabbergasted.

"I did." I clench my jaw even tighter. Damn it. Why is this so hard? My right leg bounces beneath the table as I wait for her to say something.

Silence blankets us but I watch the gears grinding in her drunken head. "Holy fuck balls," she shouts, and then slaps a hand over her mouth. As nervous as I feel inside, her reaction causes me to smile.

"I didn't know how to deal with my feelings. They scared the shit out of me. Anyone I've cared for left me or treated me badly. Then there was you and I don't know. . . we understood each other and then that kiss felt like some kind of warning like I was in too deep. I got freaked, drank too much alcohol and acted like a big jerk. It's not an excuse," I snicker. "Trust me, I know I have a problem dealing with my emotions. That's why I stopped drinking now. I can't let fear and anger control me anymore," I admit feeling sweat pop across my forehead and behind my neck. I've never worked this hard to explain myself in my life.

"Mother of all things holy. I never thought someone like you would like someone like me . . . I mean, I . . ."

"Don't stop. Say what you were going to say. If I can do this sober, you should be able to do this drunk." I hope my words are encouraging.

"I liked you, Nils, but I knew I didn't have a chance. I wasn't after a hook-up. I couldn't be like one of those girls at that frat party," she says.

"I got too drunk and didn't think of the consequences. I never seem to think of how what I do will affect someone else," I admit unable to look at her.

"If you think I'm not going to remember this tomorrow, you're wrong." She smiles slyly.

I lift my gaze and laugh. "I'm hoping you remember. Seriously," I say.

"I can't believe you wanted me. You aren't playing me now, are you?" Her brows furrow and she leans a little too close to my face, like she is trying to gauge my sincerity.

I chuckle. *This woman.* I shake my head. "No, Sierra. I'm serious about having feelings for you back then." I was never a shy guy, but this is a stretch even for me. I'm out of my element. All my old feelings have come rushing back but I am too much of a coward to admit how I feel today. Confessing the past is easier. "I kept my feelings hidden all those years ago because our parents were married, and it would have been fucking weird."

She palms her cheeks with each of her hands.

"Um . . . wow," she mutters. She stands from the table and sways.

"Easy there." I grab hold of her arm to steady her. *Don't tell me I'm making her run again.*

"I need to go to the ladies' room," she says.

"Okay." I release her. "Should I walk you?"

Her lips press together. "Um . . . no . . . I'm good."

"See you soon?" I say.

"Yup." She stumbles off. She looks like she's trying to walk straight but failing miserably.

I rake my hands through my hair and lean back in my chair. I could use a stiff drink right now.

Myles takes a seat beside me. "What did you do, Nils? It looks like you're sweating."

"I don't know what the hell I did, but I think I just got myself in deep," I say.

Myles laughs.

CHAPTER FOURTEEN

S ierra

THE BATHROOM DOOR CLOSES BEHIND ME. I'M THE ONLY ONE in here.

"Holy shit. What did I just get myself into?" I mutter to myself.

"What do you mean?" a woman asks.

My hands fly in the air and my heart jumps almost out of my chest. My eyes grow wide. I walk past a dividing wall into the sink area.

Mata. Of course.

I should've probably made sure there was no one in here before speaking to myself out loud. This must be another drunken mistake to add to my list.

"Did I just say that out loud?" I think I'm slurring.

"Yes. You're very drunk," she says.

I hiccup and laugh, then grab the counter for support. "I can't believe he liked me back in college," I say, looking in the mirror. My eyes have a red tinge and my cheeks are flushed, but for the most part I think I look okay.

"Who dear?" Mata asks.

"Does alcohol make you hallucinate?" I ask.

"No, but magic mushrooms do. Do you want me to hook you up?"

"OMG! Are you a drug dealer, too?" I take a step back from her.

She laughs. "No, it was a joke." She rolls her eyes like I should have known this. "I only smoke weed; it's good for the soul. Now, tell me what's bothering you," she insists. With her wild hair and long sari, she stands and watches me expectantly.

I don't answer. I may be drunk but something in the back of my mind says telling her my secrets is a bad idea.

She pulls a joint from her purse. "I was just going to smoke this doobie, so if it's going to take a while, I should go outside. I don't want to get in trouble by lighting up in here," she says.

I laugh. She gives me a puzzled look.

"Oh! You were serious?" I ask.

"Yes."

"I'm sorry, but I really have to pee," I point to one of the bathroom stalls and make a mad dash, thankful I'm wearing flip flops.

Hopefully if I stay in here long enough, she will get bored and disappear.

I lift the long dress up to my hips and relieve myself with a long sigh.

I get out and wash my hands.

Mata is gone. Phew!

My whole body feels kind of numb. This is freaking crazy. I don't even know what to think.

I pull the bathroom door open and it smacks against the wall. I adjust my dress and head toward the party, but I'm stopped in my tracks when I see Nils standing in front of me. Geez, he looks yummy in that tux with his hands tucked into the front pockets. His blue eyes dance as he takes me in, like he knows some funny secret he isn't going to share.

He takes a step toward me. "Are you okay?"

"Uh. Yeah, why wouldn't I be?" I ask.

"I just saw Mata walk out of the bathroom. She told me you were wasted and pliant," he says, and his lips quirk up on one side.

My eyes narrow on his mouth. "What did you say?"

"Never mind." He waves me off.

"Nils, I want to know. Tell me now," I insist.

"She said you were pliant. Like, ready for sex." He shakes his head.

My hand comes up to smack my mouth. "I didn't say anything to her."

He laughs. "Don't worry. Taking advantage of drunk girls isn't my thing."

"Oh, come on. I saw that video. Those girls could not have been sober," I say.

His blue eyes widen. I don't have a filter and probably should.

"I'm sorry." I pinch my lips together.

He waves me off. "I was more drunk than they were. They took advantage of the situation, knowing who I was. I've never taken advantage of a woman and never will. Tonight, I plan on getting you home safely and that's all," he assures me.

I don't know if I like the fact that he doesn't want to take advantage of me. He said he had feelings for me in the past. That doesn't mean they still exist today. I imagine his full lips on mine, his tongue sliding along the seam of my. . .

Nils is waving his hand in my face.

"You're staring at my lips," he says.

"Shit. I . . ."

He bursts into laughter. "You're freaking adorable." He places his arm over my shoulders. "Come on, let's get you some water."

"I don't want water. I'm enjoying this . . . buzz."

"I'm sure you are." He rolls his eyes at me and then I pull him back onto the dance floor.

MY MOUTH IS DRY AND MY HEAD POUNDS . . . I ROLL OVER TO my side and feel a hard body.

What?

I sit up quickly. "Holy shit! What are you doing in my bed?" I screech.

Nils shifts.

I check to see if I'm wearing clothes. I'm wearing one of my pajama shirts and a pair of polka-dot pajama pants. Phew!

"I . . . uh . . . are you okay?" he asks. I notice he's wearing a T-shirt. So he isn't naked either.

"OMG! Did we have sex?" I blurt. My pounding head causes me to cringe. "Ow." I press my pointer and middle fingers to my temples and rub.

"No, we didn't have sex. You were completely wasted. I drove you home but then you got sick on the sidewalk beside the entrance to your building. I didn't want to leave you alone. You didn't seem all that experienced with drinking, or after-care, for that matter," he says.

"And we didn't have sex," I confirm.

He rolls his eyes like he's annoyed with me. "I didn't want you choking on your own vomit. There was nothing sexy about what happened last night."

He stands from the bed. I think I've offended him. I take the moment to check his backside in those boxers he's wearing. Damn, he has a fine ass.

"You're leaving?" I don't mean to sound sad, but it just comes out that way.

He turns to look at me from the threshold to my door. "No, I'm going to get you water and Advil. Trust me, you'll need it," he says, and he walks out of my room.

I fall back on my pillow, nauseated. My stomach is turning, and my head is pounding. It's a horrible combination I never want to feel again.

Nils returns a few minutes later. "Here. You woke your roommate. She showed me where the medicine was. I also made you some toast. You barely touched your dinner last night," he says with a chiding tone.

I think back to the wedding. It's a bit of a blur.

Nils shakes his head at me. He passes me the water.

"Drink," he commands. "Stop. Take this." He passes me a pill. I place it in my mouth and drink more water. When I've polished off the tall glass he's brought me, he says, "Now eat the toast."

"You're really demanding," I say.

"Stop complaining. I'm trying to help you." He takes a seat at the edge of my bed. His head hangs between his shoulders.

I bite into the toast and OMG it's the best toast I've ever eaten and that's when I realize how hungry I truly am.

He takes the empty glass of water and leaves the room again. I don't know why he's being nice, but he is, and I can't say that I hate it.

He returns moments later with the glass filled.

"It wouldn't hurt if you drank more." He passes me the cup. I take it. "There. Was that less demanding?" He smirks. It's so damn sexy.

"Yes, better. Thank you." I don't know what else to say.

I finish the toast and drink more water. Nils takes my plate and the glass and places them on my dresser, then he gets into bed beside me. "You're sleeping in here?"

"Well, yeah. It's four in the morning. I've been sleeping here the last two hours," he says. "Why? Did you want me to leave?" He sounds tired and irritated.

"Well . . . no, I wouldn't want to kick you out in the middle of the night," I answer. "Not after you've taken such good care of me."

"Gee, thanks," he scoffs.

"I didn't mean it that way," I say.

"Try to get some sleep, Sierra."

"Okay." I lie back down, facing him. His eyes are closed. He's on his back. I look at the contours of his face, his sculpted cheekbones, his strong jawline. My eyes drop to his wide, muscular shoulders and chest, then trail down his sinewy and veiny arms. Even his forearms are sexy as hell. I can't believe he's in my apartment, in bed with me. My head gets foggy, but I feel so much better. I drift off to sleep.

I dream of big, strong arms wrapped around me. The rise and fall of his Adonis chest. The fresh, clean scent of his cologne, and I feel a contentment I haven't felt in a long time. In my dream, I smile because this feels right.

When I wake the next morning, he's gone. Yet a sense of fulfillment washes over me and a part of me wishes the dream was real.

CHAPTER FIFTEEN

Nils

I CAN'T STOP THINKING ABOUT HER. THE WAY THE CONFESSION about hurting her came tumbling out of my mouth has me reeling. Guilt eats away at me. I caused her to leave Minnesota, to leave her father's home. Now, here we are, together again under similar circumstances, and all I can think is how vibrant, beautiful, and amazing she is.

I step out of the shower and throw on a pair of shorts and a polo. Coach gave us a few days off, which is nice, because we have a scrimmage game coming up, along with some intense practices set up next week. The season starts the week after that.

I grab my keys and head out of town for a day of golfing with some of my buds from the team.

I've just started to drive when my cell rings. It's Fisher. I'm not in the mood to dissect my life right now, but I have no other choice. "Hello."

"Nils, it's Fisher. Is this a good time? I wanted to see how the wedding went," he says.

"Wedding was nice. I didn't touch a drop of alcohol," I say, contemplating if I should tell him about my fake arrangement with Sierra. I know he would have to keep it a secret, but he may also think I am nuts, and I don't need that.

"Good to hear. So everything was smooth?" he asks.

"Yup."

"Okay, I'll be seeing you Tuesday for your appointment."

"Bye, Fisher." I end the call and blow out a breath. That wasn't too bad.

Driving on the open road for more than an hour gives me too much time to think and my mind drifts to what Sierra said about my mother. She almost has me feeling guilty for assuming the worst of my mom—that she was with Steve for monetary reasons only.

I shake my head. I shouldn't feel guilt. The woman left me with an abusive man for years before bringing me to America, and she could have reached out to me.

She's managed to stay in touch with Sierra. Hearing that burned me. Mom cares enough to stay in touch with her ex-step-daughter and not her own son?

The night everything went down at the frat party years ago, Sierra probably went home in tears. I don't even know, because I woke in bed with naked girls draped over me. It wasn't a first for me either. What was a first was that my chest fucking hurt. A sting filled my veins—a venom I'd never felt before. I was angry at myself for hurting Sierra. Sorrow had blanketed me like a thick coat of honey. I was the bad blood in the family, I had always been. That's why I cut them off and it's not like Mom tried to get in touch anyway.

I pull into the golf club and head inside. Some of the employees know me here.

"The guys are out back by the bar," one of the ladies notifies me.

"Thanks." I tip my golf cap and head outside. "Isn't it a little early for drinks?" I say, as I walk up to their table and spot glasses filled with OJ.

"Just a little vodka and OJ," Myles says.

Matt clinks glasses with him. Being on break means they like to drink a bit.

"Hey." I fist bump Myles, Matt, and another teammate, Austin, who was traded last season.

The waitress comes up to me.

"I'll just have an orange juice," I tell her.

"Would you like it spiced up?" She smiles. She's blond and young, with a killer body and a nice set of breasts. Maybe a few weeks ago I would have been digging her and flirting, but not today.

"Just the OJ, no spice."

"Great." She grins and turns on her heel.

"Still on the straight and narrow? Proud of you, man." Myles gives me another fist pump.

"Yeah," Matt chimes in.

"Gotta do what I gotta do," I say. *Hockey is my life.*

"Is that chick on your list of things you gotta do?" Matt asks.

My brows furrow because I have no clue what he's talking about.

"The chick from Oli's wedding. The hot one with the dark hair. I was totally chatting her up. She was feeling me, and you came in and shut things down," Matt says.

I side-eye Myles because I can tell he's laughing behind his hand that's covering his mouth.

"That's Sierra, Matt. Her and Nils go way back," Myles says.

"What? Karlsson goes way back with a chick?" Austin chuckles.

I grit my jaw. "Sierra was drunk as hell at the wedding. She wasn't feeling you, Matt," I say matter-of-factly. "And fuck off, Austin." I point to Myles. "You keep your mouth shut," I say playfully, but my tone conveys that I mean business.

"Aw! Are you testy because you haven't gotten laid? Is that one of the rules of your probation?" Austin asks.

"Fuck." I rake fingers through my hair. "Why did I agree to spend the day with you assholes?"

They all laugh and so do I.

We get up and head out to the golf course where our golf clubs and balls are set up and ready for us. Matt and Austin start out and Myles and I hang back.

"What's really going on with you, man?" he asks, and I can tell he's being sincere.

"I don't know." I shrug. "The whole 'getting arrested and having my future on the line' thing is getting to me."

"But you're clear, right? Wasn't Savannah Grossi your lawyer?" he asks.

"Yeah, she was good. I need to thank Flynn for the referral. Savannah got me off the hook. Those chicks set me up and the photos and videos they had on their phone proved it."

"Does Coach know all this?" Myles asks.

"I told him." I nod. "He still wants me in anger management and he still wants me to be on the straight and narrow. He says my drinking and temper are what gets me into trouble, and I can't say he's wrong. This whole situation has been an eye-opener."

He nods and looks sympathetic. "Man, that really sucks, but at least you aren't being charged."

"Amen to that."

"And Sierra?" he asks. "I heard you two left the wedding together." He waggles his brows.

"She's my fake girlfriend and she was drunk. I was just watching out for her," I say.

"You drove her home," he says, his tone carrying innuendo that there was more than a drive home.

"You were too drunk to notice." I narrow my eyes on him.

He throws his head back, laughing. "Flynn noticed. I swear,

women notice everything. So, you're into this girl." He nods and smiles like he's proud of me.

"She's my fake girlfriend. I'm paying her to be with me," I say. If anyone will understand, it's Myles. The guy did a one-eighty when Flynn came back into his life. He behaved like an amped up bodyguard when she was around, warning us all away from Oli's hotter-than-hell sister. "I took her home. She felt sick from drinking. I spent the night in her bed just taking care of her."

"Fuck, Karlsson. You got it bad." His teeth dig into his lower lip and he nods repetitively.

"Can we be serious here? I don't know what to do. When I left her apartment the next morning, I didn't wait for her to wake up. I took off. I just. . . I don't know, got freaked?" I say.

"Have you been out with other chicks?" Myles asks. He knows me well. I can usually hook up multiple times a week if I want to.

"No. Haven't touched any girls," I say, knowing I'm digging myself deeper. "Shit that sounds awful." My face scrunches.

Myles laughs. "Only you would find falling for a chick disturbing or have you just not hooked up because of the probation?" he asks.

I repeat the question in my mind. I haven't gone this long without sex since. . . I don't know when. I think of the waitress who just hit on me back at the table. In the past, I could have flirted and possibly ended up in the employee lounge for a quickie, but I wasn't digging her because all I have on my mind is Sierra and her sweet smile. I probably just need something quick with her to get her out of my system.

"Earth to Nils." Myles waves his hand in my face. "What do you plan on doing? Don't you have a sordid past with her?"

"Dammit. Flynn told you? She promised she wouldn't."

"Man, I can be very convincing when I want to be," he says, licking his lips.

Fucking hell. I hold up my hand. "I don't want to know."

He chuckles. "Good, because I wasn't going to share. But in

all seriousness, I know what you did, and the girl has every right to be ticked off."

"We actually spoke at the wedding and I told her the real reason I lashed out at her. I had feelings for her back then and I got spooked. It's totally messed up but I'm hoping it's behind us now. We are doing this fake dating thing. We'll be hanging out a few times a week. I even made us a reservation for a dinner cruise. It should all work to clean up my image."

Myles puts a hand up in my face. "Hold up. You're going on a dinner cruise?"

"It's a crazy-ass story." I shrug, as if it's nothing, but then I begin to realize I'm doing crazy things to spend time with this woman.

"Karlsson, do I need to check you for a concussion?" he asks.

"No. It's part of our deal; she agreed to go on three dates a week with me. The dinner cruise counts toward that."

"This whole fake relationship is going to bite you in the ass," Myles says, as he swings his club.

"Bite me in the ass how?" I ask. He ignores me. "Asshole."He practices his swing a few times, and I take my club and stand off to the side. I won't fall for Sierra. This fake relationship is about me cleaning up my image in the media.

Hockey is number one in my life and I plan on keeping it that way.

CHAPTER SIXTEEN

S ierra

I throw off the tenth outfit I've tried on. "Nothing looks right." I sulk.

Sunny frowns. "I think everything you've tried on looks good." Her southern drawl is adorable.

"You should put that yellow floral dress back on," Sunny suggests. "Add a little white cardigan and you'll be good to go."

"Gah! I'll look like a schoolteacher," I say.

"Is that so bad? You said it yourself. You don't want to be like one of those puck bunnies he dates." She shrugs.

I laugh so hard my eyes tear up. Sunny is from the south. She knows nothing of hockey and puck bunnies. "I've taught you well."

She falls back on my bed and examines her nails. "I need a manicure. I also need to teach you football so we have something in common. I don't get why you want to watch a sport that takes place on the ice. It's cold. The players are probably freezing their asses off and their . . . you-know-whats are all shriveled up."

"Girl, you got it so wrong. Hockey is hot as hell. When the season starts up, I'm dragging you to a game. When those players get moving, it's pure fire on the ice. And I'm not saying that because I grew up in Minnesota where everyone is a hockey fan."

"Fine, fine. I'll watch a game. See what it's all about. Now stop wasting time. Get that outfit on and own it." She winks and stands from my bed. "I'll go wait in the living room. Someone needs to open the door for your hot hockey man."

"Ah! So, you do think he's hot."

"I'm not blind, darling. That boy is gorgeous, but it has nothing to do with hockey. He's got that bad-boy vibe," she says, fanning herself.

"It's his bad-boy reputation that has me sweating. I still can't believe I confessed that I liked him back in the day. He watched me puke the other night, Sunny." I wince and shake my head. "It's the most unattractive thing in the world."

"And yet he called to make sure you didn't forget about the dinner cruise and he'll be here in twenty. Stop pouting and get ready." She turns on her heel and bounces out of my room.

It's too hot in here. My cheeks are flushed. I slip on the dress with the cardigan. I put on some mascara and lip gloss, then slide my glasses on. I sometimes like to wear contacts on a date, but Nils doesn't seem to mind my glasses, which is better for me because the contacts dry my eyes out. I blew out my hair into loose ringlets, and I run my fingers through it to try reducing the volume. I'm as pleased as I can be with the outcome of my efforts.

There's a knock on the door. I check myself one last time in the mirror and take a deep breath as I walk to the door. I open it to a heartbreakingly handsome Nils in a fitted black T-shirt that shows off the sexy ink on his arms, and a pair of dark-wash jeans.

He's holding chocolates and flowers. His eyes graze over me from head to toe and he smiles.

"These are for you," he says, passing me a beautiful bouquet and a box of chocolates.

"You know you don't have to bring me flowers and chocolate every time," I say, because I feel bad that he's going out of his way when we aren't even dating.

"Would you actually mind taking a picture of them and posting them on your social media? It would make things look more real if we both posted about our relationship." His words make my stomach sink. It's not like I thought this was a real gesture.

"Of course. Sunny and Declan are in her room so you may want to keep it down about the fake boyfriend stuff," I whisper close to him and take in the clean scent of his cologne.

He winces.

I head to the kitchen and place the flowers and chocolate next to each other. "There we go." I take the pic and show him for approval.

He nods. "Should we head out?"

"Sure." I grin.

"You look beautiful," he says, as his eyes sweep over my body again.

"Thank you," I say shyly. Something is buzzing in the air around us tonight. For some reason, it's making everything feel different.

I hug my torso as we walk to the elevator.

"Can I hold your hand?" he asks.

"Uh . . . sure." I release my hold on myself and offer my hand.

Nils smiles sweetly. "I like that dress on you," he says.

I raise my left brow. "Really? I mean, I thought it may not be your taste."

His lips turn down. "Why would you think that?" he asks, then he rolls his eyes. "Okay, I think I know why you may think that. I have a reputation for going for a certain type. But I really am digging this dress. Those other girls have nothing on you. That dress just made my heart speed up," he says, so easily, full of confidence.

I smile. "That's sweet. Thanks, Nils."

We get into his Tesla and Nils drives us toward the pier.

WE EAT DINNER WHILE A MAN AND A WOMAN PRESENT information on time-sharing. The boat is large. The dining room is on the second floor, which provides a nice view of the lake.

"I can't believe you signed us up for this. You can't seriously be considering buying a time-share," I say to Nils before I take a bite of my chicken breast. It tastes dry and papery and I give up after two bites.

"I don't know. This guy is making some pretty good arguments. It's an economical way to travel the world," he says.

"Are you an economical guy? I mean, you drive a fancy car, and I've heard you own a crazy house," I say, forking some of the steamed vegetables, 'cause I'm starving. They're overcooked and mushy.

Nils takes a bite of his steak. "I may have overspent these last couple of years, but I realize I need to tone things down. I'm actually thinking of selling my house. Maybe getting something a little smaller, closer to the city,"

"Really? Why?" I ask.

"It's all too much, Sierra. I came from nothing. The money went to my head. I almost got myself kicked off the team because of bad choices. I have to change my lifestyle," he says. He takes another bite of steak. "This is really gross." He tosses his fork onto the tablecloth.

"My chicken is nasty, too." I laugh.

"So much for a romantic dinner on a boat," he says. "Let's just take some pics. The scenery will make for some good social media posts."

His words pierce me in an unexpected way. I know we aren't in a real relationship but when he compliments me and says sweet things, it feels real. It's hard to separate in my mind. A part of me wants to know what it would feel like to really be with him. Yes, he has a bad reputation, but he's been really nice since we struck up this deal.

You are his employee, Sierra. Don't fall for him.

I lean in and we take some pictures at the table. Then we walk around, since we aren't eating our meal. While walking around we take more pictures of the two of us against the vast expanse of the water in the background.

A couple walks by, and Nils asks them to take our picture since we've mostly been taking selfies. He starts to post on Facebook and Twitter.

#datenight

Another great night out with my girl.

He can clearly be romantic. Too bad he's only acting.

We head back to our seats and the presenters show beautiful pictures of resorts around the world. They then end their Power-Point presentation with statistics on how much money can be saved by buying into the time-share.

After dinner, there's dancing on the upper deck. The DJ plays "Just the Way You Are" by Bruno Mars. Nils twirls me on the dance floor. Then he begins to sing with his heavy accent. He's so off key.

I'm smiling so wide, I can't stop. "I don't think you have a future as a performer."

"You wound me," he says, moving his body with such ease that we fall in sync.

"Your ego is healthy. I think it can take a beating." I laugh.

"You'd be surprised," he says, and then he continues to mouth the words to me about being beautiful and being perfect.

"You're quite the charmer," I say, flirting. I just can't seem to help myself.

"You make it easy," he says.

We continue to dance to all the songs the DJ plays. There's no alcohol involved, and yet I feel light and happy. It feels like a lifetime ago that I tutored him in school.

He opens his arms, and I twirl away from him and then I twirl back into his body. "Geez. Where did you learn to dance like this?" I ask him.

"The club scene mostly. I don't know. I had to take some figure-skating classes when I was on the hockey team in college," he says.

"You're good," I say.

"I know." He winks.

The music ends and a dessert is served. A breeze brushes off the water. The sky is dark now. The presenters, along with other employees, filter through the dance floor to see if anyone wants to buy into the time-sharing.

A man comes up to Nils and me. "What a lovely couple you are." He smiles to us.

"Thank you," Nils says.

He asks the man for more information so he can contact him when he's made his decision. The man smiles like he's made the deal.

The boat docks and we head back to the car. Nils is carrying a handful of brochures.

"Are you hungry?" he asks. "Because I am starved."

"I could definitely eat," I say.

He drives away from the pier and pulls into traffic. We're only driving about ten minutes when he makes a right turn and stops at the side of the road next to a pizza truck.

"This is the best pizza in the city," he says.

"I don't know why, but I pegged you as eating only gourmet food," I say.

"I don't eat it often, and definitely not when I need to train hard, but I have the next few days off. I really want you to try this pizza," he says, sounding so sincere. It feels like he's sharing a little piece of himself with me.

We leave the car and he orders us each a cheese slice. The oil drips from the cheese but damn, does it look good. There are some patio tables set up beside the pizza truck; looks like it's parked here permanently. We take a seat.

I take a bite and moan. "This is really good."

"I told you," he says, then takes a mouthful. His eyes roll backward. *What would you look during sex when you let go?*

Heat rises up my body and pulses a beat between my thighs.

We sit quietly and enjoy the pizza. Afterward, he tells me some stories about when he first moved to Chicago. Apparently, this place was one of the first he tried. He tells me what it felt like moving to a new city on his own, and how his dreams came true when he got drafted into the NHL out of college. When we're done, he gives me a ride home.

"I'm going to have a busy week with training, and then the season starts the week after. I'd love for you to come to a home game," he says.

My insides turn to mush. I want to hate him but his revelation about liking me and feeling overwhelmed by me sits heavy on my chest. We weren't a real couple back then, only something about being with him always made me feel magnetic and charged, kind of like I do now.

"I'd really like that," I answer. My eyes drop to his lips.

His eyes drop to mine.

"What are we doing?" I ask, unable to look him in the eyes.

"I don't know. What feels right?" Our heads move together, so slowly.

"This will complicate our situation," I whisper.

"I know."

"You don't want a relationship."

"I don't have time for a relationship," he corrects, just as our lips are about to touch.

His words make me feel like a bucket of ice water has been thrown on me, and I pull away.

"I can't, Nils. I'm sorry. Kissing you would mean something

to me. I'm not the type of girl to just hook up. I don't have it in me."

His brows pinch together causing his forehead to crease. I hope he's torn, because I want him to want me.

"I like that you aren't that type of girl. I just don't want to make promises I can't keep. I need to focus on my career right now," he says, and his words sting, but I try to hide the bite they leave inside me.

"Right. That's why I'm your fake girlfriend." I smile, trying to lighten the heavy mood.

"What if I want more?" he asks.

"I'm not built that way. I'm sorry." I reach for the door handle and his hand lands on my arm. I hope he's having a change of heart.

"Have a good night, Sierra. I'll call you this week. Remember, I get three phone dates." He winks but his mood seems somber.

"I would have agreed to four," I say.

"I would have agreed to four grand," he says with a sly smile.

A smile spreads to my cheeks. "You have a good night."

"You, too," he says.

I leave the car and head straight into my apartment. *That was a close call.*

CHAPTER SEVENTEEN

N ils

THE SEASON HAS STARTED, AND THINGS ARE RUNNING smoothly so far. Daria has said she's pleased with how things seem to be progressing between Sierra and me. The senior managers also seem to be a little more chill. My social media interaction has been mostly positive, and I've been keeping sober and out of trouble.

Tonight, we're playing the Red Wings, and Sierra and her roommate, Sunny, sit in the stands watching the game. I want to be kicking ass, but we're halfway through the game and the score is zero–zero. I've got the puck with two players from the Red Wings on my tail. I'm only at center ice. No way I can take the shot from here.

Oli skates to the right and I shoot the puck his way. Crawford, a player from the Red Wings, gets the puck when Chris, a player from our team, sweeps in and steels it while I make my way closer to the net. Chris loses the puck and Crawford manages to move away. Myles sweeps in, stealing the puck. He zigzags through four players from the opposing team, and shoots it straight to me. With a flick of my wrist, I shoot the puck in the net and the crowd goes wild.

The Red Wings manage to get a goal on us when Matt leaves the net open. The rest of the game is tied. When we go into overtime, Myles scores a goal, and we win. We've had a good start to the season, but we need to get into a better groove as a team.

Coach comes down hard, and I can tell he's freaking the fuck out. It's a big fucking deal that Matt got called up from the minors at age twenty-four. He can't afford fuck-ups.

After the game, we all head to the locker rooms.

"Good game, man," I say to Matt.

"I left the net. Coach is seriously pissed," he says.

"You can't look at it that way. Think about how many goals you stopped tonight. The Red Wings are a strong team. You're new to this level of play, but I'd say you did fucking great," I tell him.

"Thanks, dude," he answers, but his head is slightly bowed as he sits on a bench in front of his locker.

"You did good, Matt. Keep up the good work." Myles smacks him on the back.

"I agree," Oli says.

Matt picks up his head and holds it high.

That's what I love about these guys. They have your back. They lift you up; they don't drag you down. Before being recruited to this team, I didn't even know that there were people like that in this world.

I head into the shower and get cleaned up.

When I leave the locker room, Sierra is there with Sunny. Seeing her makes me smile.

"Hey, you." I plant a kiss on her lips, and she startles but damn, her lips feel good. In my defense, it was a fast kiss and we agreed to those. A camera goes off behind us.

"Great game." She smiles wide. "I can't believe we're back

here; this is so freaking cool. You guys did so well. I liked the way you came around the net and stole the puck. Damn, that was hot."

Sunny laughs. "I have to admit, I didn't understand anything about hockey when I arrived here tonight, but our girl here is a good teacher. She taught me quite a bit. I was rooting for you guys."

"Thank you." I grin. I glance at Sierra. "So, you're still a big hockey fan?"

"A die-hard fan. I remember when Oli came to the AMHA to see Sloane the first time. I almost melted to the floor," she says.

"Hey, I don't want to hear how you almost melted for my teammate," I say, throwing my arm over her shoulder.

"Aw, are you jealous?" She bats her lashes.

"Damn straight I am. The only hockey player I want you melting for is me." I turn my head to look at her, and stare at her luscious body. Electricity zaps to my groin.

Damn, I want to have her wreathing beneath me so bad.

"OMG, you all are just so cute." Sunny's cheery voice breaks the moment.

I walk the ladies out to Sierra's car. I give her a quick kiss good night on the lips and tell her I will call her in a couple days since we'll be on the road all day tomorrow.

When she leaves, I miss her. I shake my head. I can't go getting attached now. My head needs to stay in the game. My focus needs to be on the career I nearly lost. Yup, that is exactly what I've got to do. I can't let my mind stray to a pretty girl with full lips and red-framed glasses.

Only, I can't help myself because that night, she's exactly who I dream about.

CHAPTER EIGHTEEN

S ierra

NILS IS AWAY ALL WEEK, BUT SOMEHOW, WE MANAGE TO TALK every night. He calls me and we sit on the phone and chat for hours. I want to tell him that he went over his three-calls-per-week limit, only I don't mind speaking with him. It's actually kind of nice to fill my lonely nights after I'm done with my schoolwork.

My cell rings. It's past midnight. I shouldn't answer, but I saw Nils had a game in New York tonight and they won. When he wins, he gets hyped.

I press the talk button. "Congratulations."

"Thanks. I'm so pumped," he says.

"I've been hearing that a lot this week." I chuckle. "You guys are doing good."

"Yeah, we've been really focused, and Matt is pulling through real nice," he says of the team's new goalie.

"I saw that. Good for him."

"It helps having my head clear, too. All that drinking and

lashing out was doing me no good. I see now that my game was suffering. My body feels so much stronger."

"I'm glad to hear that," I say, and a loud yawn escapes me.

"Are you in bed?"

"Where else would I be this time of night?" I say.

"Out with friends at a bar. Isn't that what college students do? Drink and get laid?"

"Maybe, but not this one," I say. "Besides, I'm a little older than most of the students in my class. I lost a year when I dropped out of Minnesota, and then it took me a year to apply and get into this program."

"You're far from old. Don't play that card.".

"Where are you?" I ask him, because it sounds super quiet, which means he isn't at a bar or club. I know going out used to be his post-game ritual, so I wonder how he's handling this new, calmer way of life.

"I'm in my hotel room. The guys went out for a beer, but I wasn't in the mood. I was looking forward . . ."

"What?" I ask

"Nothing. It's just better I lay low and chill. Let's talk about you being in bed," he says, changing the subject. "What are you wearing?"

"We are not going there," I say firmly, while twirling a piece of my hair with my finger.

"Oh, come on. I'm so pumped from the game and I have all this excess energy. I'm picturing you lying in your bed with your hair sprawled across your pillow, no glasses on, a little red nightie . . ."

"It's light pink, not red," I say.

He groans. Shoot. What have I done? I shouldn't have said anything.

"You're killing me, woman. Does it have lace? Are your nipples hard?" he asks.

What should I do? He's breaking down my walls.

"It does have lace," I say. "My nipples could probably cut

glass right now, but that doesn't matter; you're my fake boyfriend. You're paying me money to do a job."

"I know that, but can't we combine business and pleasure for once? I promise I can make you feel good," he says in a sultry voice.

Wetness pools between my thighs and I squeeze my eyes shut, warning myself to gain some self-control.

"We don't need the complications. You're doing so well," I remind him. I leave out the part that I am horny as hell and want to jump his sexy-AF bones.

"I don't know if you would be saying that if you saw my hard-on right now. It isn't healthy to go so long without any sex," he says. I'm surprised he's gone this long.

"You could always hook up with a bunny," I suggest. Since our relationship is fake, it wouldn't be cheating.

"I don't want a bunny, Sierra," he says. "I want you." The need in his voice turns my blood hot, and a thumping feeling travels from my chest and lands between my legs.

"You want me to sleep with you? Then what? Where does that leave me? You know I'm not hook-up material. You know what I need," I say. I pose a challenge that I want him to accept, but deep down, I know he won't.

"I have to focus on my career. You know I travel a lot. I can't deal with distractions," he says.

I want to argue that he talks to me every night and acts like my boyfriend anyway, but I don't say a word because I don't need to convince a guy that he should be with me. He should want me out of his own free will because I am his next breath. As cynical as I am about relationships, when I do fall, I want the whole love affair. I don't want to settle for less.

"Then you've got your answer," I say, trying to hide my disappointment.

The burn between my thighs hasn't subsided. Why I choose to torture myself with these calls, I have no clue. I'll just have to get myself off to thoughts of him when I hang up. At least I'll have a good night's sleep after.

"Change of subject then," he says.

"Good idea. I have the perfect topic to cool us down," I say.

"Wait." He pauses, and the minute he does, I realize what I've said. *Shit.* "You're feeling horny, too?"

I cover my face with my hand, as if he can see me.

"We're changing the subject, remember?" My heart beats fast. If he knows I want him, it will just make matters between us even harder.

"Fine. Okay," he agrees, but it doesn't sound like he wants to forget my little slip-up.

"I spoke to your mom this afternoon. I told her we've been in touch," I say, carefully.

"You didn't tell her about our arrangement, did you?" He asks the question fast, and I sense his nerves.

"No, of course not. I would never do that. I just, I don't know . . . sometimes, I talk to her and she seems sad on the phone. I thought speaking of you would cheer her up," I say.

He scoffs. "I doubt that."

"She was really happy to hear you're doing well. She said she's kept her eye on the NHL so she can watch you play."

"Who cares? Honestly, the woman turned her back on me. She hasn't tried to contact me once," he says, and I sense his anger is rising. I hate to have that affect when he's been doing so well lately.

"I'm sorry. I shouldn't have said anything. I don't want you to be angry or hurt. She just mentioned to me that she had wanted to send for you right away when she arrived in the US, but my father didn't want her to. He didn't want her dealing with a young boy; he wanted her all to himself." I sigh. My father can be a selfish bastard, that's for sure. "She had nothing, Nils. No one to depend on. All she had was my father, and she wanted to please him. I know that sounds awful, but I felt sorry for her."

"For fuck's sake," he hisses, and I hear something smash.

"What was that? What's happening?" I ask, frantically.

"Nothing," he snaps.

"I'm sorry. I didn't want to upset you. I just . . . I don't know, I guess maybe I'm projecting. I'd love for my mother to reach out to me. Even though she left me with a man who shipped me off to my aunt. I still want to see her. I want her to want to see me. It's pathetic, I know." I sigh.

"Sierra." His voice has turned soft and gruff now. "Are you crying? I'm sorry. I know it must have been so hard for you when your mom left. I wish you had this great mom that wanted to spend time with you."

"Thank you," I say softly trying to bite back tears. His words striking an open wound. "Not having a mom in my life has left a part of me always feeing empty."

"I get that. I totally do. The emptiness sucks. I'm just harboring this anger toward her. I know it isn't completely her fault, but my dad was a cruel bastard. You don't leave a kid with a man like my father. I get that your dad isn't the nicest, and he's selfish and controlling. I'm not saying one is worse than the other; I just . . . with the physical abuse he put me through . . ." His voice cuts off as the tears I tried so hard to hold at bay come streaming down my cheeks. I can't fathom what he went through. "I tried forgiving her when she brought me to Minnesota. I truly did. But then when I fucked up with you, she choose you, which is great don't get me wrong. It just would've been nice to have her support and guidance, too. Maybe I wouldn't have continued to fuck up if I had that."

"Damn, Nils, I'm sorry. I guess my own anger toward what you did blinded me from seeing the whole picture. You're right. She's your mom. She should've put you in your place but not disown you all over again. That must have been so hard. I understand she hurt you. I don't want to push you to talk to her if you aren't ready. I just thought you should know where she's at," I say, swiping at my tears.

"I know," he says softly. "I know you mean well. Damn, I wish I was there now so that I could hold you in my arms."

My heart bursts, and I know I am a goner.

"I'd like that," I say, because I can't reject him now. Not when I've dredged up his past and made him feel bad.

"I should get to bed," I say. It's getting late, and I have class first thing in the morning.

"Good night, sweet Sierra," he says.

"Good night."

CHAPTER NINETEEN

S ierra

AUNT BECCA CALLED TO SAY SHE WAS UNDER THE WEATHER, SO
I head to the supermarket and pick up some ingredients to make
a chicken soup recipe I found online. Aunt Becca has asthma, so
whenever she catches a cold or flu, it affects her way more than
it would the average person.

I use my key to enter her apartment and spot her on the
couch, wrapped in her robe and a thick blanket.

"You didn't need to come by," she insists.

"Of course I did." I head into the kitchen and set the grocery
bags on the counter.

"I don't want you catching this bug," she says, and then
breaks into a coughing fit.

"Are you using your inhalers regularly?" I ask.

"Yeah, I had just refilled the prescription when I got sick.
Lucky for that," she says.

"Do you have someone helping you out at the store? Because
I can always go in this weekend," I offer.

Her brows knit together. It's been more than a month since I got fired from the station and I'm still not working in a new job. Well, at least not one I've told Aunt Becca about. I need to come clean about being Nils's fake girlfriend, but as time passes, it's becoming harder to 'fess up.

"Have you not found a job yet? How are you getting by?" I hear the concern in her voice rising.

I take a seat in the wing chair next to the couch. There's no time like the present. Besides, I've been feeling guilty about keeping her out of the loop.

"I have something to tell you," I say carefully.

"Sierra, dear. You know me. You don't need to be scared to tell me anything," she says. I know that's true, but I feel like she may have a moral problem with what I've agreed to.

"Yes, I know . . ." I sit straight and fold my hands in my lap. My face is creased, like I'm guilty. "Remember when I lost my job at the station and got into the little fender bender?"

She nods.

"Well, I was kind of feeling a little desperate for cash and Nils made me a proposition, I couldn't turn down."

She palms her chest. "Don't tell me you had sex with him for money," she says. "Wait, that wouldn't make sense. I remember that video. That boy doesn't need to pay to get laid." She bursts into a coughing fit. I need to get that soup cooking.

"No, I didn't sleep with him for money," I confirm. "What I am about to tell you has to stay between us. It's important," I emphasize.

"You know I'd take your secrets to my grave," she says with a smile. I hate how pale she looks. I know it's just the flu, but it makes me think back to the time she was battling cancer.

"I know, that's why I need to tell you. I just can't keep it inside any longer," I say.

"Well, go on then. You're worrying me." Aunt Becca's lips turn down.

"Sorry. It's just that Nils got put on probation by the senior managers of the team. It had something to do with the sex tape we saw," I say.

A slow smile spreads her lips and she nods.

"Nils asked me to be his fake girlfriend so he could clean up his image on social media. He's been paying me every month to do the job, and it's been working out great. He posts a couple of pics of us. I've been to his home games. He's been doing really well with staying out of trouble," I explain.

"Oh, darn. This is probably why I should get on social media. To keep tabs on my niece," she laughs and it causes her to cough. "In all seriousness, Sierra, sweetheart. That wasn't what I was expecting. You know I can't tell you what to do. I mean, yeah, it must be nice to get paid to be a sexy hockey player's girlfriend. But what happens when the job ends, and he doesn't need you anymore?" She looks at me with sympathetic eyes.

"I'll have to find a real job eventually, but this has just been so great. I have time on my hands. I'm not stressing to get my schoolwork done," I explain.

"That's not what I meant, sweetheart. You're falling for him." She gives me a pointed look. "I've noticed something different about you these past couple months. You're glowing and it's beautiful, but now I'm scared he'll break your heart."

Her words cut me deep and cause my belly to dip. "He isn't the same guy he was back in Minnesota."

"Is he willing to commit?" she asks.

"It's frustrating. We get along really well. We have late-night talks when he's out of town and he comes over when he's in town. We hang out and laugh. Things between us are easy," I say. "But he's not willing to commit. He'll say he wants me one minute, and then the next, he says he needs to stay committed to his career. He was almost booted from the NHL, and it really scared him."

"What are you going to do?" Aunt Becca asks.

"I'm going to be his fake girlfriend for as long as he wants me to. Then, I guess we'll call it quits." I stand from the chair. "I should really get that soup boiling. Some broth would be really good for that cough."

I head to the kitchen and start chopping vegetables. My mind drifts to Nils. We speak every day. How can we just cut each other off, cold turkey?

At least we haven't slept together. If we had, then things would be so much more complicated.

CHAPTER TWENTY

N ils

IT'S A WEDNESDAY EVENING, AND I AM BACK IN TOWN WITH the night off. Myles and Oli went straight home to their families. There's no way I'm spending the night at home in my big, lonely house when all I want to do is spend time with Sierra. The lines of our relationship have become blurred, but I've never had such intense conversations with anyone in my life—or sexually charged ones, for that matter, either.

She has a test to study for, but I convinced her to let me come over and help her, since it's math. I'm bringing dinner, along with a bottle of wine. After months of sobriety and getting my reputation back on track, I figure a little wine with my girl won't hurt.

Only she isn't my girl. I don't allow myself to dwell on that last thought.

I knock on her apartment door with two large paper bags in my hand. She opens the door and smiles wide.

"Welcome home," she says warmly. I find it hard to breathe

as I take her in. Her words are a slingshot to my chest. *'Welcome home.'* I've never felt like I was home until now, with her.

"Let me help you with this." She takes one of the bags out of my hands.

"Thank you," I give her a peck on the cheek. It's what we've become accustomed to when we see each other.

She walks into the kitchen and I follow her. She places the bag on her kitchen table. "You look beautiful," I say, because I know she needs to hear it, and because it's true.

"Would you stop it?" She smiles, blushing. "How was the trip home?"

"Usual." I look around her apartment. "Is Sunny here?" I ask, wondering if we get the place to ourselves. Not that I'm planning anything.

"She's spending the night at Declan's. His roommate is out of town this week, and I guess they wanted privacy. She's been there since Sunday," she explains.

"Are you good staying in this place alone? I mean, do you have the proper locks on the door?" I walk over to the front door. I open and close the lock to make sure it's secure. She laughs. "I hear you," I say with a chiding tone.

"When did you become the protective type?"

I turn around and look her in the eyes. "When I met you."

Her face falls, and her hazel eyes get this glint of alarm. I was hoping my words would get under her skin not cause it to crawl. I watch her throat bob.

"Are you thirsty?"

"I brought wine, but I figure we need to study before we drink," I say.

"I just have a few things I need to go over, if you don't mind? Are you starved, or can we study first?"

"Let's hit the books. I had a late lunch," I say.

She heads to her bedroom and returns with a textbook and binder.

We spend the next hour going over calculus equations.

She's pretty good at it, but there are some complicated trig questions she gets stuck on. As I explain one equation, I take in the scent of her hair, and my eyes drop to the creamy skin of her nape. *Hmm. She's so distracting. What does she taste like?*

"Did I get it right?" she asks, pulling me from my dirty thoughts.

I clear my throat and force myself to focus. "Yeah, I think you got this."

"Yay," she cheers, and gets up from the kitchen chair. "I'll just put these back in my room."

"I'll set up dinner," I say. I turn to watch her ass as she walks away. Then I have to adjust myself for the trillionth time because my rebellious cock keeps swelling in her presence.

She returns to the table and I have the wine bottle open.

"I don't know where you keep the glasses," I say.

She opens one of the cabinets and takes some regular drinking glasses off the shelf. "This is all I've got."

"That works." I wink and pour us each half a glass.

"When did you start drinking again?" she asks, not in a judgmental way—more like she's curious.

"I didn't. I just figured it would be nice to kick back and relax with you," I say. She seems to like my answer because she smiles, and the warmth touches the gold in her eyes, making them shine.

We eat sushi and drink wine. After dinner, we drink more wine until we've polished off the bottle. I'm feeling warm and happy and Sierra is flushed.

"I think this was a bad idea," she says.

"What?" I ask, even though I have a clue as to what she is talking about.

"The wine. I'm feeling giddy." She giggles.

"If I remember from the wedding, you're a fun drunk to be around. Lucky for us, you can't drink anymore since I only brought one bottle. Just enjoy the buzz," I say.

She stands to clear the table. When she gets to the kitchen, she turns on an old CD player she has sitting on the counter.

Imagine Dragons begins to play. She starts singing and swaying her hips. I get up and we both start dancing. She laughs and I laugh, and we just enjoy the moment until I take her hand and pull her into me. Her smile fades and the flush in her cheeks brightens. With her body pressed against mine, I can't hide what I'm feeling any longer.

"Nils." She says my name as a warning.

"Stop fighting this." I gaze into her eyes and there's a silent understanding between us.

She nods, and that's all I need for my lips to come crashing down on hers. Months of wanting her come to a boil as my lips move with hers. She takes and I give. I give and she takes, our tongues swirling in delicious harmony. She tastes better than I remembered, sweet and sultry.

Her hands come up to my hair, and her fingers dig into my scalp. My hands run down her neck and wrap around her back. Her palms resting on my shoulders.

"Tell me you want me to take you to bed." My gruff voice is filled with urgency. My chest heaves and my cock pulses behind the zipper of my jeans. This isn't about my abstinence; this is me wanting her more than my next breath. Damn it.

"I want you to take me to bed, Nils. I want you so bad," she says, her voice dripping with lust and her eyes holding a carnality that makes my world tilt sideways.

I lift her in my arms and carry her to her bedroom. She giggles and her smile is infectious, but it dies the moment I place her on the mattress.

"Take off your tank top," I say, waiting.

She does as I say, and I stare at her white lace bra that is slightly see-through.

"Take off your bra." I tilt my chin to her breasts and my eyes drop to her perfect rose-colored nipples. I can't count the number of nights I got off to thoughts of her full breasts. Her chest rises and falls of at a quick pace. Her fast breaths send my own need skyrocketing. "Now the pants."

"You take something off first," she says, and she licks those pouty lips of hers. My cock pulses.

I remove my sweater and take off my jeans, leaving me in nothing but my boxers and a T-shirt. My cock stands erect and pulsing behind the waistband.

"Take off that shirt, too," she says.

I hesitate. Part of the reason I got so many tattoos was to hide my scars. The sleeve of my arms are covered in tattoos, but my chest and abdomen only have a few sparse ones. In the past, I would keep my shirt on during sex but with her, I want to feel her skin against mine. I want our bodies connected in every way. Only, I feel more naked now than I ever have.

I take a deep breath and remove my shirt.

She gasps and crawls on her knees toward me. "Are these from him?" she asks. Her touch is feather soft; her voice is silky and sweet.

"Yes. It's not something I like to dwell on or bring attention to," I say.

"I get that," she says, and she kisses me on the mouth. That small gesture makes my heart beat fast as a warmth I've never felt before floods my insides.

"Get undressed," I say more softly. I don't want to lose this moment with her. I sure as hell don't want to turn it into a therapy session.

She removes her pants and then crawls to the edge of the bed. She's about to go for my cock when I stop her. I don't know what she's planned, but I am about to blow my load without even touching her. I've been dreaming about her and getting off to thoughts of her naked body for weeks.

"Wait." I stop her hand from fisting my cock. "Lie back on the bed and touch yourself."

Her cheeks turn a cherry red.

"Don't be shy," I say softly.

"I am shy and inexperienced," she admits.

"Are you a virgin?" I ask, as I slowly remove her glasses and place them on the bed stand. I remember Sloane's mother saying something about her not having orgasmed the weekend of Oli and Sloane's wedding.

"No." Her hazel eyes are intense as she looks down at the bed. "Not a virgin. Just . . . I haven't been with many guys," she says, and I like those words very much.

"Lie back. I'll take care of you."

CHAPTER TWENTY-ONE

S ierra

SEEING HIS SCARS BREAKS MY HEART AND REMINDS ME THAT WE are two broken souls who have come together again. Is it fate? I'm falling for him and I can't seem to stop it.

He hovers above me—big, strong, and sexy as hell. I have a feeling he's used to hiding those scars. They make him more handsome than ever because they show his resilience. His tanned skin and those tattoos running up his arms are hot, but it's the searing look in his blue eyes that brings me undone.

He watches me carefully as his hands work to lower my panties. Thankfully, I put on a pair of lace panties—not that I was expecting something to happen, but it feels like we have been building to this forever.

"I want to taste you," he says. His words make me squirm.

"I can't. I mean, I've never had anyone do that before," I confess.

His chest rises and falls in a soothing rhythmic motion.

"Please let me. I need you to trust me," he says.

"I do trust you," I admit, and it's the truth. He's been so good to me these last couple months. "I'm just nervous."

"Let me relax you," he says, that accent of his sounding sultry.

"Okay," I say quietly.

He lowers his head and kisses me on the lips. I ease my body into him. Our bare skin touching ignites the flame burning low in my belly. He kisses me slowly, like he means it. His lips move to my neck, where he peppers kisses. Goose bumps erupt all over my body as he moves lower to my shoulders, spreading kisses there, too. When he reaches my left breast, the warmth of his tongue runs over my sensitized nipple and my body arches into his touch. He pays careful attention to each of my nipples, licking and sucking. Wetness pools between my thighs, and I want to moan, but I'm embarrassed from my extreme reaction. His tongue lowers down my stomach to my abdomen and then he is there, his head between my thighs as he slowly licks up my slit, then back down. His tongue runs over my clit softly, slowly, and I am a goner, as moan after moan escapes my lips. My body arches off the bed. He doesn't relent, his tongue moving torturously over my most sensitive parts.

"That feels so good." My words are lazy and drawn.

I look down to see a small smile spreading across his lips and then he licks me faster, causing my eyes to fall shut and my head to fall back. Something is building inside me. I know the feeling from when I try to get myself off. Problem is, when it's my own fingers, I get close to orgasm but can never reach that spot they call nirvana. This is different.

Nils inserts a finger inside me and my lower parts spasm. I moan so loudly, I don't recognize my own voice, and then. . . wave after wave of pure bliss. His finger pumps inside me, his tongue laves at my clit, and I ride the wave as colors spark behind my eyes.

I'm on a blissful cloud when I feel Nils's body beside me. It takes me time to return to planet earth, and when I do, I am the most relaxed person in the universe.

"How was that?" he asks, looking proud of himself.

"Perfect." I lean over and kiss him, tasting myself on his lips.

I don't want to talk. I just want to enjoy this time with him.

The kissing causes my body to heat and the pulse between my legs picks up pace. I move quickly to remove his boxers and I'm not surprised when I see his thick, smooth, long cock. The hashtag doesn't do him justice, but I get a little nervous because I've never been with anyone his size. He runs his hands up and down my ass as I move above him.

"I should get a condom," he says.

I shift to the side and he reaches to the floor to grab his jeans. He pulls out a condom.

"I always carry a condom with me, but I haven't been with anyone in months," he says, and his words ease something inside me. He rolls the condom over his swollen cock. "Do you want to ride me?"

"I'm a little nervous," I admit.

"Okay." He smiles and places a soft kiss on my nose like he thinks I'm cute. Then he hovers above me. I think he's going to enter me but his hand dips between my thighs. "You're so wet. Fuck. I don't think I'll last long." His fingers move in a circular motion over my clit and my hips begin to gyrate.

"Nils, I need you inside me," I say breathlessly.

He slides inside me, stretching my walls and filling me in the best way possible. He begins to roll his hips and the tug and pull of his cock inside me ignites a fire within me.

My breathing picks up as he grunts. My hips move, meeting him thrust for hungry thrust.

"You feel so good," he groans. And he picks up pace. At this angle, his cock presses against my clit with every thrust, and I can't take it anymore. The walls inside me begin to spasm and I let go as another orgasm hits me head-on. Nils's body jerks, and then he comes, and it's so perfect as I watch this handsome brooding man come apart for me. I hate to compare our situation to the sex tape I saw, but I do, and he is different now. He's sweet and intimate; the way he looks at me makes me feel special. I only hope that it doesn't seal my fate, and that heartbreak isn't waiting for me on the horizon.

CHAPTER TWENTY-TWO

S ierra

NILS HAS BEEN IN TOWN ALL WEEK AND HE'S BEEN IN MY BED every night except for yesterday. He said I was wearing him out and he needed to be well-rested for his home game tonight against St. Louis. I needed the space anyway so I could go job hunting. There is no way I could allow him to continue paying me to be his fake girlfriend when we are sleeping together. My Aunt Becca told me about a fair-trade coffee shop that just opened and was looking to hire. Luckily, they hired me on the spot.

I spent the afternoon training and spent last night working on a project for one of my classes late into the night. Now, it's noon on Sunday and I need my coffee fix. Trudging out of bed with my eyes half shut, I do a double take when I spot Sunny sleeping at the kitchen table. That's weird. I didn't even hear her come in this morning.

I open the kitchen cabinet quietly to take out a mug and I start our little coffee maker. Then grind some beans. Nothing like having fresh-ground coffee beans in the morning. It's the one thing Sunny and I agreed on and that's why we splurged on a top-notch machine. She shifts in the chair and lifts her head.

"Sorry." I wince.

She rubs her neck. Her blue eyes are swollen and small. Her hair is a knotty mess.

"What's going on?" I ask.

"I got into a fight with Declan," she says. "He was just being so ridiculous."

"I'm sorry. That sucks. Can I ask what happened?"

"Everything was really good. We had all this time to ourselves. We spent the whole day in bed, our first night together, and skipped classes, which I know was bad, but it was nice to have that time together. We hadn't agreed to be exclusive, but I assumed we were heading in that direction. I didn't want to seem pushy, you know?" she says, looking up at me. My stomach sinks because it sounds a lot like Nils and me.

"It's tough; I get it. I mean, it would be hard for me to really be with someone if I didn't have a commitment from them," I say, and I feel like such a hypocrite.

"You and Nils are adorable. It's so amazing that you were able to get him to commit," she says. My guilt rises. Sunny and the rest of the fandom think he and I are a real couple.

"Yeah," I say, and my stomach begins to turn. "Would you like coffee?"

She nods. "Please."

I make us the coffee and place the mug in front of her, then I take a seat opposite her at the kitchen table.

"Did you ask Declan to commit?" I ask.

She bites her bottom lip and stares at me warily. "I didn't ask him. I don't want to be that girl. I want him to want to be with me," she says, and I want to say *hear, hear,* but I keep my mouth shut. I'm feeling her pain. The past few days have been amazing with Nils, but I need more.

"I get that," I say.

"After we, you know . . . last night." She bobs her head. "He started talking about you and Nils. How it's so crazy that a guy with his reputation just gave up his bachelorhood and settled down."

"It's not like we got married." I guffaw.

"He knows that, but he was basically saying how crazy it is that a guy like Nils would want a girlfriend." She pauses and the self-deprecation that is always there somewhere inside me surfaces. I finish her sentence in my head. Why would Nils want a goody two-shoes girlfriend like me? How can I be pissed about Declan thinking that, when I've had the same reservations? Nils and I are an unlikely couple. It worked with me being his fake girlfriend but now, with all the chemistry combusting between us, I once again wonder if we could be more. Knowing the way Nils feels, it probably never will be. I don't know if I can accept that.

"Trust me, I've thought the same thing," I say, because I don't have something better. I'm so deep into the lie I'm sinking in quicksand.

"I'm sorry. I don't want to make you question your relationship. Declan is an asshole, and I told him that," she says, and I feel worse and worse by the second.

"You fought with him because of me." I swallow hard, my voice shaky.

"Not because of you, but because of the idea of you. Declan doesn't want a relationship. A guy like him never will. Where does that leave me?"

"I hate to ask this, but has he been sleeping with other girls?" I grimace. I know Nils says he hasn't, which makes it a lot easier to be with him. He'll say he only wants me one minute, and then the next, he'll say he has to focus on hockey and has no time for something real. It's so frustrating.

"I don't think so." She shrugs.

"Have you asked him about it?"

"I've asked him. He says he only wants me and that we

should just enjoy our time together, but to me, those words seem final. Like, when does our time end? And who decides?" She raises both palms to the sky and lifts her brows. "I'm getting in deep, Sierra. I've got real feelings for him. When he spoke about Nils the way he did, I felt like it was a way for him to tell me how he truly feels in an indirect way, and it stung so bad. My heart is broken. Gah!" Her head falls and hangs between her shoulders.

I stand and embrace her in a hug. What she's going through makes me think of Nils and me, and I want to kick myself because I've just set myself up for the same heartbreak. Now what am I supposed to do?

CHAPTER TWENTY-THREE

Nils

WE'RE IN THE LOCKER ROOM, PREPPING FOR THE BIG GAME tonight. St. Louis took the Stanley Cup last season, which means tonight is going to be a challenge because their goalie is so fucking good that nothing gets past him.

"Hey, man." Oli claps me on the back.

"How's it going?" I ask.

"Life is good. Sucks to be back to reality. I would have liked more time away with Sloane, but hey, we got to make a living, right?" he winks.

"I don't know. Hockey is my life, not just a living," I say. It was all I had growing up. It kept me going.

"How do you manage a girlfriend with that kind of attitude?" Matt cuts in.

"Just fine, thanks." I give him the finger and he laughs. "I'm not getting pussy whipped. Not a fucking chance."

"I heard you and Sierra did the deed. Thank fuck," he whispers.

"Fuck. I can't believe she told Sloane." I shake my head. I'm not necessarily mad. I'm just not into sharing personal details about Sierra.

"So, no more fake bullshit," he says quietly.

"No, man. That is still on," I say.

His brows furrow. "How does that work exactly?"

"Come on, don't play that card with me. She's hot. We have an arrangement, and we have some fun on the side. Everything is cool." With my skates done up, I stand and grab my helmet. "Come on, let's go kick some ass." I wave for him to come.

The team heads out to the ice. We skate our asses off. St. Louis is a strong team. We fight hard for the puck and their damn goalie blocks every pass shot his way, but then we do a play that Coach planned with me and Myles beforehand. Myles is close to the net. He's clear to shoot, but he doesn't. Instead, he skates around the back of the net, comes around, and shoots me the puck. It all happens so fast it seems like a blur, even to me. The puck flies past a player on the St. Louis team. I catch it with my stick and shoot at an angle. It hits the back of the net and we score. The home crowd goes wild and we win the game.

The first thing I do is look for Sierra in the crowd. I spot her beside Kelsey, both of them cheering and jumping up and down. I skate by the plexiglass in front of her seat and wink. The warmth in her eyes hits me in the chest.

I gave Sierra instructions to meet me by the locker room, like I usually do when she attends a home game.

I spot her when I leave through the locker room doors after changing. She's wearing a plaid mini skirt with a pair of Dr. Martens. She sees me and walks over from a spot she was waiting at, off to the side and away from the media crews.

"Hi, beautiful." My eyes rake up her body. My arm comes around her waist as I pull her in for a kiss. She lets the kiss linger and to me it feels like another win tonight. "Fuck, you look hot."

She smiles and rolls her eyes. "It's a new outfit. I'm kind of freezing my ass off, but I really wanted to wear it."

"I'm glad you did, and I'll blast the heat in the car. You're still coming over now, right?" I ask.

"Yeah, I took a cab so I don't have my car," she says.

"Cool."

We head out to my Tesla. I pull into traffic.

"You should've packed an overnight bag," I say, placing my hand on her bare thigh.

"I have a class first thing in the morning. I really can't stay the night," she says, looking out the window. "I can always Uber back to my apartment if you're tired."

"I'm not tired. I can drive you home. I'm pumped. Did you see the goal? It felt awesome," I say.

"It was an awesome play," she says, but she isn't her normal enthusiastic self. I just can't put my finger on why.

I pull up in the drive and look at her. Her eyes grow wide. My house was designed by some famous architect. It's got a smooth, sleek design with concrete, stone, and wood finishing's.

I park in the driveway.

"This is stunning," she says.

I laugh. "Let's go inside first, then you can tell me what you think."

I open the door and wave for her to step in first. I hit a set of lights in the entrance way, then I turn to watch her reaction. Her eyes are round, and she looks like she's in awe.

"Nils, this is . . . wow. The space is so functional." She walks deeper into the house and her head tilts up to the ceiling where I have a glass roof. It's one of the most impressive points in the house. On clear nights like tonight, you can see millions of stars twinkling in the sky. It reminds me of my youth in Hogsby, when I used to sneak out of the house late at night and sit in the field just to watch the stars. It was the only time I felt at peace.

"Did you buy the house ready or was it you who hired the architect?" she asks.

"I wish I could say it was me involved in the design. I bought the house ready. It belonged to a businessman who had way too much money. He was leaving Chicago to focus on his philan-thropy work. I saw the roof during the day and loved it. I came back that night and saw all the stars in the sky. Even though my hometown was a dump, something about being able to see the stars called to me. I knew it was the right house," I say. I rub the scruff on my cheek and leave out the part about how after I moved in, I realized what a mistake it was to buy such a big house for one person. Sometimes the walls echo, and the loneli-ness can be suffocating.

"It's really wonderful." Her eyes gleam. "I know it sounds crazy, but I always pictured myself living somewhere in the country. I hate how busy the city can be. This house would be perfect if it was transplanted outside the city. Imagine how many stars you'd see then, without all the city lights interfer-ing," she says, and I imagine the sky in Hogsby. She's right. There is no comparison. I would never want to go back to Sweden but the idea of living in the country somewhere does appeal to me.

"Show me around." She smiles.

I give her the grand tour from the pool and hot tub in the backyard, to the master bedroom with my king-size bed.

"You know what I want right now?" I say, stalking toward her as she stands in front of the patio door in my room that leads to a small balcony overlooking my backyard.

She turns to look at me and her eyes rake over my body. I love when she gives me that hungry look.

"What do you want?" she asks, batting her lashes. The little vixen knows exactly what I want and she's taunting me.

"I want to take you up against that window," I say.

"Hmm." She taps her fingers on her lips. "I'm guessing you must have had many girls in this room. How many have you taken up against the window?" She looks me in the eyes and my heart stammers.

"None," I say.

"None?" she repeats. "How so? I've heard about your

legendary parties. Seen Twitter feeds about you waking up with more than one girl."

I shouldn't be surprised that she knows about my antics, but in a way, I am.

"Those girls never made it to my room. I lock my room with a key during parties. No one comes in here but me and the maid," I say.

"And have you done your maid?" She raises her brows.

I place my hand on my hips and shake my head. "No! I have not done my maid. If you need to hear it, then fine," I say, sounding a little irritated. "You're the first woman I've ever had in here." The words feel gritty when they leave my lips. Why did I bring her up here? I could have taken her on the kitchen counter or on my very large couch in the family room. I could have flirted with her in one of the guest rooms and taken her on the bed there. But it's in here where I fantasize about her at night when I'm alone.

"Is that true?" she asks.

"Have I ever lied to you?" I counter.

She thinks for a second. "No. You've always been honest."

"Gee, thanks." I snicker. "Now come here."

I pull her by her waist until her body is flush with mine. She stares into my eyes and the heat in hers matches my own. I don't kiss her. Instead, I take one of her full breasts in my hand and knead it before rubbing my finger over her nipple. Her breathing changes. I handle her breasts roughly and push her bra out the way.

My mouth crashes down on hers, as hunger consumes me. Sucking on her lower lip, I kiss her breathless. We are both panting as her hands grab onto my hair and yank slightly. I love when she does that.

My hands move from her breasts, and I grab on to the back of her thighs. She wraps her legs around my waist, and her heat rubs against me through the fabric of my jeans. My mind goes to my fantasy, as I walk her to the window and press myself against her. I'm rewarded with her sweet moans as she kisses me and moves her hips against me, needing the friction.

"I need to get you naked," I mutter breathlessly into her mouth.

"Yesss," she answers, and I lower her from the window. I get to work removing my own clothes, figuring it will be faster that way. I won't have to wait as long to get inside her.

She works on removing her sweater, then her bra. The sight of her breasts makes my cock twitch. I take a deep breath. She unbuttons her jeans, then removes her panties in one fell swoop. It's only been two days since I've been inside her and yet, I can't wait to plant my cock deep inside her pussy. When we're both naked, I close the space between us and kiss her. She wraps her arms around my neck, and I take her thighs and lift her so she can wrap her legs around me.

I press her against the window, and she gasps. "It's cold."

"I've fantasized about taking you like this. I've gotten myself off to thoughts of taking you on this window. Just thinking my hand was you coating me with your juices made me so hard, I came like a fucking animal," I say.

At my words, she begins to rub herself in a quick motion against my cock. She's panting. Her juices coat me just like in my fantasy.

"I need you inside me," she says.

I don't have a condom on. For the first time in my life, I also don't have the patience to get one. "Are you on the pill?"

"Yes," she answers.

"I was tested a couple months back and haven't been with anyone but you since. Can I come inside you like this?" I ask. I surprise even myself with the request.

She pauses. I've clearly thrown her off. It seems like whatever she's thinking clouds her features and then she answers with one word . . . "Yes."

My heart gallops as I exhale. My cock slides inside her. Warmth and wetness coat me; I'm in sheer heaven. I pump inside her and she moans relentlessly, her head moving against the glass as she bobs up and down on my dick. I suck at her breasts, since my hands are being used to hold her up. Her head lolls from side to side as she makes the sweetest of sounds.

"I'm going to come," she warns. I'm right behind her. I want to say it out loud, but my balls get heavy and sparks shoot down my spine as she screams my name. I blow my load inside her. Sparks fill my vision as I stiffen and pump. Her sounds make my orgasm last longer as she spasms around me.

We both fall to the ground limp and out of breath. I've never gone bareback before, and holy fuck, was I missing out. My cum drips down her legs and something inside me makes me want to beat my chest like a fucking caveman. She's mine. *Only she isn't.*

"Let me grab you a towel," I say, trying to suppress my last thought. I trudge to the master bathroom and grab one of the clean towels hanging on the bar. I soak it with warm water and bring a dry towel too. I clean off her legs with the wet one and hand her the other to dry herself with while I get myself cleaned up.

"Come." I take her by the hand and flip my comforter over. We both get into bed. She snuggles up next to me, and I kiss the top of her head. I've never been intimate with a woman before, but Sierra makes it easy. Before her, sex was a release. A way to get off. With her, it feels like a way to be closer to her. It makes me feel good and bad. I can't understand why.

"My legs feel like jelly," she says.

"Mine too." I chuckle. "It was a hard game."

"I'm glad you think so," she says, rolling her eyes playfully.

"I can't let myself fall asleep, even though I feel like my eyes are closing," she says.

"Sleep. We can wake up extra early," I say.

She tilts her head to look up at me. "I think it would be better if you drove me home tonight, if that's okay."

I get a weird vibe from her, like I did earlier in the car. "Okay.

I can take you. Did you want to go now?" I ask, assuming she will say no.

"Yes. If we stay like this, one of us will fall asleep," she says. She moves out of my grasp. She leaves the bed and uses the bathroom and when she comes back, I want her to get back into bed with me, only she walks over to the window, picks up her clothes, and begins to get dressed. I'm disappointed.

I get dressed, too, and lead her downstairs.

"Are you hungry?" I ask her, because I am famished.

"Yes, I could eat something. I didn't have time for dinner," she explains. Her mood is solemn. I don't ask her why. I'm not sure I should.

We head to the kitchen and I make us grilled cheese sandwiches. Well, I make her one and me three. Then I drive her home.

"I forgot to mention that I got a job yesterday," she says as I'm driving.

I want to hit the brakes and say, 'What the ever-loving fuck?' but I take a deep breath and instead, I say, "Don't tell me you're quitting me."

"Very funny." She laughs. "I can't let you pay me anymore. Now that we're sleeping together, it just doesn't feel right."

My stomach sinks. "What does that mean?"

"I got a job at a fair-trade coffee shop close to my apartment," she explains.

"So, you won't be my fake girlfriend anymore?"

Her lips pinch. "Don't you think we've complicated things?"

"Things are perfect," I say.

"Look, Nils. If you need me to still help you out with the couple pics on social media, that's fine. I hate lying to Sunny about you being my boyfriend, but I've committed, so I'm willing to carry on this charade a little longer. Your rep has been cleared. You've had a great start to the season. I've seen your stats."

"But I mean, I still want to see you. Like, can we still stay in touch?" My hands grip the steering wheel tight.

"Yeah. We've become friends, I'd like to think," she says.

My brows pinch together. We are a lot more than friends. "I like our phone talks. I like spending time with you. Hell, I love having sex with you. Tonight was off the charts, am I right?" I'm stopped at a red light, so I look at her. She has her hands held together in a ball in her lap and she's chewing her lip.

"It was." She nods.

The light turns green and we are seconds away from pulling up to her apartment building. I don't know what I'm supposed to do, but I feel her slipping away.

We reach the curb.

"Good night, beautiful," I say. She leans over and gives me a closed-mouth kiss on the lips. The only relief I have is that she lingers a little longer than usual. It makes me feel uneasy like maybe she is saying goodbye.

"Good night, Nils." She leaves my car. I want to call after her. But I don't, because I think I know what's happening, and I have nothing to offer her but a good time in bed.

CHAPTER TWENTY-FOUR

S ierra

I'VE BEEN FOCUSING ON SCHOOL AND WORK THE LAST COUPLE of weeks. Nils has been on a long stretch of away games. Still, he calls me every night and posts stuff on Twitter about missing his girl, and wishing he was with me.

How I wish those posts weren't just a façade. I've completely fallen for him. I'm pissed at myself for letting it happen, when I knew he wanted nothing more than a fake girlfriend and a warm bed.

Sunny told Declan she doesn't want to see him anymore, and he didn't come running after her. I'm afraid if I say the same to Nils, he won't come running after me either, and where will that leave me?

I've gone and fallen in love with the jerk. I can't picture my life without him. I wait for his nightly calls. Sometimes, he calls after midnight if he's had a late game, but without fail, he always calls. It's confusing, because he says he's attracted to me and doesn't want to sleep with other women, and the sex between us is the best I've ever had. I think he feels the same, minus all the intense feelings I've developed.

He's going to be home tomorrow, and he told me to clear my schedule in the evening so we could have dinner together. I made sure to get the assignment I was working on out of the way just so I could spend time with him. It's messed up. I don't know what to do.

I can't share my thoughts with Sloane because she basically went apeshit when I told her we had sex. Yes, she wants us together, but she wants Nils to be committed to me. Only that isn't happening because, as I've learned, commitment isn't his thing.

After picking up some groceries, I head home. I place my items on the counter and I realize I have a message from Nils.

Nils: What do you want for dinner?

Me: I'm making us dinner.

Now that I'm not under his employment, this isn't one of our designated dates and he doesn't need to feel obligated to pay.

Nils: Let me bring takeout. You work hard enough as it is.

He has a point, but after treating me so many times, I'd feel better if I made him dinner.

Me: I'm cooking. What time do you plan on coming by?

Nils: I can be there by seven.

I look at my phone. It's five.

Me: Perfect. See you then.

Standing by the stove, I feel torn. Yes, I've been sleeping with him, even though he isn't willing to commit, but now that feelings are involved, something has shifted.

As I sear the chicken breasts in the pan for the chicken piccata, I make a decision. I can't sleep with him anymore. My heart breaks as my mind and heart process exactly what it will mean, but I don't have a choice. I can't continue making love to him, knowing he doesn't feel the same way. It will implode eventually, and I want to have control over when it ends. As it is, I'm in too deep.

When dinner is cooked, I take a shower and wash my hair since I hate smelling like the food I've cooked. I slip on a pair of panties, joggers, and a loose grey T-shirt when the doorbell chimes. Wearing a completely unsexy outfit won't keep his advances at bay, since he clearly wants to have sex with me no matter what I am wearing, but feeling unsexy may help me reject his advances when they arrive. And I know they will arrive. I could sense his tone was needy during last night's call.

I saunter over to the door with wet hair, no makeup, and a heavy heart. When I open the door, I am met with a smiling Nils. He's holding a bouquet of pink roses and a box of Godiva chocolates.

"We aren't in a fake relationship. You didn't have to do this." I lean up and press a fast kiss to his lips.

His arms snake around my waist and he pulls me flush with his body.

"I wanted to do this. I can tell you like flowers and chocolate," he says, pressing his lips to mine.

"The chocolate is going to add to my already curvy hips," I say. I pull away from him.

"I love your hips; they're sexy as hell." He looks around the apartment. "Are we alone?"

I can read his mind; it's easy. "Sunny is out. I'm guessing she'll be back around midnight."

He nods and smiles. "Good. I've missed you so hard."

My hand comes up to caress his cheek. I love touching him, being with him, talking to him. I'm going to miss this.

"Hope you're hungry," I say, walking into the kitchen. I place the chocolates on the counter and get the flowers set up in a vase. I place them on the side of the table.

"It smells really good," he says.

"I made chicken piccata. I hope it turned out good because it was my first time trying this recipe," I say.

"Just smelling it, I can tell it will be delicious," he says.

"Thank you." I place it on the table. Nils sets the cutlery and plates.

We sit to eat. He compliments me repeatedly. Other than thank you, I don't say much. I don't know what to say.

After we finish eating, I stand to clear the plates off the table. He stands, too, and places his hand over mine.

"Let me get this," he says. "You cooked. I'll clean up."

I don't know why those words surprise me, but they do. Nils and I grew up in dysfunctional families. To say we had bad role models is an understatement. The fact that he is being so sweet makes what I am about to do even harder.

I help him clear the table. He insists on washing the dishes. He tells me about his time away. I tell him I was able to watch a few of the games.

"I did well on the math test you helped me out with. I just got the mark back," I say.

"Good." He gives me a one-word answer that sounds tense. I've been less than talkative all evening and I know he senses it.

The air in the kitchen suddenly feels dense and my chest constricts.

"Do you want to tell me what's going on with you?" His voice is filled with concern. I'd expected him to maybe be irritated because I've been shut down since he arrived, but he isn't.

I take a deep breath. *You can do this.*

"I don't think we should see each other anymore," I say quickly. He flinches. The sting of my words reverberates in my chest. My heart splits in two.

"Are you serious?" His face contorts. "Why?"

"Why?" I repeat. "Because we aren't going anywhere. This whole 'fuck buddy' situation we have going on is messed up. I told you from the start that I'm not okay with no-strings-attached sex. I just can't do it anymore."

He snickers, loud and ugly. "Fuck buddy, huh?" he says, like the words taste bad on his tongue. "You damn well know I don't treat you like a fuck buddy."

I fold my arms over my chest as anger builds inside me. "Oh, really? Explain it to me, Nils. We have these intense talks like we are good friends. I've told you things I've never shared with anyone else—"

"I have, too."

"We sleep together, Nils. A lot, and it's great, but it needs to end because I'm not built for this." A lone tear I was trying to hold in escapes and slips down my cheek.

"Don't do this, Sierra," he pleads. His blue eyes look pained, but he isn't offering an alternative, and I won't ask for one.

"I just did." I hold strong. My chin is slightly tilted up. I can't break. Not now. He can't know that I've fallen so utterly, deeply in love with him that I can't think straight. He doesn't feel the same way. I won't be rejected.

"What about our friendship? You just want to throw that away?" His voice shakes, and his eyes fill with tears. I hate that he's hurting. As much as I see his pain, he won't give me what I want.

Hold strong, Sierra..

"I don't want to end our friendship, but I don't see another way. I need you to leave, Nils. Please," I plead, working hard to keep my voice even, when I'm only moments away from breaking.

He gives me an incredulous look and picks his car keys off the counter. He turns away from me and stalks out of the apartment.

I follow after him to lock the door. My heart is splitting in two. Did I just make the biggest mistake of my life? I wasn't expecting it to hurt so bad.

I head over to the couch and cry my eyes out. Love hurts. I should have never gotten myself involved with him to begin with. Given our history, it was always going to be a recipe for disaster.

I head to the kitchen and grab a bottle of the cheap red wine I bought at the supermarket. I was going to serve it with dinner, but then thought it would send the wrong message, and I needed a clear head. Now I just don't want to feel anything at all.

I turn on Netflix and find a romantic movie because I am clearly a glutton for punishment. Then I pour my first glass of wine and drink it down too fast. I pour another as I watch *Return to the Blue Lagoon*. Being stranded on an island would suck, but I like how the characters love each other so much. Then, when that woman comes from the mainland and tries to take poor Richard away, my blood boils. I think of all the relationship-haters Nils and I had. There are going to be lots of women to pounce on him now. Will he revert back to his old ways and sleep with random women? The thought turns my blood cold. Yet, I know you can't cage a wild animal and expect to tame him. That's why I had to let Nils go, because he could never be what I need him to be.

CHAPTER TWENTY-FIVE

N ils

#RELATIONSHIPSSUCK. I TWEETED THOSE WORDS A WEEK AGO. Now, the bunnies are hot on my tail, sending me private messages. I don't want any of them, but I would just love to fuck Sierra Cole right out of my system.

I lace up my skates for tonight's game. I've wanted to drown myself in all the alcohol, but I haven't touched a drop all week. The temptation is strong. I still can't believe Sierra cut me off the way she did. Everything was going so well.

"Karlsson," Myles shouts. "We gotta move."

My mind snaps back to reality. I stand, grab my stick, and head out to the ice for tonight's game against the Minnesota Wild. Fitting it's the team she cheers for. Out on the ice the anthem sounds, and I look out to the stands, wanting to see her face, but of course, she isn't here.

I've picked up the phone to call her every night, but I haven't put the call through. She doesn't even want to speak to me. I know she wanted me to say that I would be in a relationship, that maybe we could see where our torrid little affair would lead us, but I can't say something I don't believe. I'm not relationship material. Besides, I've been having my best year in hockey yet. My stats are way up, and I need them to stay that way. I'll never do anything to risk my career again.

The bell sounds. Myles and a player from the other team start us off. Myles gets the puck first and shoots it out across the ice. We dash toward it like a bunch of mad men. The puck goes to Oli. He veers off to the right, shoots past Johnson from Minnesota, and straight to Chris. Chris gets hold of the puck. I wait closer to the net. Sears, a player from the other team, is hot on his tail. He's a hulk, and sometimes plays dirty.

Sears steels the puck from Chris and the other team takes it across the ice. They shoot, and Matt saves the day. The crowd goes wild and the game moves on.

Sweat drips down my face. I'm fucking tired, and it's not even half-time. I haven't slept well all week. I look out to the stands to the area where Sierra used to sit for home games. Kelsey, Sloane, and Flynn are here tonight. *Fucking great.*

Oli shoots the puck my way and I miss. Johnson flies past me sneaks up on Austin, steals the puck, and takes off. *Motherfucker.* Oli speeds off; Myles is already at Johnson. He steals the puck from Johnson, punting it back across the ice. Oli catches it and passes to Dave. Dave gets close to the net but doesn't have a clear shot. He takes the puck around the back of the net. When he reaches the front of the net, fucking Sears is in his way. I skate toward mid ice in time for Dave to make the sweetest pass my way.

I shoot and score. Only the excitement I usually feel after scoring just isn't there.

～

I'M SITTING ON THE BENCH, GULPING DOWN WATER AT HALF time when Oli glares at me. "What was that?" he asks.

He's referring to the pass I missed because I was daydreaming about seeing Sierra cheering for me in the stands. "Nothing." I shrug. "I'm human."

"Don't give me that bullshit. I've been playing with you long enough to know that you spaced. Why? You've been acting weird all week," he says. I turn to look at him and see the concern on his face.

"I'm fine, Oli. Drop it." I don't mean to snap, but I do. *Great.* Now my fucking anger is returning. Sierra had eased my anger like a balm. No, it wasn't her. It was Fisher. He did a good job, refocusing me. I should increase my sessions

The bell rings and we head back out to the ice.

CHAPTER TWENTY-SIX

S ierra

"HOW ARE THINGS GOING WITH SCHOOL?" AUNT BECCA ASKS, as I sit across from her at the kitchen table making jewelry. Since she was sick, she's fallen back on her orders. It's my third time over here this week making jewelry.

"Same old. I'm working on a big assignment. It's pretty cool. We have to create an addition to a house. It can be anywhere in the house," I explain.

"Which area did you choose?" she asks.

"In the drawings they gave me, the kitchen was super small. The space wasn't functional at all. I created an addition to the kitchen using all glass walls. I also included some solar panels on the roof. Environmentally clean building is the way of the future," I say, trying to sound cheerful.

"I like your optimism. Still with all the high-rises being built, we are a long way off from sustainable architecture," Aunt Becca replies.

"Agreed," I say, and pick up a stone. When I look up, I see concerned hazel eyes watching me.

"Do you want to tell me what's going on with you? I mean, I could guess. And don't get me wrong—I love it when you come over—but sitting here for hours on end making jewelry isn't like you. What happened to your job? Did you get fired?"

"I didn't get fired. I've been calling in sick," I admit, my shoulders hunched forward.

"Are you okay?" She furrows her brows.

"I'm not sick. I ended things with Nils," I say, as the all too familiar burn rises in my chest.

"Oh, honey." She stands and walks around the table to give me a hug. I force the tears to remain at bay. "What happened?"

"Nothing." I throw my hands in the air dramatically. "He didn't want to commit, and I told him I couldn't do what we were doing any longer."

"What did he say?" she asks.

"He didn't want things to end, but he also didn't want to commit. That was two weeks ago. I was hoping he would have a change of heart and realize he can't live without me, but clearly he can, so . . ."

"Breaking up is hard to do." Aunt Becca's lips turn down. "I had a beau once. We were best friends, and it turned into more. Then we went off to college and went our own separate ways. We drifted apart. I began traveling; he joined the workforce. I checked him out on Facebook a while back. He's a CEO of some corporation." She laughs. "Could you see me with a CEO?"

"Yeah. I mean, why not? Don't they say opposites attract?" I ask. Nils and I were nothing alike and somehow, we worked. The chemistry between us was undeniable, or so I'd thought.

"In certain cases, and in others, not so much," she says.

"Is the guy married?" I ask.

Her nose scrunches up. "I don't know if he was married but his relationship status showed single."

"You should totally reach out to him. What happens if he's the one?" I ask.

She shakes her head, laughing. "You're such a romantic, dear niece. Life isn't a romance movie. We aren't just going to pick up where we left off. Besides, I'm pretty sure that certain relationships have an expiry date."

She's cynical, and it reminds me how I used to think in the pre-Nils era when I didn't believe a relationship could last. When I didn't want to get myself in deep for fear of getting hurt. Somehow, Nils got me to overlook everything I believed. We are two opposites who meshed. Only, it wasn't lasting. *Nothing ever is.*

CHAPTER TWENTY-SEVEN

N ils

IT'S THANKSGIVING, AND I FIND MYSELF SITTING AT OLI AND Sloane's dining table with the rest of the usual gang, minus Sierra. Oli and the guys know we broke things off. The ladies know, too. Sloane called me out just before Halloween. Told me she thought I was a wuss. I didn't argue with her. I just didn't say anything at all, so she dropped it.

During our hearty turkey dinner, I lift my beer. "Thanks, guys, for having me over again. I'm thankful to have friends like you," I say to Oli and Sloane.

They both smile and mutter something along the lines of me being family.

After dinner, the kids are playing with toys in the family room while the adults sit back, too full of all the good food. A memory of Sierra having dinner here the weekend of Oli and Sloane's wedding pops into my mind. The ridiculous dancing we'd done with Quinn. The way she came to help me get Mata to her hotel room when she was stoned off her ass. The way Sierra just seamlessly fit into my life.

"You want to come outside?" Oli stands and asks me.

"It's freezing," I say.

"We got heaters on the deck. It's a nice night," he says. He tells Dave and Myles to join us.

We sit in a row on his Adirondack chairs and stare out to his backyard. It's big with lots of greenery, considering how close it is to the city. I take a deep breath and inhale the cool, crisp air.

"How are things going?" Myles asks, looking at me.

I sip my beer. "Alright."

Silence ensues. It lingers a while longer than I'd expected it would. These guys are usually a talkative bunch. If we have nothing to discuss, we talk hockey, plays and what to watch out for next game.

"Nils, don't take this the wrong way . . ." Oli breaks the silence.

"Okay." I laugh at the serious look on his face.

"You think that maybe you were affected by the whole Sierra breakup . . . like, a little more than you're letting on?" Oli continues hesitantly, like he's walking on eggshells.

My brows knit together. "We were never together. It wasn't a breakup."

"Your game has been off," Dave says.

Don't I fucking know it. Coach came down on me this week. Asked if I was drinking and partying again.

"I just haven't been sleeping well," I answer easily, leaving out the part that I miss Sierra. I won't admit those words out loud. I don't need her. I'm used to being on my own.

"Is it because you've started hooking up again?" Myles asks. "I'm only asking because I care, man. We all see something off with you."

"Why does it matter if I'm hooking up with chicks?" I ask, instead of answering. I don't want to admit that I haven't had sex in weeks because the only girl I want has booted my ass.

"It doesn't matter," Dave says, trying to maybe ease the tension I feel building in the air. "It's just that you've missed plays, you've lost the puck way more than you usually do, and your stats are down."

I shoot out of my seat. "Thanks for bringing my flaws to my attention. It's not like you guys don't have bad weeks. Why are you raining down on me? It isn't exactly fair."

Oli stands from his chair. "This isn't an attack. We think you're hurting over Sierra. Sloane said she ended things between you guys. It wasn't you."

"So?" My voice grows louder, as my irritation heightens. "Why the fuck does it matter who ended things? It's over. I had nothing to offer her. I have to focus on my career. I was almost booted from the team. I almost lost my spot in the NHL. My life was this close to going down the drain." I pinch my pointer finger and thumb together.

"I get that, man. I do. We are all human. Fuck-ups are part of the game. But for me, when I'm having a lagging week, it's because Sloane is sick, or Quinn had a fever the previous night. I also need to be on top of my game because I have a family to support, and hockey is all I know. I can't afford fuck-ups either," Oli says, staring me down.

"Fair enough. That's why we work our asses off," I say.

"Yeah, but having a woman in your life doesn't prevent you from being at the top of your game," Dave says. He was the first of the guys to get married and have kids. He's also a few years older than us.

"I get what you guys are saying. I appreciate that you care, but I'm fine. Sierra and I are very different people; it would never work," I say, feeding them the line I've been feeding myself. I barely believe it. The truth is, we worked just fine.

"Have it your way." Oli claps me on the shoulder and sits back in his chair. I take a seat too, and we discuss next week's games, which are out of town. I enjoy the night with my friends and tell myself it's enough for me. I don't need any more than this.

It's a lie.

CHAPTER TWENTY-EIGHT

S ierra

IT'S A WEEK BEFORE CHRISTMAS, AND I WALK DOWN THE BUSY streets, getting my shopping done after class. Half the year is over. Another half to go, and I will officially graduate.

Dad had called last night to ask if I would come home this year for Christmas, but I wasn't in the mood to spend the holidays with a man who didn't give me his love and support when I needed it most. Besides, flying home costs money I don't have. Even though I'm sure Dad would pay my ticket if I did decide to go home. I just feel like I don't want to go out of my way to see him. Especially when I have Aunt Becca here in the city. She has a group of friends who spend Christmas together, and so I'll spend the holiday with them. It's what I do every year.

My cell rings in my coat pocket. The weather is below freezing. Sloane's name lights up my screen and, as I say hello, my breath mists the air in front of me.

"Hey, babe," she says.

"Hi! I'm out Christmas shopping. Why did I leave it to last minute?"

"Because you're a rock-star student. How was the model you built?" she asks.

"It was freaking amazing. I'll have to send you pictures," I say.

"Please do." She pauses. "I don't want to keep you. I just wanted to see if I could convince you to spend Christmas with us."

She asked me a month ago for the first time. Now she calls me at least once a week to see if my decision has changed.

"You're so funny. I do appreciate your efforts, but it would be really awkward," I say. Nils never contacted me after our dinner together. I told him we were done, and he was out the door. No way do I want to see him. At least not for a few years.

"I get it. I do. Maybe if you bring a date it wouldn't be so weird," she suggests.

"Only I'm not dating anyone," I remind her.

"What about that friend of yours from school? Klause," she says. She knows he's a German citizen and that he's here on a student visa, meaning he has no family or ties to the city.

"I wouldn't want to give him the wrong impression. He tried hitting on me when we first met, and I put him in the friend zone," I explain.

"That's perfect, then. Bring him as a friend," she says.

"I promised Aunt Becca I'd do Christmas with her and her friends," I counter.

"Aunt Becca was doing Christmas with her friends before you ever moved to the city. They won't miss you" She giggles.

"Gee, thanks," I say in mock offence.

"Oh, you know what I mean." She sighs. "You can't hide from him forever, and we want to spend time with you. Kelsey and Flynn were just asking about you too," she says, pulling out the big guns.

I cave. "Okay. I'll come. It's nice of you to include Klause. I don't think he had anywhere to go. I'll ask him and get back to you."

"Yay," she squeals. "It's going to be awesome. Seriously. We do Christmas special around here."

I don't ask her what she means, but my heart feels warm and fuzzy from her words. I like spending time with them.

"I can't wait," I say.

"Me too. I'll call you soon with the deets," she says.

"Thanks. Take care." I end the call.

Now I have more gifts to add to my list. After finding gifts for Aunt Becca, Sloane, Oli, and Quinn in a department store, I bump into Sunny.

"Fancy meeting you here." She's holding hands with a guy.

"Reed, this is my roommate, Sierra," she says, and her cheeks are flushed. I had no clue she was seeing someone.

He shakes my hand.

"Nice to meet you," I say.

"You, too," he says. He has a kind smile. He looks like the bookish type—the complete opposite of Declan, who was rougher around the edges, with tattoos and a chip on his shoulder.

"Reed was just helping me pick up some presents," Sunny explains. I know she's heading home on Friday.

"Yeah, I was out doing some shopping myself," I say holding up all the gift bags in my hands. The moment is kind of awkward. I want to ask her why she would hide her new relationship from me, but it will have to wait. She gives me a half hug, since I have my hands full, and tells me she'll see me later.

I walk home, since I don't mind walking in the cooler weather and taking my car would have been a disaster with parking this time of year. I call Klause on my way. He's initially hesitant about joining me, but when I mention having Christmas with famous hockey players, he says it sounds like an experience he will never forget. I don't say it out loud, but I think it's going to be an experience I will never forget either.

CHAPTER TWENTY-NINE

S ierra

I'M LYING ON THE COUCH HAVING A *HOW I MET YOUR MOTHER* marathon on Netflix when Sunny slips through the door. She tiptoes to the kitchen. I pause my show.

"Oh, no," I call out. The girl has some explaining to do. She pauses mid-step. "Get yourself over here and tell me who that boy was, and why you were holding hands," I say with a playful tone.

She pinches her lips together and gives me a look that oozes guilt.

"I can explain," she says, batting her eyelashes while using that sweet southern accent of hers.

I lie back on the couch. "I'm all ears. This should be good."

"I wasn't hiding Reed from you. It's just that things are new between us. I didn't want to introduce him to my friends just yet," she begins.

"He's super different from Declan and Tino, and, who was before that?" I tap my finger to my chin.

"He is different. I'm doing an experiment," she says.

"Care to elaborate?" I raise my brows. *This should be good.* "I mean, I get it. You don't necessarily need to have a type. Nils was very different from the other guys I dated."

She takes a seat beside me on the couch and crosses her legs. She's sitting sideways, looking at me. "I know," she says. "But I have a type, Sierra. It's the bad boys with tattoos who like to party that get my skin hot, but you know what? Those boys only lead to broken hearts, so I told myself I'm changing my type to the bookish guys. No tattoos. No ladies' men."

"I get where you are going," I say. "And you are attracted to Reed?" He isn't a bad-looking guy, it was just . . . maybe I'm not used to seeing her with that type. It sounds awful.

"Hmm." Her lips pinch together. "I'm really trying to be. He's sweet and a gentleman. He wants to see me and spend time with me."

I call bullshit. Something is off. "He wants to hold your hand. You two looked like the sweetest couple," I say, mocking her southern accent—which I truly love, so much.

"Ha ha. We've been on a few dates. He's nice to talk to but I don't feel that electricity with him. Do you know what I mean?" She looks to me intently.

"I do." I didn't feel the buzz of electricity like a live wire until I hooked up with Nils.

"I need to tell him that I see him more as a friend. I just really liked the idea of him. If I could fall for someone sweet and dedicated, it would be a dream come true."

"Yeah, but chemistry is a vital aspect of the equation," I remind her.

"Fucking chemistry." She falls back on the couch and kicks her legs out like a toddler. I understand her frustration.

"At least you're trying to meet someone. That's a good start. I have no interest in dating at all," I say.

She ends her faux tantrum and places her hands behind her head so it's perched up and she can look at me. "I know it's hard, but you need to get back on that horse and ride." She stands up and begins to dance and sing "Old Town Road" by Lil Nas X.

I burst into laughter. "OMG you've totally lost it."

I'm laughing so hard I can barely breathe but she did get me to laugh. It's been a while, and it feels damn good.

"Glad to see you smile. Now, get up and join me." She waves me over.

I can't leave her hanging, so I stand, and we both sing, "Old Town Road" and dance. If anyone walked in now, they would think we were crazy. *Okay, we are crazy.*

I tire out first—after we repeat the song five times—and fall back on the couch. Sunny falls next to me.

"I agreed to go to Sloane and Oli's for Christmas," I blurt.

Sunny's eyes widen. "You're kidding me. Will he be there?"

"Yup. Sloane recommended I bring a friend just so that I have back-up. I asked Klause," I say.

Sunny gets a knowing look on her face.

"What?" I ask.

"Nothing," she answers, snapping her mouth shut.

"What?" I nudge her.

"Nothing. I just want to meet Sloane one day. She sounds like my kind of girl."

"And why is that?" I ask. Sloane is amazing, but I'm missing something.

"Because the girl's got tricks up her sleeve. I'm digging it." She begins singing and bobs her head to, "Old Town Road" again and that's when it hits me.

I'm screwed.

CHAPTER THIRTY

Nils

I'VE BEEN LUCKY TO GET AN INVITATION TO OLI AND SLOANE'S the last few years for Christmas. Before them, I had spent many alone.

I arrive a little late, since I did my Christmas shopping last-minute. I see Myles's SUV and Dave's car parked outside, right beside Sierra's. I'm surprised she came tonight. I know Sloane invited her for Thanksgiving, and she declined. Sloane hadn't mentioned that she would be here.

Oli comes to the door wearing a ridiculous red and green Rudolph sweater. He, Sloane, Flynn, and Myles wear the same sweater every year. It looks totally weird, but it gives them a sense of family, and I dig being around that kind of loving and commitment.

"Hey, man. Merry Christmas." Oli gives me a bro hug.

"Merry Christmas," I say. I pass him a bunch of gift bags.

"All for me? You shouldn't have," he jokes.

"Fuck you," I whisper, knowing not to swear loudly in case the kids are nearby.

I walk deeper into the house and I'm greeted by the usual crew, who stand up to hug me.

Matt is here tonight along with Dave's sister, Kierran, whom I've met a couple times before. I shake Matt's hand and give Kierran a wave. That's when I spot Sierra sitting on the couch. Beside her is some guy I don't know.

My blood turns hot and my muscles tense. Did she bring a fucking date? He sure as hell looks her type—bookish, smart. Their glasses practically match. I will myself to maintain control and not have a fit. I go over the steps Fisher taught me in my head.

First, I ask myself why I'm so angry. I don't have a right to be. We aren't together. It doesn't fucking mean my feelings for her just stopped. Seeing her is like a knife to the heart.

"Hi, Nils," she says from her spot on the couch. "This is Klause."

I've heard that name before. I think the douchebag is in her classes.

"Nice to meet you," I say. I'm actually picturing punching the guy out, which I know is really fucked up. I won't do it. I won't ruin everyone's Christmas.

"Yeah, you, too," he says, giving me a friendly smile.

"Okay, everyone come sit down," Sloane says.

We all head over to the large dining table and take our usual seats. The wait staff she hired comes around to offer champagne and set water pitchers on the table. Sloane tells Kierran to sit beside me and Matt on her other side. It leaves two seats open on the right side of me. Fucking hell. Sierra sits next to me and Klause next to her.

Sloane says grace and some of the kids sing Christmas songs, then we dig into our meal.

"Everything is really good," Flynn says.

"Thanks, schnookums. I used a caterer. Things have just

been so crazy busy. The publisher I'm working with is giving me the tightest deadlines," Sloane rolls her eyes.

"Everything is amazing," Flynn says.

"Catering is awesome," Myles says.

Dave and Kelsey are busy helping their kids eat, and Oli and Sloane are focusing on feeding Quinn. Matt and Kierran have struck up a conversation next to me.

"You look so familiar," she says to Matt.

"Yeah, well, you've probably seen him on TV," Dave jokes.

"Ha ha." She mock laughs. "Seriously, though. Do you have a brother or father working for one of the teams?" Kierran asks, her brows furrowing together.

Matt's jaw tenses. His eyes move from side to side quickly. I wonder why he looks like a cornered mouse.

Kierran redirects her attention on Matt. "Sorry, did you say something? My brother tends to be annoying most of the time." She laughs.

Truth is, I'm surprised Sloane is cool with having Kierran over, knowing her and Oli hooked up in the past. Sloane had caught Kierran coming on to Oli when they were together, and it led to a big blowout. Apparently, Kierran was drunk and getting over a breakup but still, that's got to sting. Just like it fucking hurts me now seeing Sierra with a date. I throw back some wine, knowing it isn't the best choice given the situation, but old habits sometimes die hard.

"Matt, what's up with you?" Dave asks.

Matt drops his fork on his plate. "Nothing, man. I never told you guys, but Daniel Sears is my half-brother," he says, and the table falls silent. I look at the guys and we're all pretty much sporting the same dropped jaw.

"So what?" Sloane says, breaking the silence.

"Sears is one of the top players in the NHL," Matt explains. Matt was only recently called up from the minors. "I don't make it public knowledge that we're related," he explains, his cheeks looking a healthy pink.

"Okay, well no big deal," Sloane says.

It is kind of a big deal. We just played him a few weeks ago. Sears was being a big asshole. He was riding the puck hard to get through the net and Matt blocked his every advance.

"I dated Daniel." Kierran drops her head.

Dave hisses something under his breath that sounds profane even from where I'm sitting. "Are you kidding me?"

"Look, it doesn't matter who your half-brother is," Sloane says looking at Matt.

Kelsey rubs Dave's shoulder and whispers something in his ear.

"Or who you dated," Sloane says, looking to Kierran. "Let's focus on happy things, like who is coming to the shelter to deliver all this food?"

The rest of the gang chimes in that they're in too. I don't hear a word come from Sierra's mouth until she says, "Can you please pass the stuffing?"

It's sitting to the left of me, so it would make sense I pass it to her. It takes me a moment to make a move. I lift the large platter and hold it out for her.

She shifts in her seat and our thighs rub. Electricity zaps through my body. She's wearing one of those plaid miniskirts she likes to wear. It's green and red. Her dark stockings are incredibly sexy, since she has the best legs. I remember what it felt like having those legs wrapped around my waist.

Fuck, I miss her. Wait! What?

"Thank you." She smiles uneasily, and then turns to Klause. "Can I pass you some?"

The smile she gives him is way brighter than the smile I got. It pisses me off.

"Sure, thanks," he says with a heavy German accent.

When they are done putting stuffing on their plates, I ask if anyone else wants any. The platter gets passed around.

Klause fills up Sierra's glass with wine, and I tense. She drove here. Is she going to let him drive her car? *She better not.* How long have they been together? Why didn't Sloane mention any of this to me?

We finish dinner and move on to dessert.

"I'm stuffed," I say, leaning back in my seat. I do a minor side glance to see Kierran and Matt are in deep conversation with their heads close together. I'm not sure what that's about. I look to my right, and Sierra is standing up and leaning over the table. She's wearing a cropped red sweater that reveals less than an inch of her creamy skin, and my fingers ache to touch her in that small spot. *What the fuck is wrong with me?*

The waitstaff clears the table and then sets up dessert. Sierra and Klause laugh beside me at some story he's telling her, and I feel like the odd one out.

"How is everything going, Nils?" Sloane asks innocently, even though something tells me the woman can read my distress. *Did she set this up?* She better not have.

"All is good. Everything was great. Thanks so much for having me," I say. No way am I calling her out now. Besides, I really do appreciate being included in their holidays.

After dessert, the waitstaff packs up the abundance of leftovers.

We all sit in the family room, waiting. Sierra is holding Quinn. She coos at her and makes funny faces. I can't stop watching her.

Klause reaches over and whispers something in her ear. My anger kicks up a notch. I don't want him anywhere near her. My mind spins, wondering if he's touched her, been inside her. Has he made her come?

She nods and then passes Quinn over to Flynn. Sierra stands from the couch and he follows her. He thanks Sloane and Oli for being such hospitable hosts. And then he heads for the door. But Sierra didn't say goodbye, so I'm sure she isn't leaving.

Just then, the doorbell rings. Sloane stands and heads to answer it.

"Is there more company coming?" I ask Flynn.

"Babysitters for the kids. It's too late to take them out now," she explains.

Matt and Kierran walk into the room and take a seat in the spot just vacated by Sierra and Klause. I'm itching to go to the door and ask her if she has feelings for him. That would be fucking crazy though. She made up her mind.

"Guys, we are going outside." Oli stands.

"It's freezing. Are you crazy?" Myles snaps.

Oli eyes him weirdly and he relents.

"Think this has something to do with you, Karlsson." Dave jabs me in the ribs.

"You come too," Oli says to Matt.

We follow him out to the second-level deck. He turns on two heaters, but they aren't warm yet, so it's freezing.

"Have a seat, boys," Oli says. There are only four Adirondack chairs and five of us.

"I'll stand," I offer.

"You sit," he says demandingly. "I'll stand."

"Fucking hell, man." I shake my head, laughing. "You think you've become a shrink now because you've got the perfect family," I chide him. When I first met this guy, he was a fucking mess, holding on to all kinds of baggage concerning an accident that involved his parents.

"Don't start, Karlsson. I know you well enough to see that you were about to lose your shit in there," he calls me out, and I can't argue.

"So what?" I say.

"You fucking want her? Then claim her," he says.

I grit my jaw. "She's with that guy. He's fucking perfect for her. I guarantee he wasn't thinking of smashing my face in like I was his. I'm messed up."

"We are all fucking messed up," Dave says. "Just 'cause we're making millions every year doesn't change who we are or where we've come from. Did you see that Williams was arrested last week? There is always someone in the league getting themselves into trouble. We are exceptional at a sport. Doesn't mean we've had an easy life. Also doesn't mean we don't deserve better," he finishes, and fuck, he's got me there.

"What is this about?" Matt asks.

"Karlsson and Sierra," Myles explains.

"Look, Karlsson. I know you think I'm some goody two-shoes with a perfect life, but that's just a story I've been selling. It's fucking crazy but it turns out that Kierran is a physical therapist. She's worked with my brother and dated him. That's how she caught onto the resemblance," Matt explains.

"First of all, I never said you were a goody two-shoes. All I said was that you have your shit together. If you don't, that's cool too. You've been bringing it on the ice. That's what counts," I say.

"Your stats are down. You did way better when you were with her, Karlsson," Myles says and then raises his brows.

"What the fuck am I supposed to do?" I ask.

"What do you want to do?" Myles asks in challenge.

"I obviously want her, okay? My life has been crap without her. Should I grovel? Tell her to break up with the guy?"

"He's just a friend. Had nowhere to go for the holiday," Oli explains. His words ease something inside my chest.

Sloane opens the door. "Kids are settled. We are good to go."

Oli shuts off the heaters and we all head inside and pack up Myles and Oli's cars with the food. Sierra and I ride with Oli and Sloane. Kierran, Matt, Flynn, and Myles ride with Kelsey and Dave, since Kelsey drives one of those mom-mobiles.

Oli plays music. He and Sloane don't say much. Sierra and I sit on opposite sides of the back seat. I want to reach out and touch her thigh, but I have no right. Tension crackles between us—or maybe it's just me feeling the tension. When we arrive, I turn to look at her. I want to tell her I made a mistake, but I'm still not sure I can be the man she needs.

CHAPTER THIRTY-ONE

S ierra

WHEN KLAUSE SAID HE WAS LEAVING, I GOT NERVOUS. HE
knows that Nils and I broke up. I'm pretty sure all the Black-
hawks fans followed Nils's dramatic tweets about how heart-
broken he felt. A part of me wanted his feelings to be real but
those words were posted for the sake of ending our fake relationship.

When the guys went outside, the girls told me to come
upstairs with them while they got the kids settled and then they
huddled around me. They said it looked like Nils was going to
lose his cool over Klause. They totally think he has feelings for
me, which is nuts. He never fought for us.

Sitting in the backseat of Oli's SUV, I was beginning to think
that all our friends were in on some master plan to get us back
together. The air in the car is tense. This whole evening has been
nerve-wracking. Maybe it's because I've noticed Nils's jaw
ticking and red rising in his cheeks.

We arrive to the shelter. I gaze sideways before leaving the car and catch him staring at me, the same pulsing tension radiating from his jaw. I wish he'd say something. *Anything*. I wore a little mini number knowing he likes me in this kind of skirt. I can't help but want to cause some kind of reaction from him. Maybe I did get a reaction, since I caught him staring.

Oli and Nils walk around the SUV to the trunk to get all the leftovers. Apparently, this is a ritual they do every year since Myles proposed to Flynn one Christmas Eve. Sloane and I carry some smaller parcels inside. The rest of the gang arrive about the same time.

The volunteers get all the food sorted and then we are handed aprons. We stand in a line to serve the food but there are too many of us so some of us are just standing around. Myles, Oli, Dave, Matt, and Nils are all serving.

"This is really amazing," I say. "Before my mom left, we did Christmas. I mean, the dinner, and opening presents the next morning. When I moved to live with Aunt Becca, she wasn't too big on the holiday, but she and her friends would get together and have a festive meal. They had no presents or tree."

"Oli and I didn't celebrate Christmas for years after our parents died," Flynn says.

Kierran and Kelsey remain quiet.

"That's why we make it extra special now," Sloane says.

"Thanks so much for including me." I hug her.

My cell rings. The screen says No *Caller ID* and I pick it up. "Hello."

"Is this Sierra Cole?" A woman's voice speaks through the phone, sounding very professional.

"I'm Nurse Kent calling you from Northwestern. Maria Karlsson was admitted to the trauma unit. She's in a critical condition and has you down as next of kin." A chill runs down my spine.

"Oh my, is she okay? I mean . . ." I mutter.

"It would be best if you could get here as soon as possible," she replies.

"Okay . . . yeah . . . on my way," I say.

"Thank you. Please come through the ER," she says, and the call ends.

"What is it?" Sloane asks.

I palm my chest as tears begin to spill from my eyes. "There's been an accident. Nils's mom is in a critical condition. She's here in Chicago. I don't know what she's doing here," I whisper. He's only standing a few feet away.

"Shit. Take our car," Sloane offers as she digs into her purse. She pulls out the keys.

"Thanks," I say in a daze. I haven't spoken to Nils in months, but he needs to know.

I walk over to him, and my whole body is shaking. I place my hand on his shoulder and he turns to see who's touching him. He gives me a wary look.

"I need to talk to you now. It's important," I say.

His lips turn down. "What's going on?"

"I need you to come with me, please," I say biting back tears.

"What's going on? Are you okay?" He pulls off the sanitary gloves he was wearing and whips off the apron, too. I grab his hand and pull him outside.

"Sierra, what the hell is wrong with you?" he says in a tone that tells me he thinks I'm crazy. We leave and the cold winter air hits me like a ton of bricks. I left my jacket inside the shelter.

"There was an accident, Nils. I'm not sure what happened, but your mom is in critical condition. I know she would want you to be there," I say quickly. My heart is beating so fast, I fear it may explode.

He pulls his hand out of my grasp and runs his fingers through his hair.

"We need to go," I say.

He stares at me blankly.

"Come with me, please. Tell me you want to see her. This may be your only chance. Do you want to let it pass you by?"

Nils stands frozen. I'm not sure what he's going to do. Then he says, "Okay."

"Okay," I repeat. "We need to take Oli's SUV. I hope I can drive it," I say. I'm used to driving my little Toyota, and Oli has a hulk of a car.

"Give me the keys. I'll drive," he says. We run to the SUV. "What hospital?"

"Northwestern," I say.

"I thought you said she lives in New York," he says.

"She does. I don't know why she's here," I explain.

He presses the gas pedal hard.

I just hope we make it in time.

CHAPTER THIRTY-TWO

N ils

"SHE WAS WALKING ACROSS THE STREET WITH A FRIEND. A CAR ran her over," the nurse explains. "She has internal bleeding. She's been to the OR, but she has a brain bleed that hasn't been contained yet."

"Yet?" I ask.

"The neurosurgeon is on his way. It being Christmas Eve, he was off. We didn't have another doctor to take his place," she explains.

"Okay." I use hand sanitizer and put a mask over my face. Sierra does the same and we head into the ICU.

My heart shatters when I see how banged up my mother is. Something inside me breaks. I walk over to her bed, and the smallest of whimpers escapes my lips.

She opens one eye, since the other is swollen shut.

"Nils," she says, even though it looks like it hurts her to speak. She turns her head. It looks like she spots Sierra beside me. "You brought him."

"We were at the same place," she explains.

"Thank you," she mutters. "I'm so sorry," she says, and it looks like she's trying not to cry, but even crying seems to cause her pain.

The hospital door opens, and a man walks in. I eye him. He isn't dressed like a doctor.

"I'm your mother's friend, Max," he says, extending his hand to mine.

"Nils." I shake his hand. "I don't understand. Why is she here in Chicago?"

"She had this crazy idea of spending Christmas with you. She chickened out and didn't contact you. We ate dinner in our hotel room, since everything was closed. Then we decided to take a walk. We were crossing the street when a guy came out of nowhere and ran her over. I thought she saw him coming fast around the corner or else I would have hung on to her. It just all happened so fast, you know. One minute we're talking; the next I'm dialing nine-one-one," the man explains.

Hearing Mother had come here to see me for Christmas tugs at something in my heart. I think back to the talk I had with Sierra months ago about getting in touch with Mom. How sorry she feels for having left me. I know people make mistakes. I have a list of my own to deal with.

Sierra's hand rests on my shoulder, giving me comfort.

"I'm going to go ask the nurse when they are expecting the neurosurgeon," she says against my ear. I'm so happy she's here.

"Thank you," I say, feeling a responsibility for my mother I haven't felt in a long time. As a kid, I had wanted to protect her from my demon father, and then my anger over her leaving me ruled my life.

"P-please forgive me," Mom says.

The guy—Max—stands beside me. "She told me all about you. I know what happened back in Sweden. She feels terrible for leaving you. She found herself leaving one abusive relationship only to get involved with a man who wanted to control her every move," he explains. "She wanted to come here to explain to you that she's sorry. That she misses you terribly," Max says. He seems like a genuinely nice man but Mom clearly didn't tell him that she chose someone else's daughter over her own son. Or that she never tried to contact me at all. Not even on my birthday.

"P-p-please," my mom mutters.

My head falls between my shoulders as a tear slips down my cheek. I don't remember the last time I shed a tear, but I must have been a very small boy.

"S-so many mistakes. S-sorry. So s-sorry," Mother murmurs. Her words hurt. They don't feel therapeutic. *What happens if she dies right now?*

I lift my head and take her fragile hand in mine. "I forgive you."

CHAPTER THIRTY-THREE

S ierra

AFTER GIVING ME A RUNDOWN ON MARIA'S PROGNOSIS, THE nurse says, "They are prepping the OR now. Doctor Strauss is one of the best in Illinois. She'll be in good hands."

"Thank you." I sigh.

I head back into the room and call Nils outside.

He walks my way and swipes at a tear. When we are on the other side of her hospital room door, I update him. "He's the best, Nils. They don't know if there will be lasting damage, but this doctor is the best. They feel very hopeful," I say.

He doesn't say a word when he leans down and wraps me in the tightest hug. "I've missed you so damn much," he says.

The confession sucks the air out of my lungs.

I don't say anything. I just hold him tight.

"I don't want her to die," he croaks.

"I know," I say, and my tears begin to flow again. "She has a good chance of survival. Let's pray she makes it."

The nurses arrive. Nils and I break apart.

"We're going to take her now," a female nurse says.

We watch Maria being wheeled off. They direct us to a waiting room. We take a seat. Max says he's going to get coffee.

Nils and I sit side by side. He doesn't breathe a word, but he holds my hand tight, and I pray that Maria makes it through because my wish tonight for Nils is to have his mother back.

CHAPTER THIRTY-FOUR

N ils

"SHE'S GOING TO BE ALRIGHT," I TELL SIERRA, LIFTING HER UP in my arms and swinging her in a circle. "The doctor said she has a long road to recovery. She will have to do physical therapy and work with an occupational therapist. They don't know what her mobility and speech will be like, but there isn't any brain damage."

"That is such good news," Sierra says, sounding cheerful.

I place her back down on her feet. It's close to six in the morning. We spent the night on a hospital chair, and the doctor delivered the news to me while Sierra remained fast asleep beside me.

I set her down. "I would have never made it through last night without you here by my side."

"Don't be silly. You would have been just fine. You always are," she says.

"Let me rephrase." I press a finger to my lips and think of better words to express what I want to say. "I want you by my side always, Sierra. I'm so in love with you. I'm sorry for being slow and taking so much time to realize what was in front of me all along."

Her jaw drops. Her glasses aren't on straight, and I level them on her face. "There. That's better."

"Can you go back? I don't think I heard you right," she says.

I throw my head back and laugh. "You're adorable. I said I love you. I think I always have. I just didn't understand what all my feelings meant. I want to be with you forever. I don't want anyone else to have you. Damn, when I thought of that guy from last night putting his hands on you, it made me crazy. You're lucky I didn't punch him out."

"Klause and I are just friends. He never had hands on me, and you know you can't just punch people out," she says, lifting her finger like she's admonishing me.

"I've been through anger management. See? It's working. I didn't punch him out. Thoughts don't count," I say.

"So you love me, huh?" she asks playfully.

"With all my heart," I say, leaning into her. I pause before our lips touch, and she pouts. "It would be nice if you said it back," I say, lifting my right brow.

"I love you, Nils. I think I fell in love with you back in Minnesota, then I fell in love with you all over again in Chicago," she says.

"I know I was an idiot. Mata said your vagina was singular and I didn't believe her," I say.

Her hazel eyes turn so round they look like they are going to bug out of her head. "She said *what?*" she screeches as her checks flame red.

"The night of Oli and Sloane's wedding. When you went into the bathroom, Mata told me I need to take care of your vagina because it only wants me." I chuckle. "I told you that she said you were willing and pliant. I just didn't tell you what she said before that. The woman has some good intuition."

"You . . . you . . ." She smacks my chest playfully.

"Aw, come on, beautiful. Don't be embarrassed. I like that you are mine. That I am the only one who can get you all hot and bothered," I whisper against her ear. When I look down to check out her nipples, which are pressed against me, they are sharp points. "I can't wait to get you in bed. I love you."

I kiss her hard, sucking the air from her lungs because she *is* the air I breathe.

My life, my heart, my everything.

"I love you too, Nils. So, so much."

EPILOGUE

As I cut up fruit and set it on our kitchen table, I hum the song from our wedding. Even though it was a year ago, the memories are fresh in my mind. Sauntering over to the pantry, I grab the granola and make my way over to our fridge. I take the yogurt out and set it on the table.

Nils is upstairs getting ready. I hear footsteps, which means he's out of the shower. I fry up some eggs and turkey bacon. After our sex marathon last night, I'm starved, and I'm sure Nils is, too.

With a full spread on the table, I start the coffee machine just as my husband walks into the kitchen. His hair is wet, and he's wearing a pair of lounge pants low on his waist.

I grab two cups from the cabinet and pour the coffee.

He wraps his arms around me from behind and peppers slow kisses down my neck. "Hmm, you taste good. I'm hungry as hell."

I spin around to face him, and I'm met with his hard cock pressed against my belly. "Really?" I look down to his swollen member. "We just finished making love." I giggle.

"Knowing I'm going out of town and leaving you makes me want to have as much sex as possible," he says.

"Let's eat first. I don't want our food getting cold." I pat his chest and he groans.

"Okay, beautiful." He walks over to our kitchen table and takes the seat beside mine.

We bought a piece of property outside the city when we first got together. I was the primary architect, and Nils and I went through exactly what our dream home would be. It isn't as large as some of the homes on our street, but it exudes the warmth we wanted to feel inside it with wood trims, large expansive windows, and an open-concept layout. It's good the neighbors are far away because we've made love against almost every window in this house.

"How long will you be gone for?" I ask.

"Four days," he groans. "I wish you could come with me." He frowns. Sometimes on weekends I am able to get away and watch him play in other cities.

"We have a big project. I told you. It's the first of its kind in Chicago. It's important to me," I say.

When I finished my degree, I landed a job in a prestigious architectural firm. We will be designing the first eco-friendly low-rise building in Illinois. A technology firm commissioned the project, and they want to set a new standard in the industry for reducing the emissions of greenhouse gases. It's truly very exciting.

"I'm excited for you," he says, giving me a warm smile.

"Thank you."

We both devour our food and drink our coffee. It's these normal life situations with him that I crave. It isn't about him making me feel wanted either because I know in his eyes, I am beautiful and that's all I need, but this sense of belonging and family has me feeling at peace.

I end up on his lap. My arms wrap around his neck and our lips brush in soft strokes against one another. His tongue slides against mine, and that wave of heat that always sucks me under when we touch flows over me like a tsunami. I twist myself a little so that I can sit on his lap, facing him, my legs dangling either side of his waist. His swollen cock pulses against me. I'm wearing a nighty with no panties. My wetness rubs against the fabric of his pants.

"Nils," I moan.

"What do you want, beautiful?" he asks, his tone gruff and raspy.

"You, inside me." I whimper, rubbing myself unabashedly against him.

He removes his hands from my waist, and I stand to give him leverage to remove his pants. With his cock free, he slides inside me. I rock against him. He hisses and groans, his carnal pleasure evident on every part of his face. He thrusts his hips into me, and my need grows. The orgasm I want so badly is threatening to take over, and I shut my eyes as my head falls back.

"Yesss, baby. Ride me," he says.

I shudder, my body exploding with sparks of heat and lust, as I ride out every wave of bliss. Nils's body contracts, and his hot cum pours inside me, making everything feel so much more intense. When we've completely ridden out the last of the shockwaves of our orgasm, I fall limp, resting my head on his shoulder.

"Kick ass this week," I say, pressing a kiss to his neck. Goose bumps pebble on his skin.

"You know I will," he says. As much as he pouts about leaving me, he's been at the top of his game, which is good, because the Blackhawks just extended his contract. It was a relief because Oli, Sloane, Flynn, Myles, Dave and Kelsey aren't far away, and they are our family.

Nils's mom went back to New York after she spent months in physical therapy here in Illinois. She will have a limp for the rest of her life, but we are grateful she made it through because it gave her and Nils a chance to grow closer.

I speak to my dad about once a month. He is who he is. Nothing is going to change that. I've learned that you can't teach a person how to love or how to care. At the end of the day, they are who they are. For me, it's been more about acceptance and letting go, not holding a grudge for his past behaviors.

Nils and I get cleaned up after remaining stuck together on the kitchen chair for far too long. I hope this month I will become pregnant. We've been trying for six months now, with no luck. We went to a fertility clinic to get tested, but the results showed that we are both able to make a baby, which means we just need to be patient. We have all the time in the world. At times, I stress about not getting pregnant, but I try to follow the doctor's advice and tell myself it will happen when it's meant to be. For now, I have what I need.

My crazy life brought me to this moment, to this man, and he is my everything.

Stay tuned for Kierran and Matt's story coming 2020.

Flip the page to read an excerpt from The Truth About Us: A Brother's Best Friend Romance!

THE TRUTH ABOUT US: A BROTHER'S BEST FRIEND ROMANCE
SYNOPSIS
She was my best friend's little sister—forbidden.

Jolie Campbell was my solace in a dark life. Jolie was my first love, my first kiss. She was a soothing balm, loving me, keeping me from sinking in a ship of life that experienced storms daily. I promised her forever but I should've known better.

I made mistakes and ruined everything. Jolie is my favorite memory and my biggest regret. My need for her hasn't faded even after all these years. She loved me for who I am. There was never a choice about moving on. I'll always be alone. It's what I deserve after leaving her the way I did.

UNTIL FATE HANDS ME A SECOND CHANCE. A FUNERAL BRINGS me home to a place I swore I would never return. My memories and mistakes come crashing down on me before the plane even lands. I want to keep my distance from Jolie but my old feelings return like a tidal wave sucking me under while breathing life back into me. I tell myself to keep my distance from her. That no good could come of us, but she's too hard to resist and I want my second chance with the only girl I ever loved. Too bad fate has other plans. . .

FLIP THE PAGE TO READ AN EXCERPT!

PROLOGUE

C hristmas
    Ten years ago

Two days till Christmas and I wait anxiously by the window.
When will he be here?

I stand up and sit back down. Excitement courses through
me. It makes my heart beat fast. As I stare out the window small
flakes fall ever so slowly. It's so pretty, adding a magical essence
to this time of year.

The gloomy wintery day isn't a downer at all because Griff is
home visiting from College in Florida. We will be able to sneak
time alone together. That is, if my family stays out of the house.
If my brother Logan ever caught on to what was going on
between Griff and me, he would lose it. Griff has been his best
friend since kindergarten. And if Daddy ever found out, all hell
would break loose, but we are careful . . .

I text Griff. Everyone left more than an hour ago. This is
quality alone time for us.

When are you coming? Dad is out of town.

Griff was my first kiss junior year of high school. He was a
senior. That kiss locked our

fate. Since then, I've only wanted to kiss him.

Not a good idea. I see your brother all the time. He's my roommate. We need space from each other. I can't just come over and hang with you. Even though I can't wait to kiss you.

Grr.

Logan isn't home and neither are Jenn and Mom. Everyone is out for the day.

Now that changes everything. See you soon!

Yesss!

I squeal. I've crushed on him since I was young. Never in my wildest dreams did I think he would fall for me, the simple sister. Jenn is beautiful. A human version of a Barbie doll with blond hair and blue eyes. I am simple with my chocolate-brown hair, green eyes, and naturally tanned skin. We barely look like siblings, but that's because Logan and Jenn look more like Dad with his Scottish background, and I look more like Mama with her Italian heritage.

I jolt from a knock on the door and stand quickly from my seat. As I bolt toward the door, my smile spreads across my cheeks. Excitement gets my blood pumping hard and it feels like I'm going downhill on a roller coaster, my breaths coming fast and my heart beating rapidly.

OMG. He's finally here. I haven't seen him since he left for college with Logan at the end of August.

I fling the door open and gasp as Griff stands tall and handsome in the doorway. His aquamarine eyes sparkle. His lips tug up at the corners.

"Jojo," he says breathlessly, taking a step inside.

"No one's home," I assure him, taking him by the hand and pulling him over the threshold. My family isn't expected back until tonight.

He's shivering. "C-Close that door so I can get my lips on you," he says, his voice horse. Boston is experiencing an abnormally cold winter and Griff doesn't own a car.

"You're ice." I wince.

"So warm me up." He sticks his hands under my shirt, resting them on my hips. They are so cold, I squirm out of his reach.

"Hey, get back here." He laughs. "I want to kiss you so bad."

I can't resist snaking my arms around his neck. Our lips touch and a familiar heat sparks inside me, spreading like wildfire through my body. His cool hands run up and down my back but I no longer care. I want to kiss him into tomorrow. Kissing Griff is the best drug. It's been so long.

He breaks the kiss and gazes around with anxious eyes. "Where's your dad?" He is always paranoid when we hook up at my house, but we don't have many options for privacy.

"Out of town, I told you, and Logan is out with some friends. Said he wouldn't be back until much later."

"Yeah, he texted me earlier. Some of the guys from the team were getting together," he explains.

"Didn't you want to go see them?" I ask, knowing better. I just want to hear him say the words.

"There's no place I'd rather be than here." He kisses me again, kicking off his shoes and backing me deeper into the house. My eyes open as he walks me toward the family room.

"We are going to need more privacy than this," I say into his lips.

"Oh yeah? What did you have in mind?" he asks with a hint of intrigue.

"For starters, we need to go to my room and close the door. You know the neighbors can be nosy." I remind him, because Mrs. Saloway is constantly on the deck in her backyard even in winter and somehow, she is always looking around. Mom just mentioned to me the other day that she asked her about the new plant on the left-hand corner of the room.

"Your room, huh? I'm liking the sound of that." Griff's grin closely resembles that of a Cheshire cat. It floods me with need. I grab his hand and take the stairs quickly to my room.

"Eager much?" He laughs.

"You have no idea." I smile deviously. I wonder what his reaction will be when he finds out what I have planned.

After climbing on my bed, I place my head on the pillow, and Griff cuddles up beside me.

"How's school going? You have a lot of work to do over break?" he asks.

As a senior, I've been working my ass off. If I want to get into Harvard to do an undergraduate degree in history, I need to have top marks.

"I've got work," I answer, not wanting to get into details. "But I was hoping we could focus on other things right now," I say, using my finger to caress some exposed skin on his neck.

His face flushes, and I'm sure his blood is running south.

"I'm liking the sound of that." He smiles, his voice low and gruff.

It takes mere seconds for our bodies to meld together. Our lips brush and heat overtakes us the way it usually does. He rolls on top of me and uses his arms to prop himself up so I'm not crushed beneath him. He smells like fresh shower gel and Griff. I inhale, marking his scent to memory, knowing he'll be leaving soon. Two weeks of break will fly by, and I'll have to wait for Easter to see him again. For more stolen moments.

His tongue sweeps inside my mouth, wet and messy. My hands run up his back and lower to his behind while his hand skates under my shirt. His eyes open when he finds me bra-less. His thumb gently rubs my nipples, giving attention to both of them, and I let out a moan.

"You have no idea how much I missed that sound," he says. "I'm rock hard." He winces, as if he didn't mean for the second part to escape. "I'm sorry."

"Don't be. Knowing you want me makes me crazy." Sparks of heat shoot between my thighs.

He slides his finger inside my flannel pajama pants. "Fuck, you are so wet," he growls.

"Yes," I moan, moving my hips. I need him so much. I reach for his belt and unbutton his jeans.

"Jolie, what are you doing?" His tone is scolding, but I'm five weeks away from my eighteenth birthday and I want this.

I blow out a breath.

"What?" he asks.

"I want us to sleep together." There, I said it, and I feel so much lighter. His eyes widen. He needs some convincing.

I press my pelvis into the hardness of his crotch. He groans and rubs at his eyes.

"I love you. Is that not enough?" I ask with a pout.

He stares at me, his gaze filled with agony. "I would love to sleep with you, Jolie, but not yet. I want to be something, establish myself when I make you a promise of forever."

"You already made me a promise of forever," I remind him playing hard ball.

"I did," he agrees, rubbing my back.

"I'll be eighteen soon enough," I preen. "I'm ready. I want you. I need to have something to remember you with when you're away at school. I want to feel you inside me."

An animalistic rumble vibrates his chest and leaves his mouth. "To hear you say those words . . ." He flips me on my back and presses his hard length into my belly. "You're going to be the end of me. I can't say no to you." He grinds his length into me and I whimper. I manage to read between the lines of his words.

"My dad is on another continent. We have the house to ourselves all day."

We grind into each other. I moan.

His resolve weakens as he cups me behind my head and brings his lips to mine. We've always been hot for each other, but now it feels like a new fire has been lit and burns wild between us. As we kiss hungrily, my breath is sucked away. We work frantically to get each other's clothes off. Naked, we continue to dry hump. Why are we dry humping? Our clothes are off. Still, it's such a turn-on feeling his skin rub against mine, and I think I may come so I take a breath and look down. I've never seen his penis. It's bigger than I thought.

"What?" He laughs.

"It's big." I have no frame of reference. His is the first penis I've seen.

"Having second thoughts?" He cocks his left brow.

"No." My answer is fast.

I slowly touch him, and he groans. I wrap my hands around his cock and pump.

He groans and gyrates his hips beneath my touch. "Jesus," he hisses. "You're going to make me come."

He places his hand over mine to stop the movement and flips me on my back, hovering above me. My nipples strain beneath his stare. He doesn't leave me hanging long as his hot mouth connects with my nipple. My body feels too hot. Need throbs painfully between my thighs as I run my fingers through his hair.

"Griff," I moan, needing something.

"I know," he answers with a raspy voice. His kisses move lower and lower . . . until his lips connect with warm flesh. I moan so loud I'm sure the house rattles.

"You sure we're alone?" he asks, looking up to me from between my thighs.

I blush, and I'm unable to formulate a sentence. He has never gone down on me before and his warm tongue against the most tender parts of me makes me detonate like fireworks on the fourth of July. I am going to explode as my heart pumps fast, and my skin is slick with sweat. "Don't stop," I groan.

Griff chuckles. "Wasn't planning on it."

Colors. . .lots of beautiful colors and rainbows fly past me as I climax.

"I want inside you. Problem is I don't have any condoms." He frowns.

"I have a box," I say, and his eyebrows almost hit his forehead.

"What?" he asks, as if he didn't hear me right.

"I told you on the phone I wanted this." I don't know why he is so surprised.

"I thought I was dreaming," he answers with a snicker.

"No." I lean away and reach into my side table where I have a full box of condoms I bought from the pharmacy last week. I pass him the box, and he cusses under his breath as he sheathes himself. I watch him intently. With the condom on, he hovers above me and kisses me softly, tenderly.

"I love you so much," he whispers.

"I love you," I answer.

"Forever," he says.

My heart bursts because college hasn't changed him. He is still different from the rest of the teenage boys I know. He doesn't only want in my pants. Our hearts are connected in a way that's hard to describe.

We were friends first. He's been there at so many important moments in my life and we are here now, sharing this special moment.

"Forever," I say as he slowly enters me, and a slow burn of pain crawls up my spine.

"I'm sorry. I'm trying to be gentle." He grits his jaw tight.

"This is perfect," I assure him even with my eyes squeezed shut and my breath held. If I tell him it hurts, he will stop.

"You're perfect and mine, always." His movements quicken, and the burn I felt before turns to white sparks. Need like I've never felt before blazes through me and I begin to move with him. I take what he is sharing: his love, devotion, everything, us, forever. My orgasm comes spiraling, surprising the hell out of me. Just as I let go, Griff falls with me. We fall together.

I'm so sore, but I also know I have him for a limited time. He gets up briefly to dispose of the condom and I watch the clench of his bare behind as he walks to the trash can next to my desk. Everything about him is perfect, from his heart to his muscular build, and when he turns around and smiles, my heart bursts a little further.

He climbs back into bed and I lie in his arms, sated, for I don't know how long. I roll on top of him and we begin to kiss. His arms wrap around me and with our naked bodies pressed together I feel him lengthening and that blazing need I felt before returns, but he doesn't initiate anything more.

"I want you again," I assure him.

"I don't want to hurt you," he sighs.

"You won't. I need you," I say.

He groans. "You don't know how much I want that."

"So have me. We don't get a lot of alone time together. We need to take advantage." I try to convince him. It isn't hard. He flips me on my back and his head dips down between my legs.

His tongue caresses my clit back and forth, and it doesn't take long for me to writhe beneath him. I begin to moan.

"I want to make you come like this but I am greedy." He stops and pulls the condom box off my side table. I watch him roll the condom over his length as my insides contract, and I feel bereft of his touch.

He rubs me with his fingers a little, spreading my wetness, and then he thrusts inside me and my eyes snap shut. His movements are hungry and both our bodies are coated in a sheen of sweat. My hips begin to move with his and my chin tilts back, and I come. The feeling is euphoric. Griff picks up his pace and stiffens inside me. I open my eyes and watch him come undone before me. I revel in the thought that I can make him completely come apart.

"How am I going to be without you until Easter?" He falls on the bed beside me, panting.

"I don't know." I can't imagine him leaving to go back to school. I want him more now than I did before. "Maybe I can come out there to visit for a weekend?"

He cocks a brow. It's my senior year and I've been working extra hard. Logan is his roommate; it was a far-fetched thought.

"I wish you could." He kisses the tip of my nose.

"I should get up." I sit and throw the blanket off me, and my eyes widen at the sight of blood between my legs.

Griff hisses beside me. "I'm sorry," he says.

"You have nothing to be sorry for," I answer fast. I don't want him going inside his head; he has a tendency of tearing himself down.

"Let me grab you a warm cloth," he says, and he climbs out of bed and heads into the washroom attached to my bedroom.

He returns with a warm cloth and slowly cleans off my thighs before cupping me between my legs. His touch is gentle, and the warm look in his eyes makes me fall even harder for him. "I hope I didn't hurt you. I feel bad for making you bleed."

"I'm pretty sure bleeding comes along with taking one's virginity and you shouldn't be sorry. Today was perfect." I lean forward and press a kiss to his lips.

"We should probably get these sheets in the wash," he says.

"Definitely." I don't want Mom coming home and finding them. I spring into action, throwing the pillows off my bed and gathering the sheets.

I put on the T-shirt I was wearing before and the pajama pants, and I saunter down the hallway to the laundry room. I start the machine right away.

When I return to my room, Griff has his clothes back on.

"I better get out of here. I hate to leave you but we both have these stupid smiles on our faces. I want to stay and say hi to your mom but she will know we had sex." Griff laughs, looking a lot more relaxed.

I walk over to the mirror in my room. He's right; my cheeks are a healthy pink and I'm grinning from ear to ear. "I look like I just got lucky." I giggle.

"I'm the lucky one, Jolie," he says, making my heart feel so full. He kisses the side of my neck and shivers roll down my spine. "When is your dad expected back?"

"I don't know the exact time. Mom said he was on a late flight, and he would be taking a cab home," I answer. It is only five in the afternoon. We have plenty of time. "Today was perfect."

"It was. I plan on having more perfect moments with you over break," he says, and we begin to kiss again and that sparks fire..

When my fingers thread through his hair, he pulls away. "I better go. If I kiss you like this a little longer, we are going to end up back in that bed, and I'll have you whimpering under me."

I want to tell him I'm too sore for a third round, but I don't want him feeling bad. Today was perfect.

I kiss him and slide my tongue in his mouth. He moans.

"I need to go. I have to leave." It is taking all of his willpower not to take me to bed again and that makes my ego soar.

"When will I see you?" I ask.

"Stevenson is throwing a party tomorrow night," he says. Mark Stevenson was on the football team with Logan and Griff. I'd heard he had stayed in town and went to Boston U. "I wish you could come with me," he says, rubbing his hands up and down my waist. "Your brother will be there."

"Will Jenn be there too?" I ask, trying to hide the bitter taste I feel on my tongue. Jenn gets to hang out with college guys and do fun things while I will be stuck at home watching some old nineties movie. If only my friends wanted to go to parties too.

"I'm guessing she might be," he says sympathetically.

"Why does she get to go and I don't? It isn't fair." I cross my arms over my chest, knowing I sound whiney but not caring.

"Logan expects her to get drunk and act like an ass. And if you're there, I will want to be with you. I don't have to go," he says.

"It's not like we can hang out anyway," I answer. "Dad will be home. He hasn't been home in a week. I'm sure he'll want to spend time with Mom," I say, even though that isn't always the case. Sometimes Dad is gone for a week or a few days, then comes home and spends most of his time in his office at the

university. He and Mom don't have the most romantic of relationships.

"Maybe we should just tell Logan the truth about us," I
suggest.

"What if he tells your dad?" Griff sounds terrified. "I don't
want to think what would happen then."

Logan is Dad's clone. He looks like a young Chris
Hemsworth. He also idolizes our father and wants to be a
Harvard professor like him. Dad isn't home often but when he is,
Logan tries to do everything to soak up his attention.

"You have a point. I don't know that my brother can be trust-
ed." I grunt.

"I'll see you Christmas Eve. Your mom invited me over," he
says apologetically. I know he wants to spend more time with
me. Our situation sucks. "I should go. I hate to leave. I wish we
didn't have to hide . . ."

"I know." I can read his nerves. If Dad comes home, this
won't look good.

Dad doesn't like Griff hanging around me. He made that
clear when he found Griff teaching me how to slow dance in our
basement when I was in eighth grade. Griff had been a freshman
and he was just a friend helping me out, but maybe we had
always been more than friends and Dad saw it.

"I love you." Griff presses his lips to mine and closes his eyes
like he's cherishing the moment. I close my eyes and enjoy his
lips on mine.

"I love you," I answer. "Come, let's go eat something," I say,
knowing Mom always has home-cooked food ready in the fridge.
Griff grew up with an alcoholic father who did a shit job at
taking care of him. He probably doesn't have food at home now,
and being a student, he is on a tight budget.

We sit in the kitchen and I warm some of Mom's mac and
cheese. The way he quickly eats tells me he is hungry. I hate
knowing he hasn't eaten, and internally, I chide myself. I should
have brought him to the kitchen before taking him to my room.

He didn't even say anything, because he probably wanted to spend our alone time together in private. At least if someone comes home now, it won't look so bad.

When he finishes eating, I pack him a ham and cheese sandwich for later tonight and walk him to the door. We kiss and say goodbye. I am sure we will sneak more perfect moments over Christmas break.

Only we don't, because on Christmas Eve, when he is supposed to join us for our usual festive dinner, he doesn't show.

Logan gets a text saying Griff is back in Florida. Apparently he had applied for a job at Universal Studios and it came through early. He started work right away.

Griff doesn't answer my calls or the million text messages I send. He's vanished from my life and I don't understand why . . .

Ten years later

"Hey, Jolie, how about we go to that hot new bar tonight? The client that was just here invited me, but it's not a date. I could really use you as my wingwoman." My best friend Michelle pushes out her lower lip.

"You know a hot new bar isn't my scene." I scrunch my nose at the mere thought of having to get dressed in some trendy outfit and wear high heels. The last time I was out was approximately three months ago, for my twenty-eighth birthday. Michelle and our other friends literally tricked me into going out with them.

"So the wingwoman argument isn't working?" Michelle's lips quirk on one side.

"Sorry, babe." I shake my head and smile. She's a good friend for trying to get me to go out, since I have a tendency of staying home all weekend. "I have fifteen minutes until my next client. I was going to grab a cup of coffee and snack. I'm exhausted. I got caught up in a really good book last night about a highlander pirate." I waggle my brows.

"Bleh. You and your books." She waves me off. While I like to read about happy ever after, Mich is out there trying to find hers. I think it's great but after everything I've been through, a book boyfriend is playing it safe, and I like safe.

A customer walks up to the front desk, a credit card in hand. Mich's disappointment with me transforms into her full-wattage smile. I'm thankful to be saved from one of her lectures on how I'm throwing all the good years of my life away by reading books and not living life. I don't see it that way.

I lived to the fullest. I married young. My husband was an NFL star who unexpectedly died too young. Now, I prefer to spend my time working as an aesthetician at a posh Manhattan spa. My job isn't the most fulfilling but it gives me a stable income.

After grabbing a quick coffee and power bar, I head back to

my room to prep for my next client who has booked a one-hour massage.

I go through my routine of laying out fresh sheets and towels, and I light an aromatic lavender candle. My life is predictable and stress-free, just the way I like it.

"Mr. Reynolds is on his way to you." Mich's voice comes through the intercom speaker on the phone in my room.

I press the red button so that she can hear me talk. "Thanks Mich."

"He's so hot," she says with a long drawl. "Like seriously. Holy shit. It isn't fair you get to touch all that male hotness," she whispers, and I shake my head as a slow smile forms my lips.

Mich is twenty-nine and single. She moved to New York City five years ago from a small town in Nebraska. She wants to settle down with a man, but so far has had no luck finding someone suitable.

The spa has a strict policy about employees dating clients but Mich just likes to look and not touch, which explains why she is drooling over the client about to enter my room.

I press the red button again. "You're incorrigible and he'll be here any minute, so buzz off," I say playfully, and just as I release the red button, the door to my room opens and there stands Mr. Reynolds, all piercing blue eyes and muscles that go on for days. With a towel wrapped around his torso, not much is left to the imagination. Mich is right. He's a hottie. As a single female who hasn't gotten laid in more than three years, my jaw should be dragging along the floor. My heartbeat should kick up a notch, and my woman parts should say, 'Hello there. Come to mama.' I should be flushed for sure- and I feel nothing.

"Hello, Mr. Reynolds, I'm Jolie. I have you booked in for a one-hour Swedish massage," I confirm then smile. Taking a step back, I allow him to climb on my table. His towel remains wrapped around his waist and I'm relieved, since some clients prefer to remove it. I usually don't mind because it's a part of my job, but Mr. Reynolds is a very handsome man. What if I do suddenly develop an attraction to him based on the feel of his tense muscles beneath my fingertips. Shit. That can't happen.

My thoughts make me anxious and I cough to clear my throat. "Excuse me," I say, and then I begin to work his neck and shoulders. "Let me know if you would like more or less pressure."

"That's perfect. He smiles, flashing perfect white teeth. My husband was also a handsome man but given he was a professional athlete, his teeth were far from perfect. It's been two years since he died. I wish my thoughts didn't somehow always lead to him but how could they not?

I nod and apply some heated lotion to my hands in order to warm them up. Starting at his shoulders, I try to release his tension with my fingertips.

"You have a good touch," he says, and for the next hour, I work on his tense muscles. He remains quiet and my own mind drifts to more mundane things, like the highlander book I am reading, what I will make for dinner tonight, and my cat Sasha. My quiet and simple life makes me content.

At the end of the hour, I realize he's fallen asleep.

"Mr. Reynolds," I whisper while wiping my hands on a towel.

His eyes flicker open and clear aquamarines stare at me causing me to startle. A color like his is rare and for a split second, they remind me of Griffin Campbell's, my first love.

My heart skips a beat. I take a deep cleansing breath. That's weird. I haven't thought about Griff in years. I try not to think of him at all. Logan is still in touch with him and he will sometimes mention him but I never ask. Even though my brother will just throw things out there, like the fact that Griff moved to LA or that he has some big job in Hollywood. Good for him. My family never knew we had a thing and after the way he left, I didn't want them thinking poorly of him even though I shouldn't have cared.

"Sorry about that." Mr. Reynolds smiles bashfully. Something about his looks are so similar to Griff it makes me feel uneasy. This has never happened before.

"Don't be. It means I did my job." I grin.

"You definitely did. I'd like to book with you again?"

"Sure."

He stands, rooted in his spot. This is the point where he is supposed to turn and leave only he isn't leaving. His brownish-colored brows bunch together.

My eyes sweep over his body. It's smooth and sculpted to perfection. Something resembling attraction sparks inside me. So what if he's my type. This is definitely not happening. I haven't been on a date since my husband passed. I'm not ready. Even the slight attraction I feel right now causes guilt to claw inside me.

"Can I ask you out?" he says shyly. It surprises me that a guy like him can be shy about anything. It makes me think that maybe he's a nice guy.

"I'm sorry. We aren't supposed to date our clients," I answer, figuring it's the easy way to let him down. He isn't the first person to ask me out at work, and other than with a few persistent guys, my excuse works like a charm.

"I can ask for someone else next time. That way I won't be your client," he suggests.

That's sweet of him. But my tattered heart is in too many pieces to even try to date. I have never been one for one-night stands so Mr. Handsome and I aren't happening.

"That's sweet, but I'm not available," I say carefully. This is my second line of defense.

"Okay, well maybe I'll see you around then and hopefully by then, you'll be available," he says and smiles, and a cute dimple pops on his cheek.

"You never know." I smile to keep things friendly. I still hope he'll leave me a tip on his way out, and I don't want to get in the way of that.

I'm not going to tell him that I don't think I will ever be

emotionally available again, even though that's the truth. I'm happy living a simple single life. I have good friends and a cat who loves me, and that is all I can handle.

"You have a great day Mr. Reynolds," I chime.

"You too." He grins and leaves through the door.

I quickly prepare for my three o'clock. My cell buzzes in the front pocket of my pants. I usually don't answer the phone while working but a quick peek tells me it's Mom. Shoot. She knows not to call during the day.

I ignore the call and change the bedsheets, then warm the wax. My cell phone continues to buzz. It's a few minutes before three, so I quickly pick up the phone.

"Mom I'm just about . . ." I whisper when I hear a loud gasp.

"Oh dear," Mom cries. Her sadness seeps through the line and my heart sinks. *Oh no.*

"What happened? Are Logan and Jenn okay?" I ask frantically about my siblings.

"It's Kip," she croaks, referring to my stepdad.

"Mom what happened? Is Kip okay?" My heart beats too fast. I had a similar phone call when my husband died. The familiarity causes a cold sweat to break over my body as the memory of Mason's mom calling me, frantic over the phone, surfaces.

"He had a heart attack. He died. He was playing squash at the club and just fell. Didn't open his eyes again," Mom continues to weep and it feels like someone has speared me in the chest. Breath is sucked from me. Bitter memories of death surface in my mind as Mom sobs for her husband.

My client enters the room wearing a robe.

"OMG, are you okay? You look as white as a ghost," she asks. She is a twenty-something woman I wax on the regular. Her father owns some posh hotel chain, and she's a bit of a spoiled brat.

"My apology." I swipe at tears I didn't realize were falling. "I . . .uh." My brain isn't working enough to tell me what to do.

"You know what?" she says, sounding nasal. "I'll just come

back another time." She points to the door behind her and turns on her heels and leaves the room.

Shit!

"Jolie, are you there?" Mom's voice breaks through my muffled thoughts.

"Sorry. What can I do? What should I do?" Gah! I feel like a helpless wreck. When did I become this much of a mess?

"I need you to come home. I have to plan a funeral," she cries some more. "I can't believe this is happening to me again," she bellows. Dad died unexpectedly in a car crash. We had all been sideswiped.

"I'm so, so sorry." I snap out of my daze. "I'll book a ticket. Do you have anyone with you?"

"Rick and Agnes are here at the hospital. They are going to take me home," she explains, and I'm relieved she's with friends.

"Okay." There isn't more to say.

I remember people telling me how sorry they were when Mason died. He had been a big star, and his death was all over the news. Nothing could comfort me back then.

I have to go to Mom. "I'll get there as soon as I can. You take care of yourself."

"Thanks, Jojo bear," she says, calling me by my childhood nickname. And with that, she ends the call.

I tidy my room and shut off the wax warmer like I do at the end of a shift. I gather all the dirty linens and put them in a bin, and head for the reception to find Mich.

When she sees me, her brown eyes brighten. "How was Mister Tall, Dark and Handsome? Did you see the color of his eyes?" Her tone bleeds excitement until she really looks at me, and her face falls. "What happened? What's wrong?"

I swallow, rubbing the back of my neck, trying to keep my shit together. The waiting room is full of patrons. I walk behind the front desk and over to Mich, and whisper in her ear that there is a family emergency.

"I need to leave," I say.

"Okay. Take care of you," she answers, rubbing my shoulder.

"I also want to quit," I suddenly say, surprising even myself.

"Um, what?" Her brows furrow.

"I don't want to work here anymore," I say to her, since she is one of the managers of the spa which is owned by a hotel chain.

"Sweetie, why don't you go take care of your family thing? We can talk more about this another time," she says softly so no one can hear.

I blow out some air.

Hearing of Kip's death, so sudden, without warning, makes every synapses in my body fire on alert. My husband died without warning and my father did, too. It reminds me how unpredictable life is, and I don't want to spend another minute wasting mine or living a life I don't love. I may still be hurting from everything I've been through, but living a safe simple life isn't making me happy.

"Mich, I appreciate that you're letting me go, but I am telling you right now to find someone to fill my spot," I answer, because even though I hate to leave her hanging now, she needs to know she has to find a new aesthetician.

"You're in shock. It's understandable. Go take care of your family and we will talk soon," she says, but she is starting to look at me like I've lost it, and I begin to think maybe I have. Having to face so much death is draining and sad, and makes me want to curl up in a ball.

"I will call Heidi to come get you," she says, referring to one of our friends who works at a restaurant nearby.

"I'm okay," I assure her. "I'll head home and make arrangements to fly to Boston."

"Okay. Call me and let me know when you arrive," she says.

"Will do," I agree. I don't think she has taken my resignation seriously, but I need to leave.

My heart beats fast as I look out the cab window on the way to my apartment. Mom must be crushed.

Her and Dad had what I think of as a loveless marriage. It

isn't something we openly speak of at home, but there were signs, like Dad working all the time. They didn't do couply things like some of my friends' parents, but they didn't fight either. My parents' marriage had solidified my thoughts about true love being nonexistent if people could fall so easily in and out of love. Love wasn't real.

Then Mom went and married Kip. I didn't spend much time with them, but I knew enough of their relationship to know Mom began to blossom and I began to believe again.

After Griff ripped my heart out and stomped on it, I'd begun to think that maybe what we'd shared wasn't love—maybe it was just lust or a bad crush. My entire senior year of high school had been spent reliving our last moments in my mind while barely trudging through school. Dad had been on my case about my grades, so I still tried to get on the honor roll. By spring, I had admittance to Harvard.

I'd stumbled upon Mason one night over spring break—or more like he stumbled upon me. We became quick friends. Then Dad died and I did a one-eighty. I applied to Brown and left with Mason the following September.

It took time for our love to sprout. It was different than what I had felt for Griff. It was rooted in mutual adoration and respect, and I'd thought it must be true love. But he didn't make me burn the way Griff did. Mine and Mason's chemistry wasn't scorching hot, but it was real, dependable. It was true love because what Griff and I shared wasn't, and so, in my young mind, it all made sense. Funny how death has caused old memories to surface.

I usually take the subway home from work because it's more cost efficient. This cab ride is going to cost me a nice buck.

The cabbie pulls up in front of my apartment building. I pay him and exit the car. In the elevator heading up to my apartment, I pull up Google. I quickly search for flight options.

Sasha greets me at the door, rubbing her face along my leg. She purrs as I pat her head. Leaving my front door open, I walk to see my neighbor, Mrs. Montgomery, two doors down. She is an elderly woman who is lovely to talk to, and she loves Sasha. Her own cat died last year, and when I need to head out of town, she's always up for babysitting her.

Sasha follows me, and I knock on her door. She doesn't leave me waiting.

"Jolie." She smiles. Her long white hair is twisted in a bun at the back of her head. "I just made some fresh banana bread. Can I offer you a slice?"

"I would love to but I'm kind of in a bind." My nose scrunches. "I need to head back to Boston. My stepdad passed away unexpectedly."

She gasps, palming her heart. "Oh dear. That's terrible. Do you need me to watch little Sasha?" She speaks of Sasha like she is a little baby, and I love that.

"Please. I don't know how long I'll be gone. My mom needs me. I just bought a large bag of food so she should be good for a few weeks," I explain. "If I'll be gone longer, I can order more and have it shipped."

"Of course, but how long do you plan on heading out of town for? I mean, I don't mind taking care of Sasha, but don't you need to get back here for your job?" She raises her brows.

I may have mentioned to her how I left for Brown with Mason on a whim decision when Dad died, and I left Texas on a whim decision when Mason died.

But this isn't the same thing. Kip and I weren't close and . . . I'm doing it again. I'm running.

"I quit my job," I mumble, because she is onto me. She can see I am running and now, through her wise eyes, I see it too. I still don't want to talk about it right now.

"I thought you liked that job," she persists, sounding like a concerned mom.

"I did." My voice rises a few octaves too high. "I can't explain now, but I will. My mom is on her own, and she sounds like she is a mess. I need to go to her."

"Okay, dear, but think hard on it and consider your options before making rash decisions. You've been happy here, and don't worry about little Sasha. She will be well taken care of."

I lean in for one of Mrs. Montgomery's hugs. The woman hugs with her whole heart, wrapping her arms around me firmly while rubbing my back in an assuring way. Her hug manages to make the loneliness I feel dissipate for a short time while instilling strength in me.

"You'll be just fine, Jolie. You are one of the strongest people I know," she says and I want to believe those words because she is wise and has so much life experience. "You may be crazy for quitting that job. It paid well, but you're resourceful. You'll figure something out."

Her confidence in me makes my heart warm. There is a reason I am quitting my job. I want to follow my dreams and even though it's a rash decision, my dreams were made when I was a little girl. I just put them on hold, and hearing about Kip's death reminds me that life is too short. The time has come to do something for me. Mrs. Montgomery's right; I will figure out a way.

"Thank you, and that's the plan," I finally pull out of her embrace and give Sasha's head one last rub. I swear it's as if she knows I'm leaving her.

I speed walk back to my apartment and pull my suitcase out of the main closet. The last time I used it was a year ago when I went for a girls' weekend with my friends to the Hamptons.

I open my suitcase on my bed and begin to dump my summer clothes inside, along with all my bras and underwear. There is no way I would ever want to move back to Cambridge, Massachusetts. The town holds too many memories of my child-hood. Too many good times I spent with Griffin Campbell. Even now, a whole decade since he walked away, I can't wrap my head around why he would leave me the way he did. It was so cold and callous. Something I didn't believe he was capable of, but then again, I may have just been a bad judge of character.

This trip home isn't going to be easy. That's the reason I've stayed away.

With my bags packed, I call the airline. It takes forever to be passed through to an operator. When I finally get through, the news isn't favorable. All flights are booked. The representative recommends heading out to the airport and trying to get a standby seat.

I change out of my work uniform and throw on a pair of jeans, a white T-shirt, and my yellow chucks. I don't have time to shower because I could be missing an opportunity to catch a flight, and I am anxious to get to Mom. I still smell of the lavender oil that I used on Mr. Reynolds. Hopefully it isn't too strong, I barely notice it anymore.

I cab to the airport and head inside. A loud yawn escapes me, and I look to my cell to see it's five o'clock in the evening. My eyes tear up. I start my day by jogging the streets at six a.m. By this time of day, when I usually leave work, I'm ready to pass out. I need coffee or maybe an extended nap.

A coffee stand catches my attention, and I dash straight toward it. Standing in line and having to wait for caffeine is a nuisance but it is also my top priority.

My eyes feel as if they will lull shut. The emotional weight of all the stress is causing me to crash.

I people watch as I wait my turn. My gaze lands on a tall man who reminds me of Griffin. I haven't thought about him in so long—I don't know why today, of all days, my mind is playing tricks on me. Maybe it's because I am heading home for the first time in years.

While waiting for my coffee to be made, I watch the tall man talking on the phone. He's dressed to the nines in a three-piece suit. Griffin was always the laidback type, but he was also a student back then.

Geez, I really have to stop thinking about him. He's part of my past I've worked hard to forget. Going home now is about Mom, not me facing old demons.

The man turns around and his eyes search around and lock on mine. Air is sucked from my lungs as the most piercing blue eyes I've ever seen take me in. He's just as shocked as me. His head tilts to the side and he blinks too many times. My heart begins to hammer in my chest.

This. Can. Not. Be. Happening . . .

I'm not ready. I pull my gaze and completely ignore him like I would a stranger. After not seeing him for ten years, that is what he is to me—a stranger.

ACKNOWLEDGMENTS

Thank you, first and foremost, my reader! Your love and support mean the world to me. Your time is valuable and I thank you from the bottom of my heart for choosing to spend your time with my words.

Thank you to my wonderful editing team, Lauren Clark and Carmen Jenner you both made this a better book with your attention to detail. Honey Palomino thank you for your attention to detail and for being the last eyes on this novel. Thank you to Robin Harper for making all the wonderful graphics.

Thank you to Sarah Hansen for another amazing cover. Thank you to my agent Stephanie Delamater Phillips for always being there when I need you and being a rockstar.

To all the bloggers I can't thank you enough for all that you do. You guys are the true rockstars and I thank you from the bottom of my heart.

To my family thank you for your continued love and support. Love you all so much.

ABOUT THE AUTHOR

R.C. Stephens is a top 100 Amazon best selling author.

When she isn't in her writing cave she is raising three lovely children with her adoring husband.

Her books are filled with humor, heartbreak, emotion and true love.

Born and raised in Toronto, she loves the winter, but Spring and Fall are her favorite seasons.

Keep up with R.C. by signing up to her newsletter-http:// rcstephens.com/newsletter/

ALSO BY R.C. STEPHENS

Big Stick: A Big Stick Novel 1

Butt Ending: A Big Stick novel 2

The Truth About Us: A Brother's Best Friend Romance

Fraud: A Romantic Suspense

HALO: A Military Romance

Mr. All Wrong: A Billionaire Romance

Mr. So Wrong: A Billionaire Romance

Dick: A Bad Boys Novel

Where Promises Die: A Small Town Rock Star Romance